Cat & Cat

3. MY DAD HAS A DATE... EW!

CHRISTOPHE CAZENOVE
HERVÉ RICHEZ
SCRIPT

YRGANE RAMON
ART

PAPERCUTZ
New York

To my parents,

To Kali & Toudougras, Patate & Pitou, Crocopik.
To China, Stormy & Oswin for that so very personal support.

To the whole crew of purrers, to all loving creatures.
To those who take care of animals.
To Chloe & Oboe, Farley, Pip & Sophie, Maya; to the late, undefeatable Pipo.
To friends & readers who keep this series alive,
To Pierre.
Thanks.

- To Charlie
www.yrgane.com
www.yrganeramon.com

- Sarujin & Théo Grosjean for their help with prep for colorization for this book.
www.sarujinsworks.blogspot.fr
www.loyd.fr

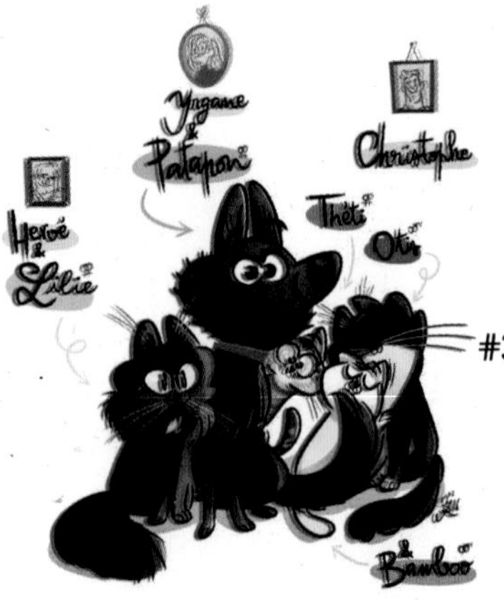
Yrgane & Patapon
Christophe
Hervé & Lilie
Bamboo

* The Authors' Pets *

Cat & Cat

#3 "My Dad's Got A Date… Ew!"
Christophe Cazenove &
Hervé Richez – Writers
Yrgane Ramon – Artist
Joe Johnson – Translator
Wilson Ramos Jr. – Letterer

Special thanks to Catherine Loiselet

Production – Mark McNabb
Managing Editor – Jeff Whitman
Editorial Intern – Eric Storms
Jim Salicrup
Editor-in-Chief

Papercutz books may be purchased for business or promotional use. For information on bulk purchases please contact Macmillan Corporate and Premium Sales Department at (800) 221-795 x5442.

Hardcover ISBN: 978-1-5458-0551-0
Paperback ISBN: 978-1-5458-0552-7

Printed in India
September 2020

Distributed by Macmillan
First Papercutz Printing

Cat & Cat

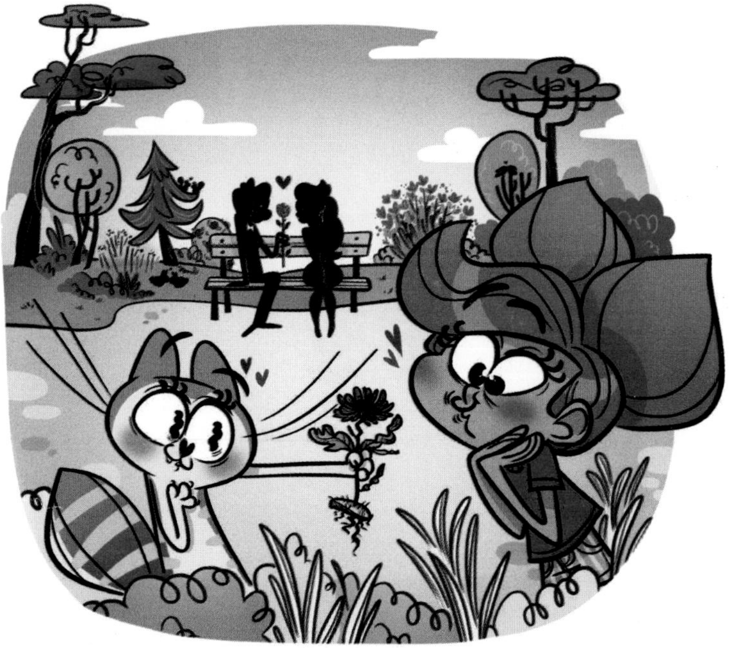

PAPERCUTZ

MORE GREAT GRAPHIC NOVEL SERIES AVAILABLE FROM

PAPERCUTZ™

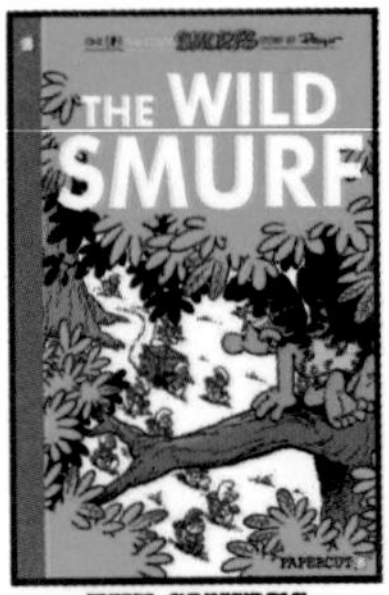
THE WILD SMURF
PAPERCUTZ

THE SMURFS

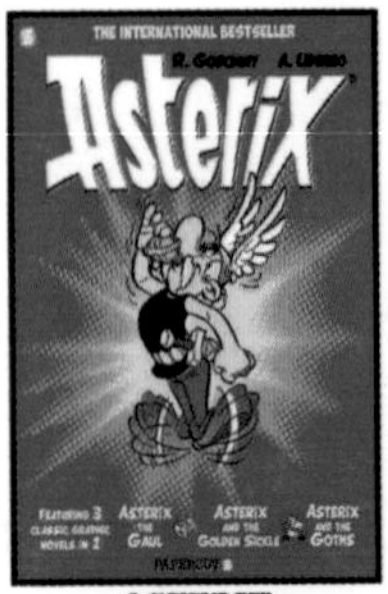
THE INTERNATIONAL BESTSELLER
R. Goscinny A. Uderzo
Asterix
PAPERCUTZ

ASTERIX

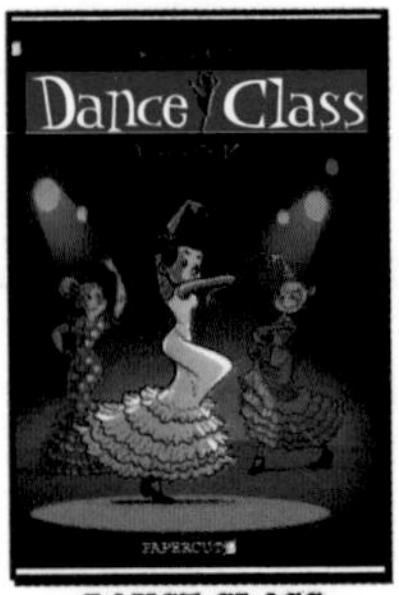
Dance Class
PAPERCUTZ

DANCE CLASS

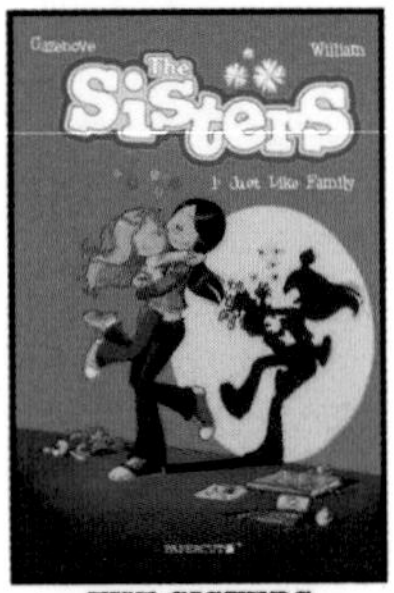
Cazenove William
The Sisters
PAPERCUTZ

THE SISTERS

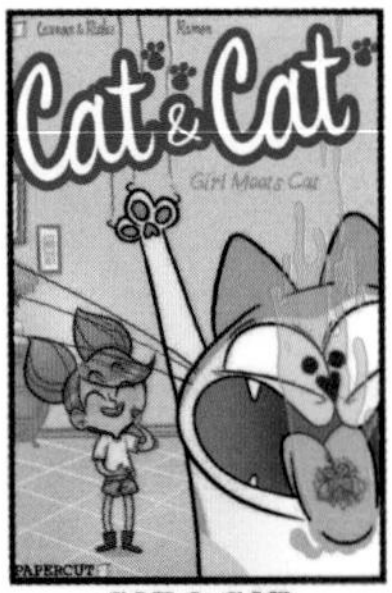
Cat & Cat
PAPERCUTZ

CAT & CAT

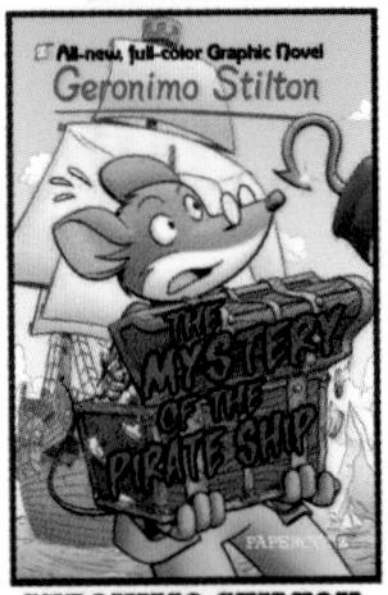
All-new full-color Graphic Novel
Geronimo Stilton
The Mystery of the Pirate Ship
PAPERCUTZ

GERONIMO STILTON

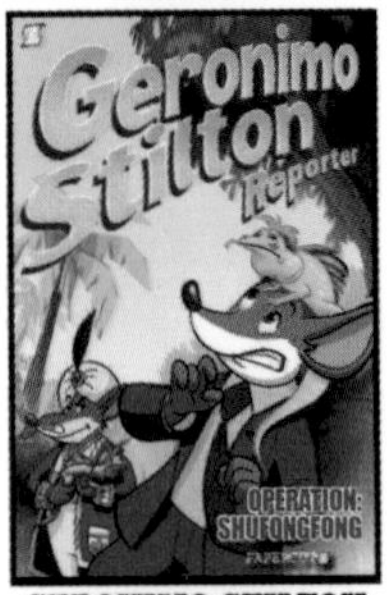
Geronimo Stilton Reporter
OPERATION: SHUFONGFONG
PAPERCUTZ

GERONIMO STILTON REPORTER

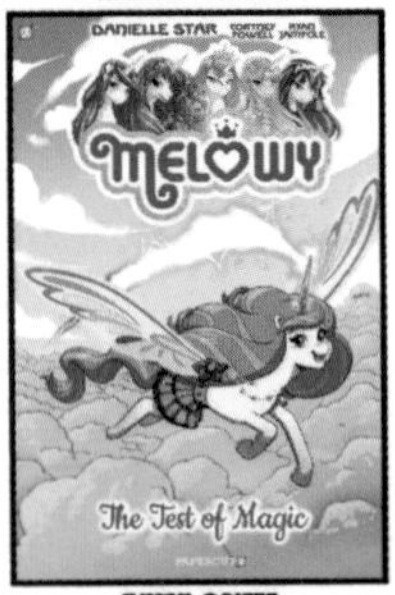
DANIELLE STAR
MELOWY
The Test of Magic
PAPERCUTZ

MELOWY

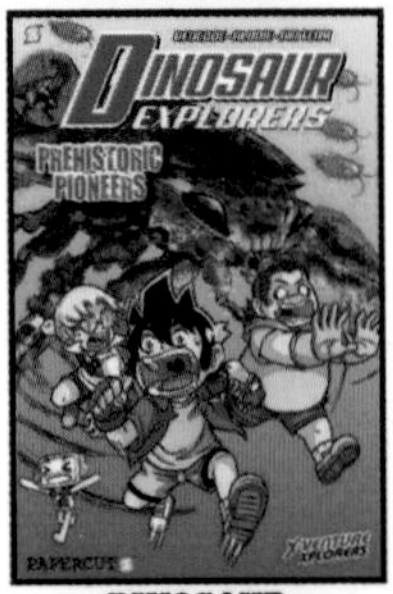
DINOSAUR EXPLORERS
PREHISTORIC PIONEERS
PAPERCUTZ

DINOSAUR EXPLORERS

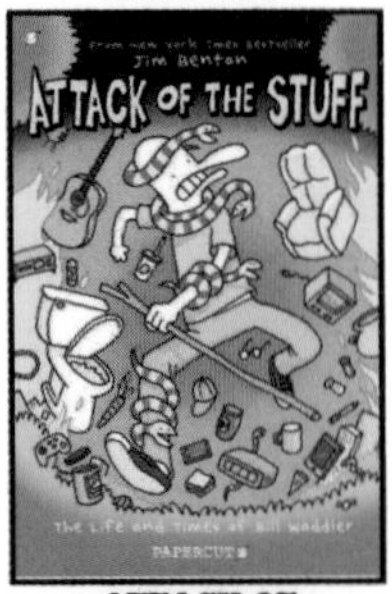
Jim Benton
ATTACK OF THE STUFF
PAPERCUTZ

ATTACK OF THE STUFF

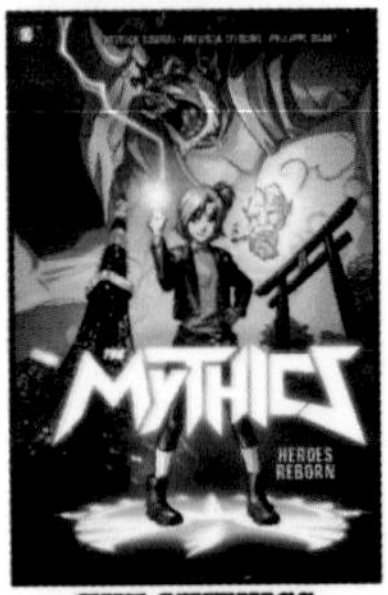
MYTHICS
HEROES REBORN

THE MYTHICS

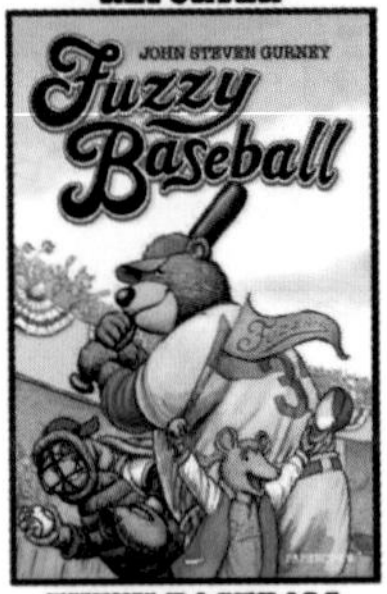
JOHN STEVEN GURNEY
Fuzzy Baseball
PAPERCUTZ

FUZZY BASEBALL

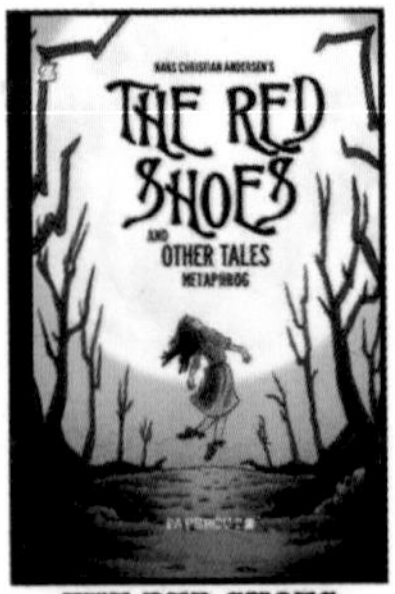
HANS CHRISTIAN ANDERSEN'S
THE RED SHOES
AND OTHER TALES
METAPHROG
PAPERCUTZ

THE RED SHOES

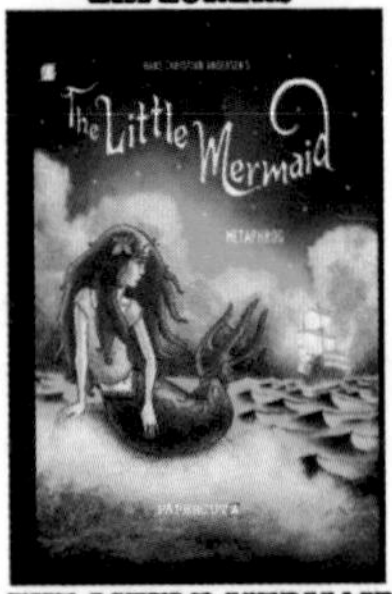
The Little Mermaid
METAPHROG
PAPERCUTZ

THE LITTLE MERMAID

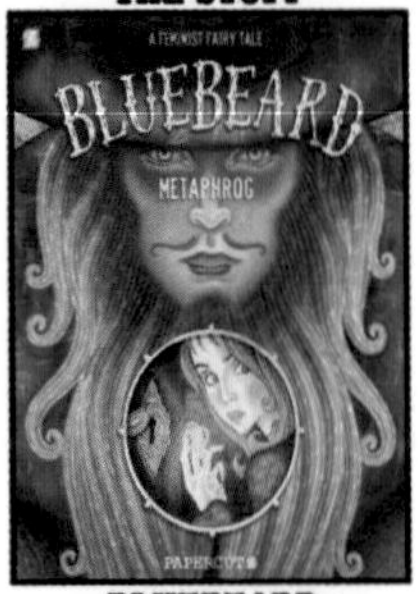
A FEMINIST FAIRY TALE
BLUEBEARD
METAPHROG
PAPERCUTZ

BLUEBEARD

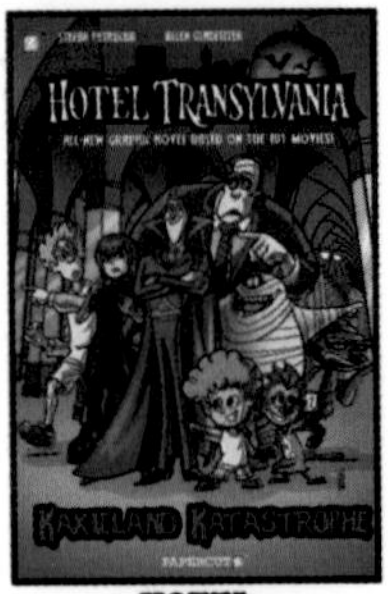
HOTEL TRANSYLVANIA
KAKIELAND KATASTROPHE
PAPERCUTZ

HOTEL TRANSYLVANIA

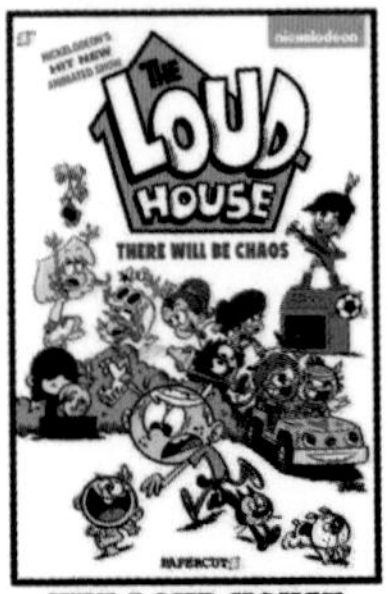
nickelodeon
THE LOUD HOUSE
THERE WILL BE CHAOS
PAPERCUTZ

THE LOUD HOUSE

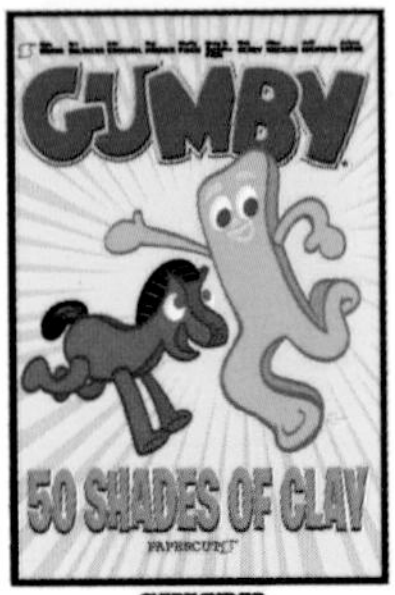
GUMBY
50 SHADES OF CLAY
PAPERCUTZ

GUMBY

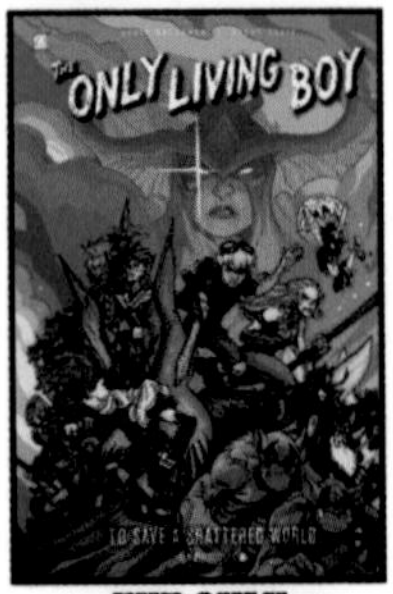
THE ONLY LIVING BOY
TO SAVE A SHATTERED WORLD

THE ONLY LIVING BOY

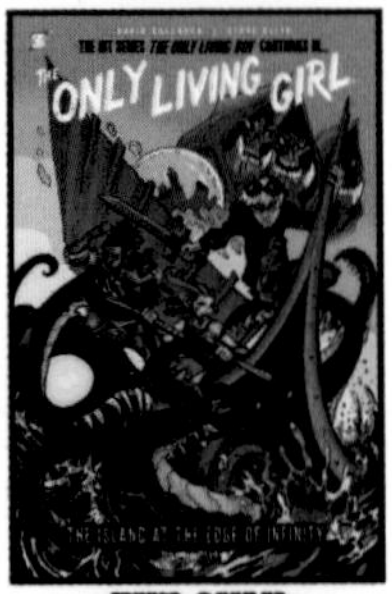
THE ONLY LIVING GIRL
THE ISLAND AT THE EDGE OF INFINITY

THE ONLY LIVING GIRL

Go to papercutz.com for more information

Also available where ebooks are sold.

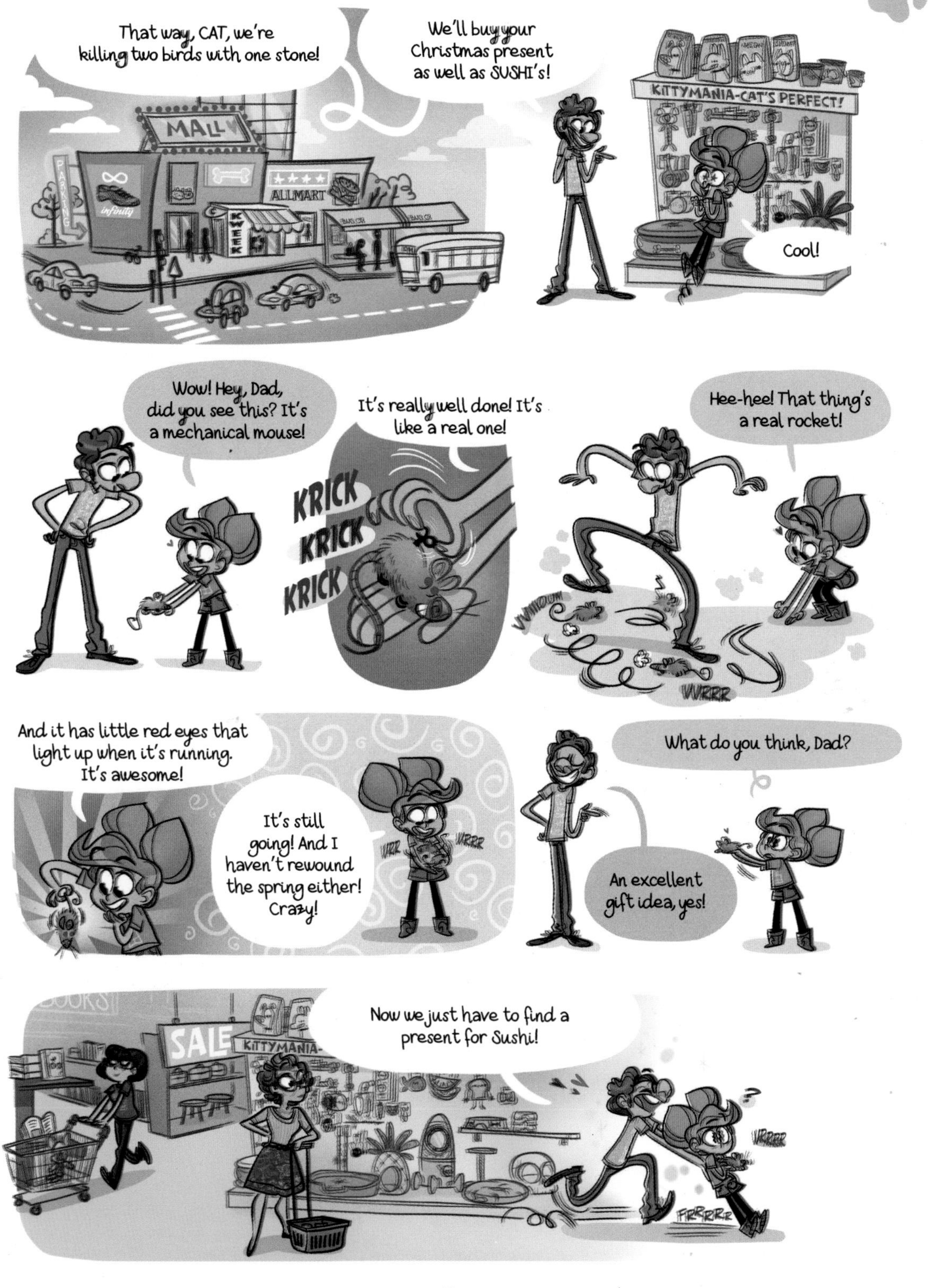
That way, CAT, we're killing two birds with one stone!
We'll buy your Christmas present as well as SUSHI's!
MALL
PARKING
infinity
ALLMART
KWEEK
KITTYMANIA-CAT'S PERFECT!
Cool!
Wow! Hey, Dad, did you see this? It's a mechanical mouse!
It's really well done! It's like a real one!
KRICK
KRICK
KRICK
Hee-hee! That thing's a real rocket!
VVRRR
And it has little red eyes that light up when it's running. It's awesome!
It's still going! And I haven't rewound the spring either! Crazy!
VRRR
What do you think, Dad?
An excellent gift idea, yes!
Now we just have to find a present for Sushi!
BOOKS
SALE
KITTYMANIA-
VRRRR
FRRRRR

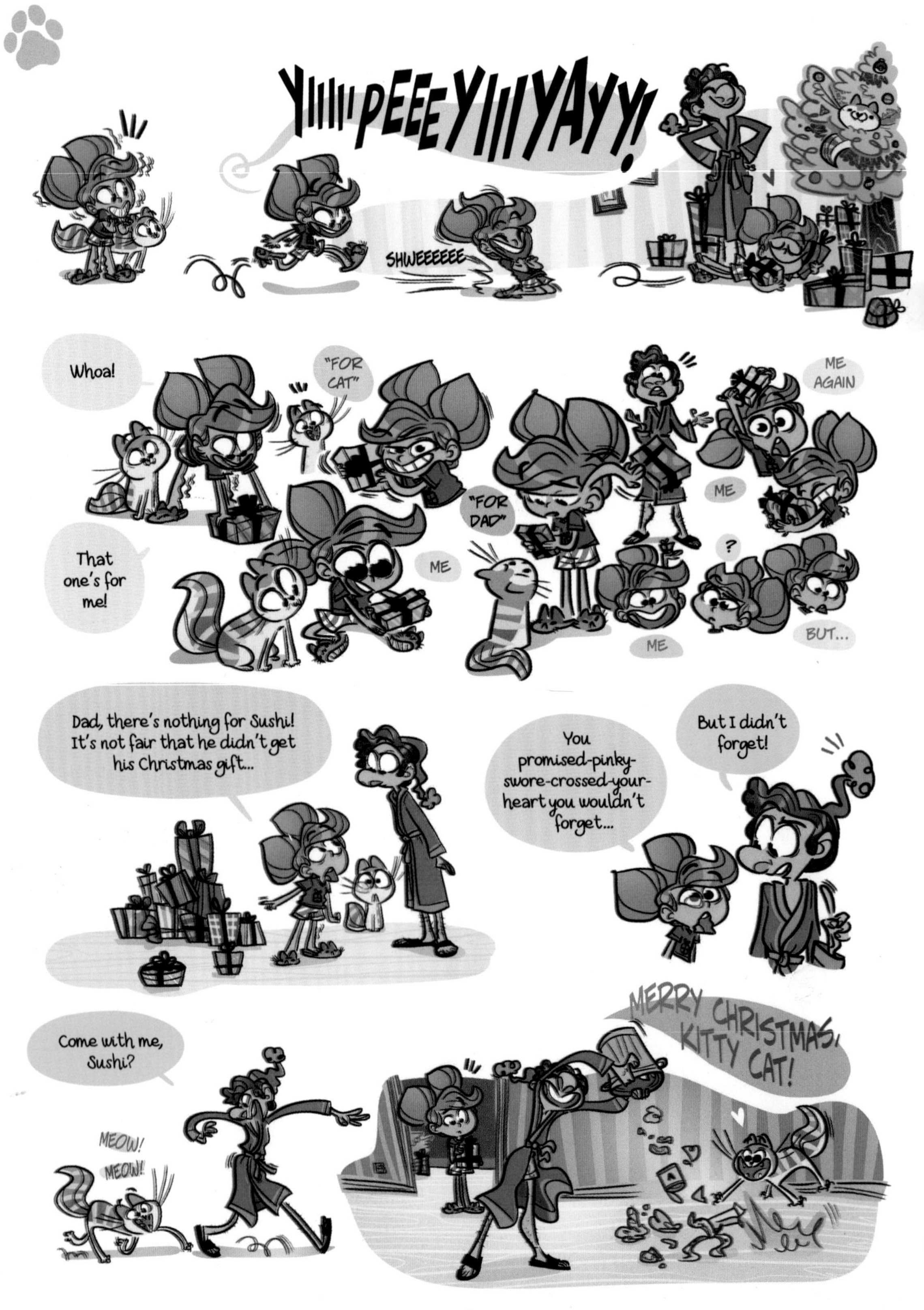
YIIII PEEEYIIIIYAYY!
SHWEEEEEE
Whoa!
"FOR CAT"
ME AGAIN
"FOR DAD"
ME
That one's for me!
ME
?
ME
BUT...
Dad, there's nothing for Sushi! It's not fair that he didn't get his Christmas gift...
You promised-pinky-swore-crossed-your-heart you wouldn't forget...
But I didn't forget!
Come with me, Sushi?
MEOW!
MEOW!
MERRY CHRISTMAS, KITTY CAT!

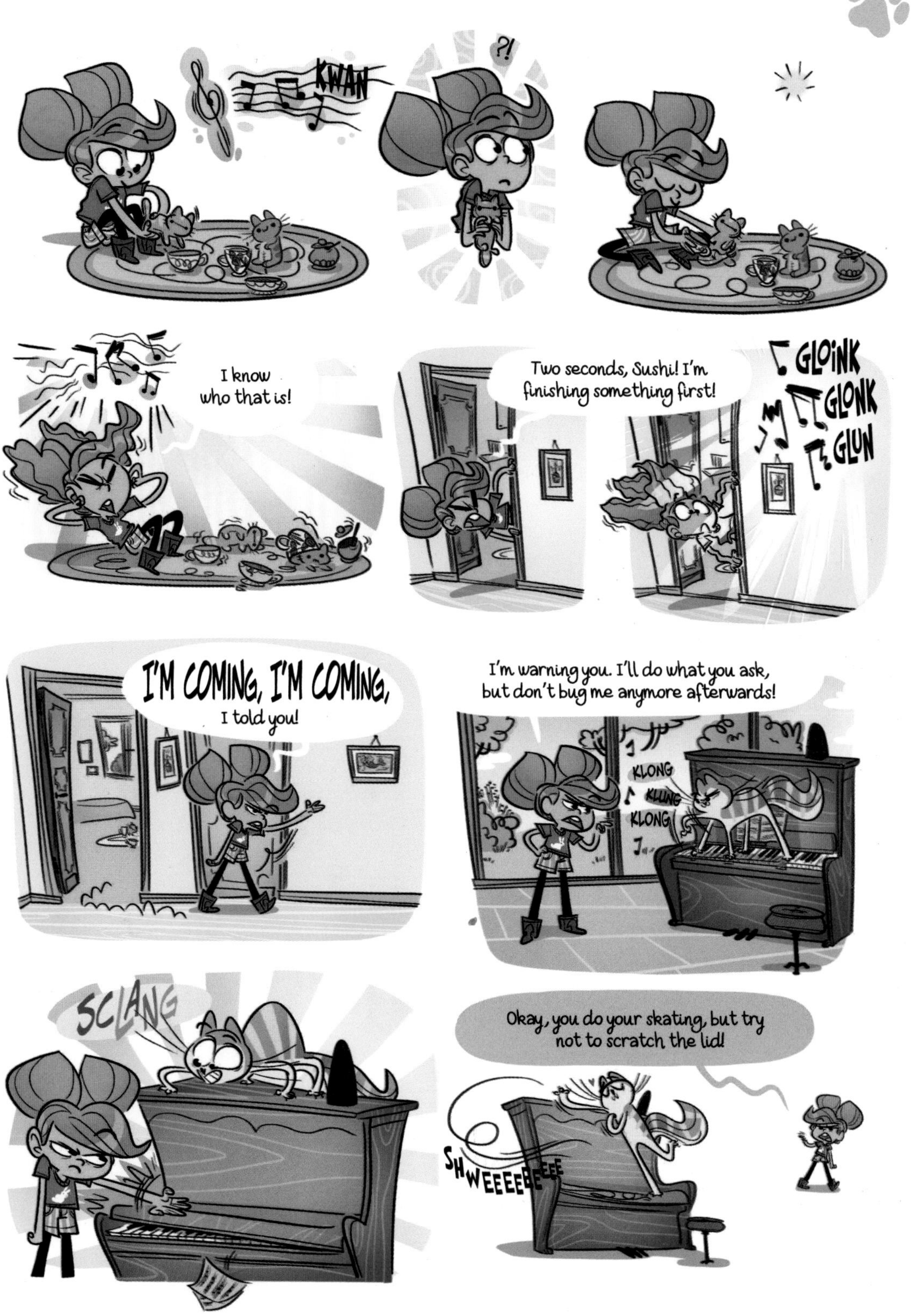
KWAN
?!
I know who that is!
Two seconds, Sushi! I'm finishing something first!
GLOINK
GLONK
GLUN
I'M COMING, I'M COMING, I told you!
I'm warning you. I'll do what you ask, but don't bug me anymore afterwards!
KLONG
KLUNG
KLONG
SCLANG
Okay, you do your skating, but try not to scratch the lid!
SHWEEEEEEEEE

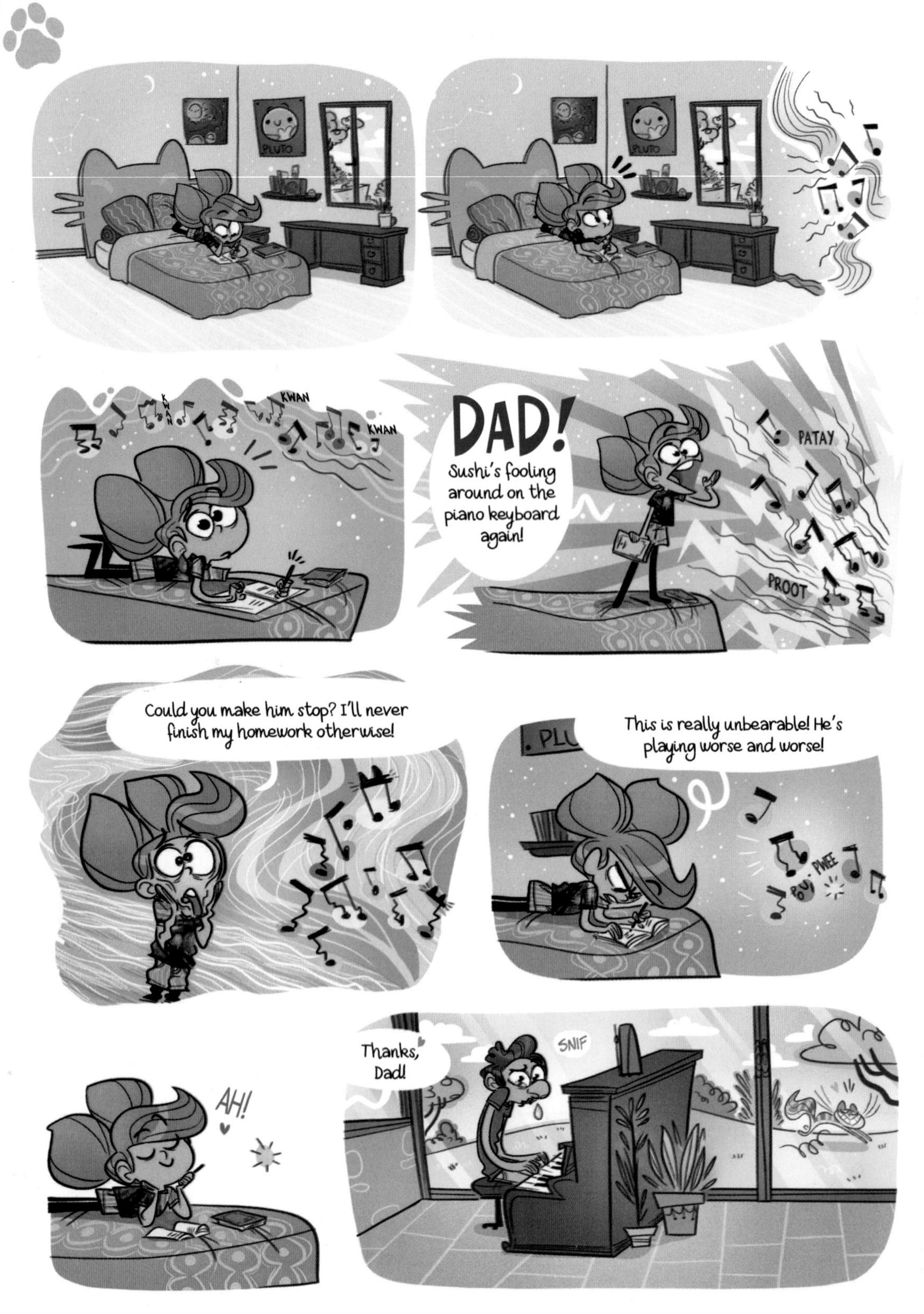

KWAN
KWAN
KWAN
DAD!
Sushi's fooling around on the piano keyboard again!
PATAY
PROOT
Could you make him stop? I'll never finish my homework otherwise!
PLU
This is really unbearable! He's playing worse and worse!
PWEE
AH!
Thanks, Dad!
SNIF

The best moment of the day...

Ohh, I hate toys in my bed!

PWEET

≥Eeeeekk!≤ And right beside the butter, too!

≥Pfff≤... and another one...

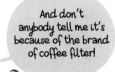
And don't anybody tell me it's because of the brand of coffee filter!

Caaattt! That's it...

...I'm tired of finding Sushi's toys EVERYWHERE in the house!

SQUEAK

Hey, I bet you there's one in my briefcase, too!

You lose! That's not a toy!

SHBAM

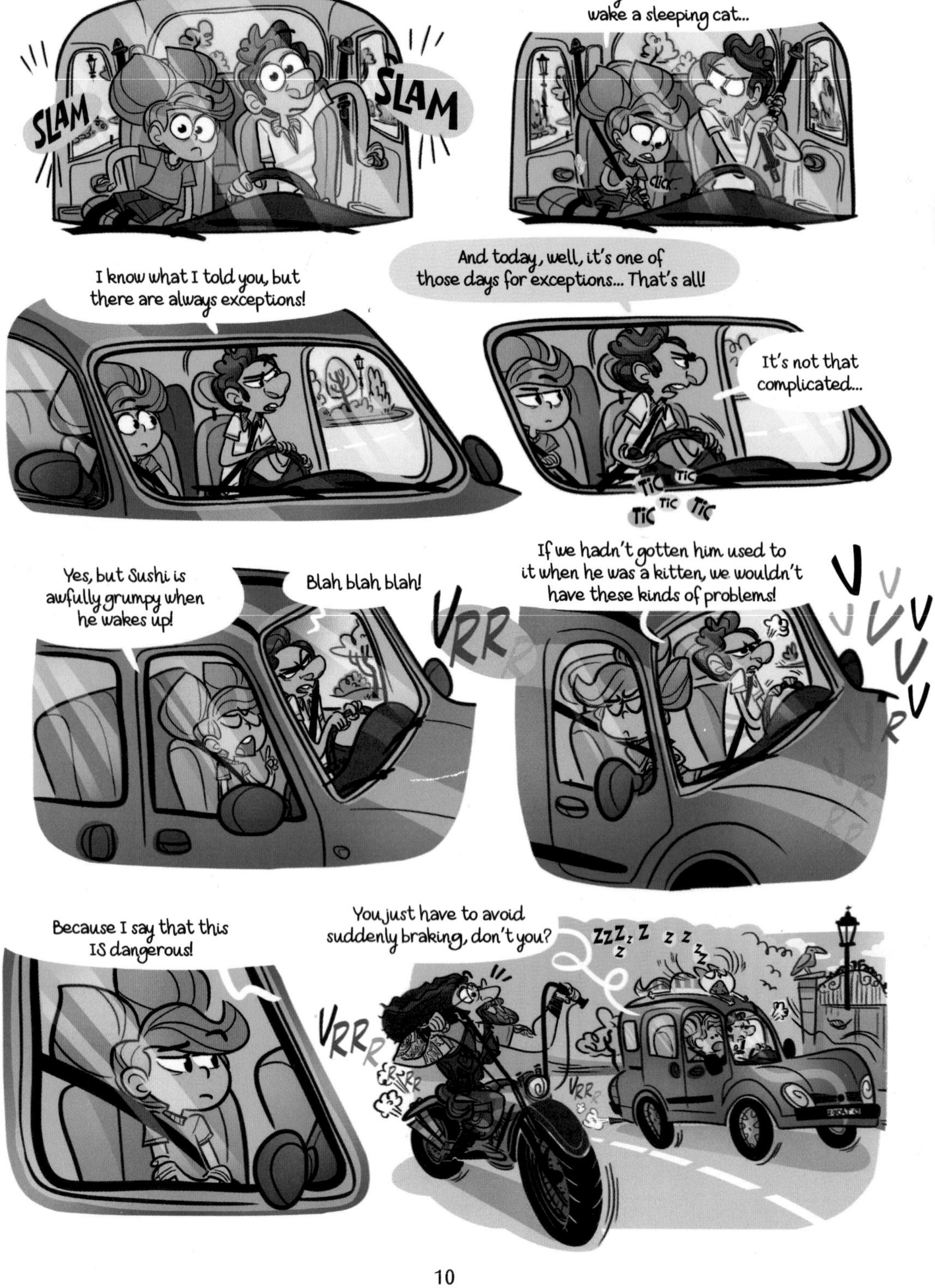
SLAM
SLAM
You always told me me to never wake a sleeping cat...
CLICK
I know what I told you, but there are always exceptions!
And today, well, it's one of those days for exceptions... That's all!
It's not that complicated...
TIC TIC TIC TIC TIC
Yes, but Sushi is awfully grumpy when he wakes up!
Blah blah blah!
VRRR
If we hadn't gotten him used to it when he was a kitten, we wouldn't have these kinds of problems!
Because I say that this IS dangerous!
You just have to avoid suddenly braking, don't you?
ZZZ Z Z Z Z
VRRR
VRRR

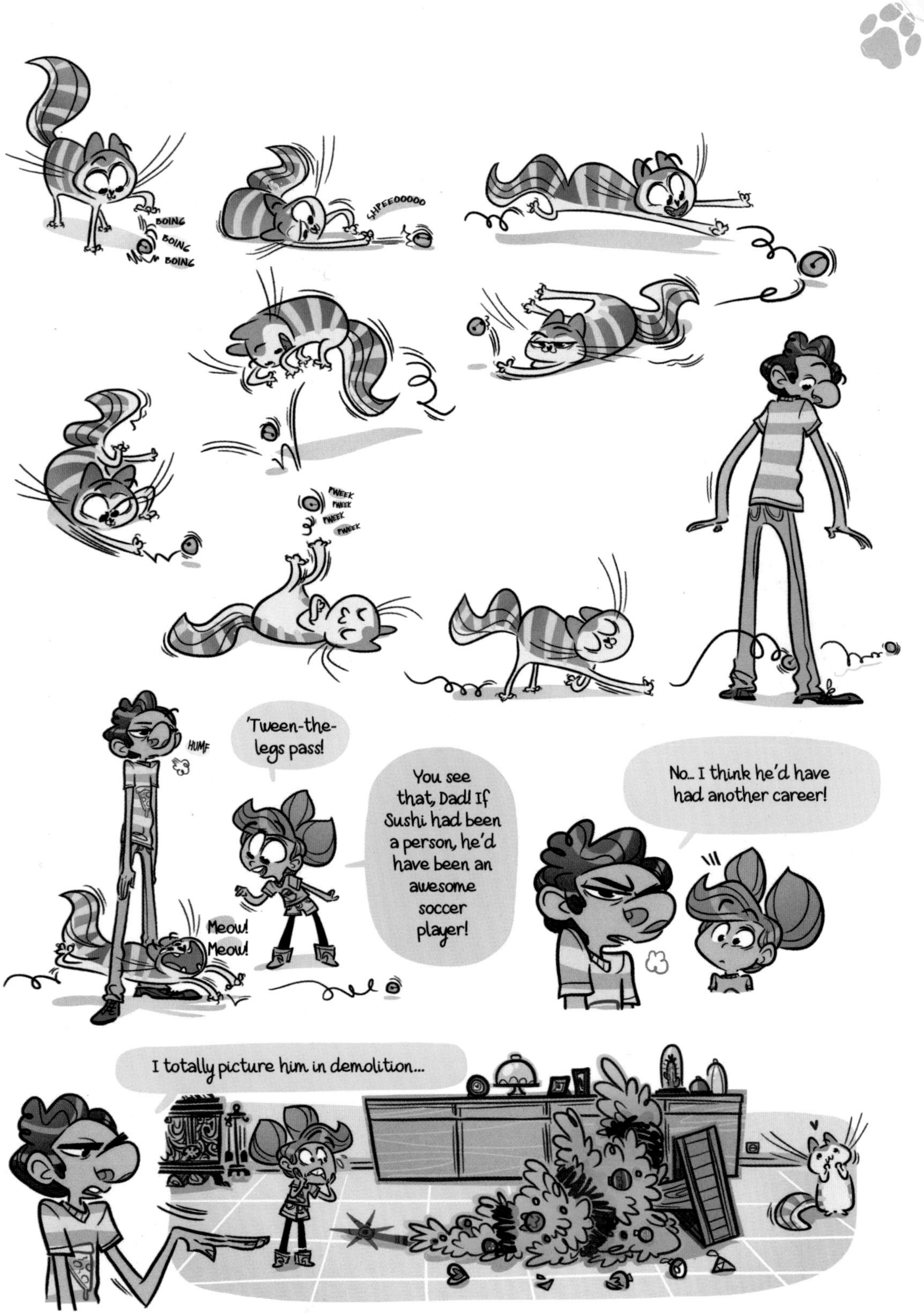
BOING
BOING
BOING
SHPEEOOOOO
PWEEK
PWEEK
PWEEK
PWEEK
HUMF
'Tween-the-legs pass!
Meow! Meow!
You see that, Dad! If Sushi had been a person, he'd have been an awesome soccer player!
No... I think he'd have had another career!
I totally picture him in demolition...

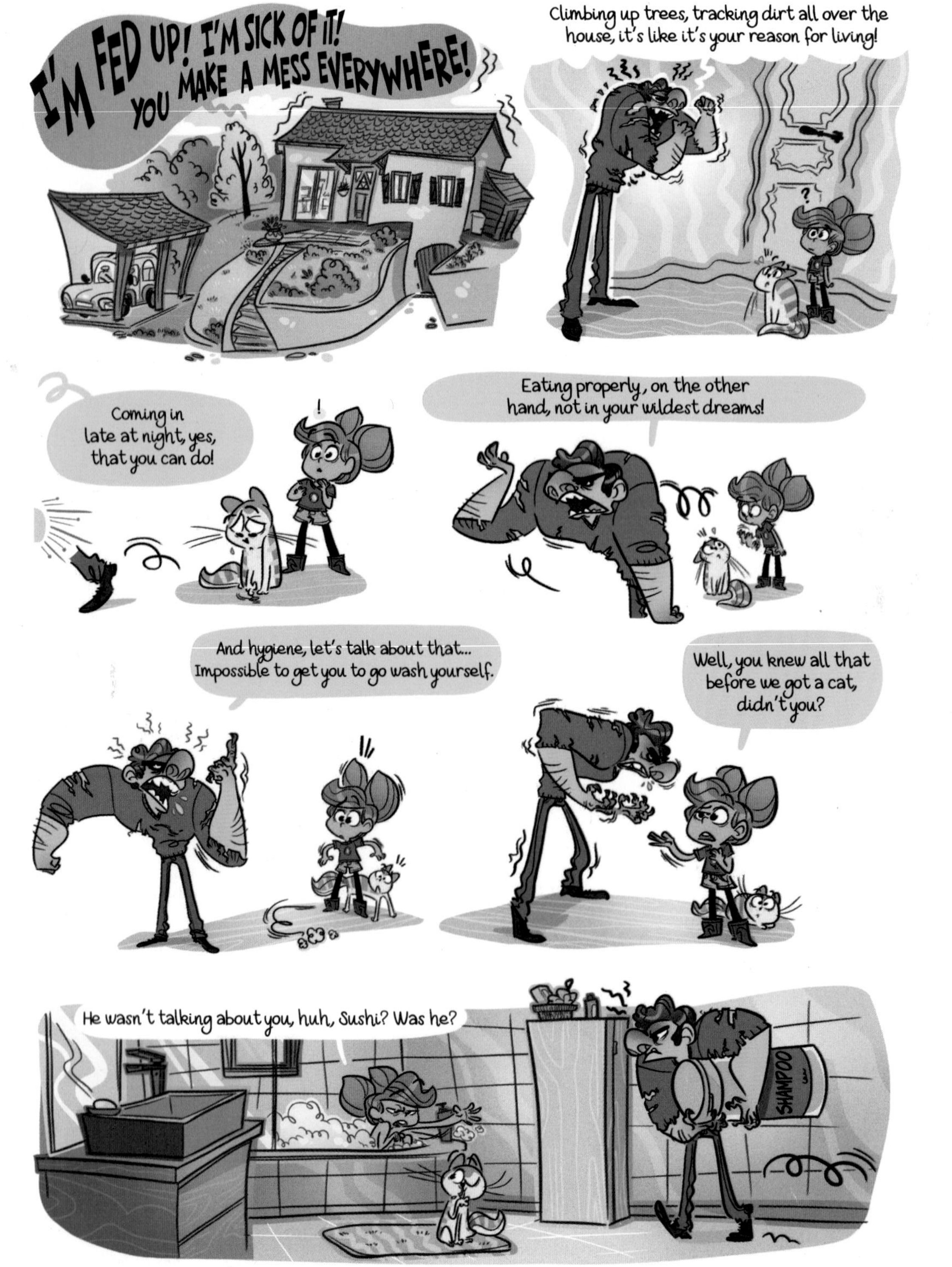
I'M FED UP! I'M SICK OF IT! YOU MAKE A MESS EVERYWHERE!
Climbing up trees, tracking dirt all over the house, it's like it's your reason for living!
?
Coming in late at night, yes, that you can do!
!
Eating properly, on the other hand, not in your wildest dreams!
And hygiene, let's talk about that... Impossible to get you to go wash yourself.
Well, you knew all that before we got a cat, didn't you?
He wasn't talking about you, huh, Sushi? Was he?
SHAMPOO

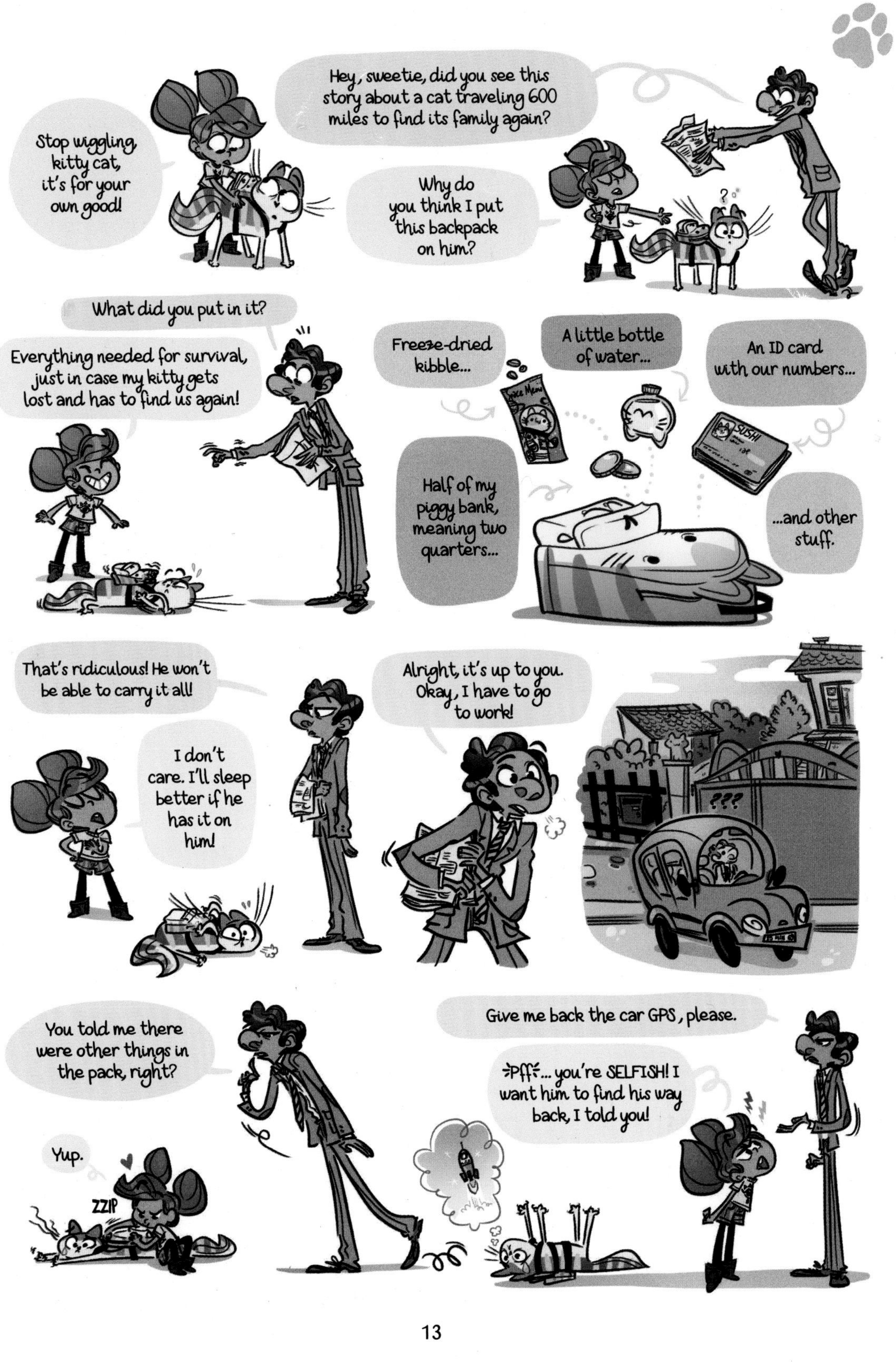

Stop wiggling, kitty cat, it's for your own good!
Hey, sweetie, did you see this story about a cat traveling 600 miles to find its family again?
Why do you think I put this backpack on him?
What did you put in it?
Everything needed for survival, just in case my kitty gets lost and has to find us again!
Freeze-dried kibble...
A little bottle of water...
An ID card with our numbers...
Half of my piggy bank, meaning two quarters...
...and other stuff.
That's ridiculous! He won't be able to carry it all!
I don't care. I'll sleep better if he has it on him!
Alright, it's up to you. Okay, I have to go to work!
???
You told me there were other things in the pack, right?
Yup.
ZZIP
Give me back the car GPS, please.
Pff... you're SELFISH! I want him to find his way back, I told you!

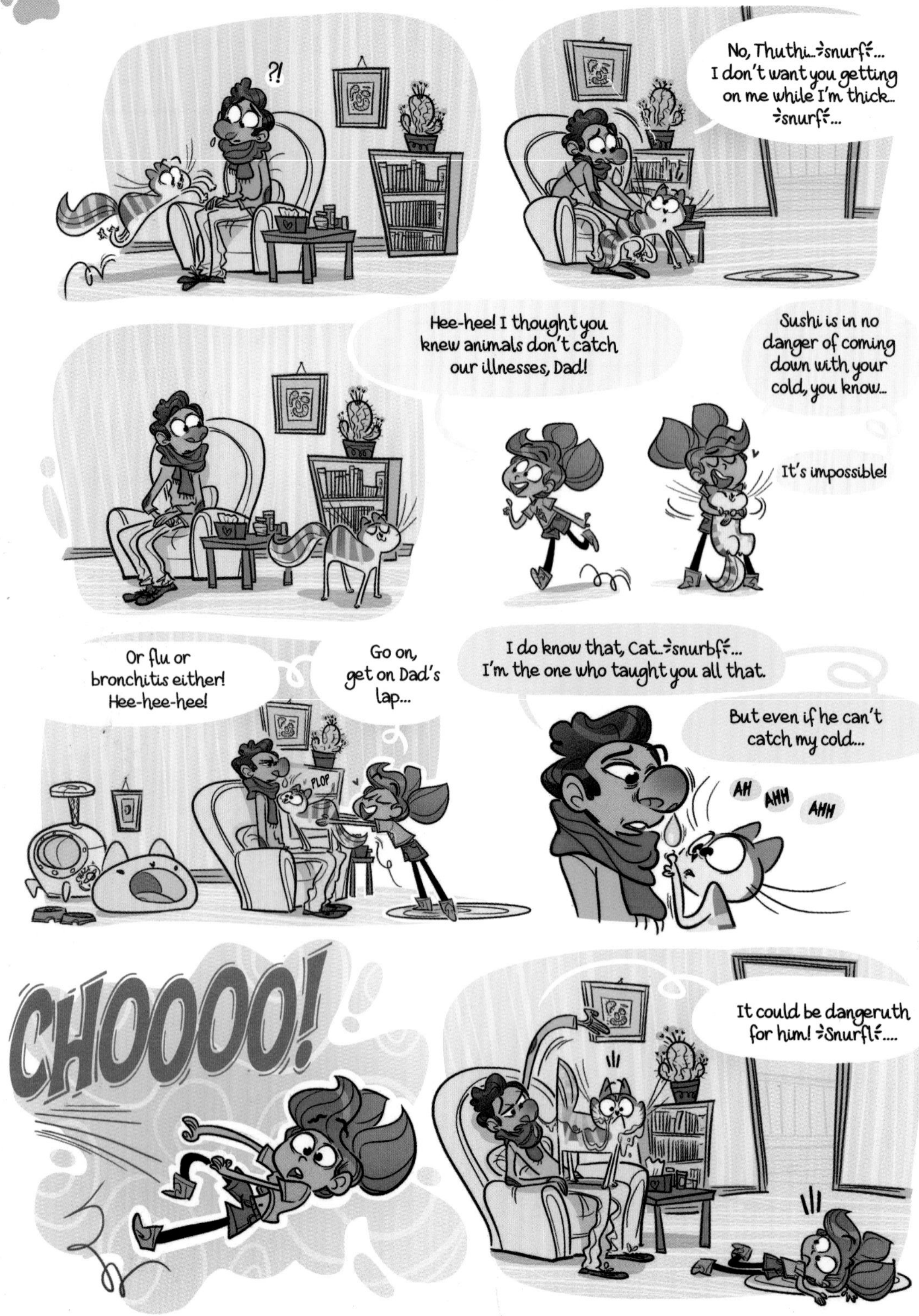
?!
No, Thuthi... snurf... I don't want you getting on me while I'm thick... snurf...
Hee-hee! I thought you knew animals don't catch our illnesses, Dad!
Sushi is in no danger of coming down with your cold, you know...
It's impossible!
Or flu or bronchitis either! Hee-hee-hee!
Go on, get on Dad's lap...
PLOP
I do know that, Cat... snurbf... I'm the one who taught you all that.
But even if he can't catch my cold...
AH
AHH
AHH
CHOOOO!
It could be dangeruth for him! Snurfl....

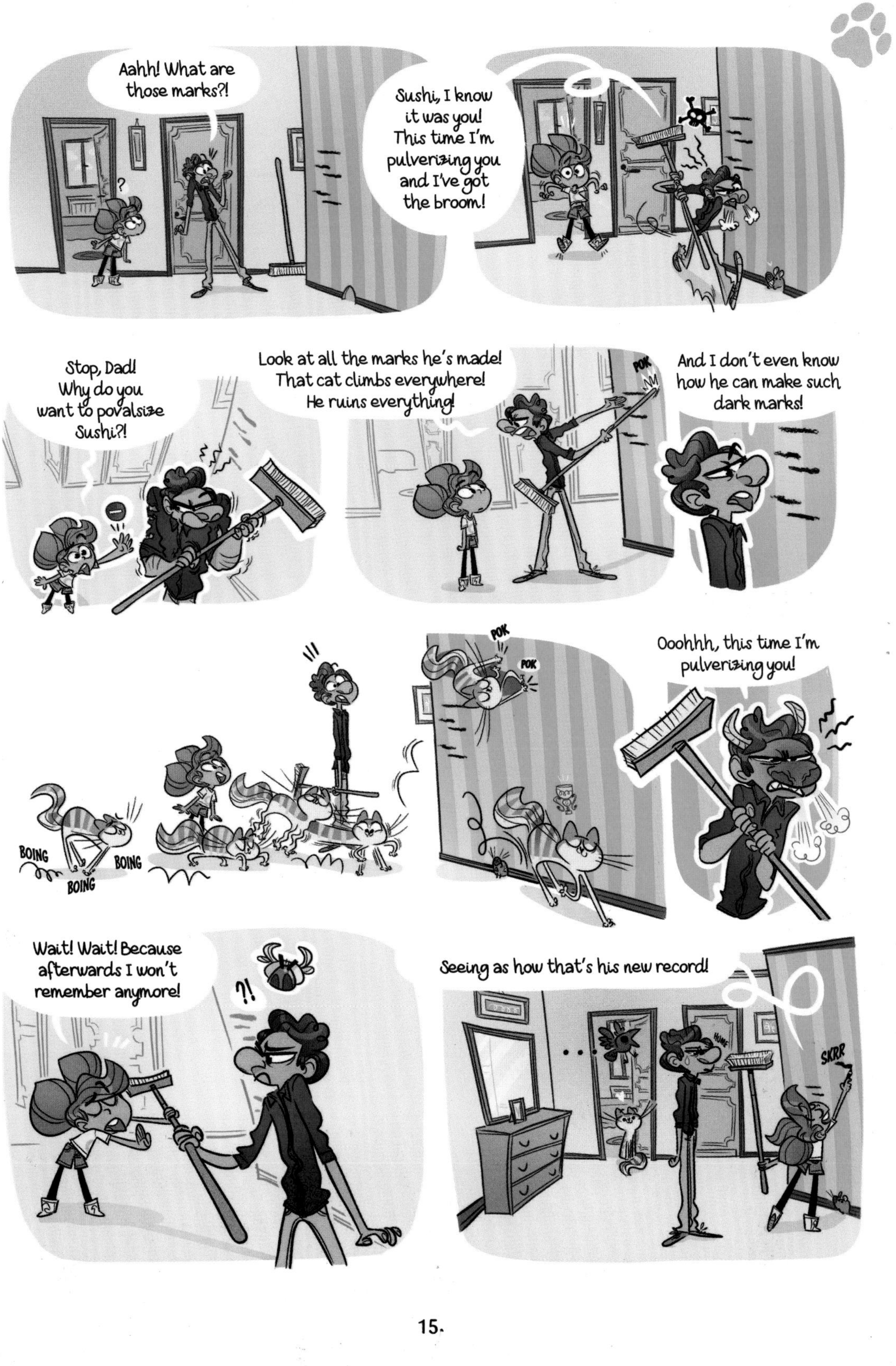
Aahh! What are those marks?!
?
Sushi, I know it was you! This time I'm pulverizing you and I've got the broom!
Stop, Dad! Why do you want to povalsize Sushi?!
Look at all the marks he's made! That cat climbs everywhere! He ruins everything!
POK
And I don't even know how he can make such dark marks!
BOING
BOING
BOING
POK
POK
Ooohhh, this time I'm pulverizing you!
Wait! Wait! Because afterwards I won't remember anymore!
?!
Seeing as how that's his new record!
...
HUMF
SKRR

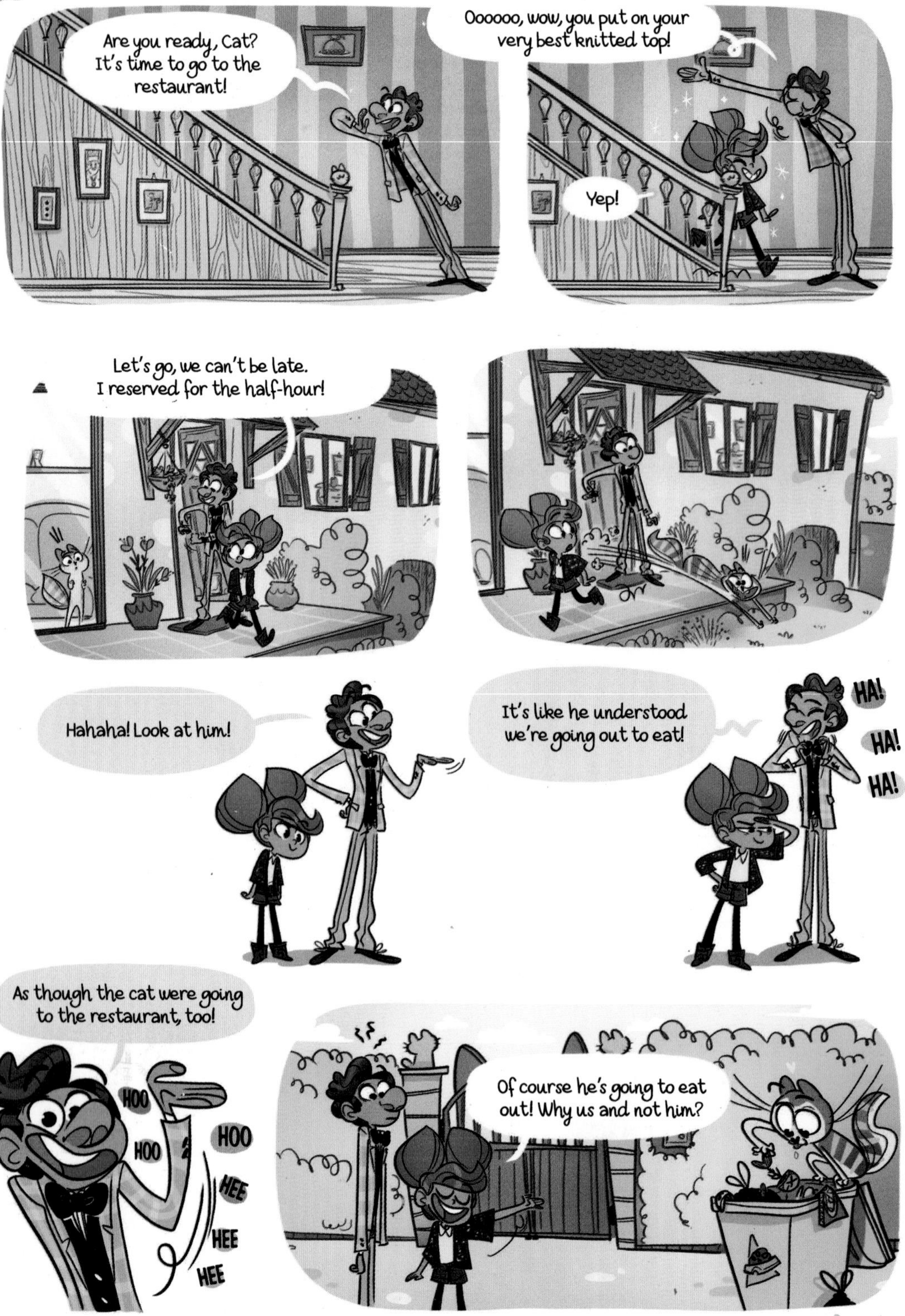
Are you ready, Cat? It's time to go to the restaurant!
Oooooo, wow, you put on your very best knitted top!
Yep!
Let's go, we can't be late. I reserved for the half-hour!
Hahaha! Look at him!
It's like he understood we're going out to eat!
HA! HA! HA!
As though the cat were going to the restaurant, too!
HOO HOO HOO HEE HEE HEE
Of course he's going to eat out! Why us and not him?

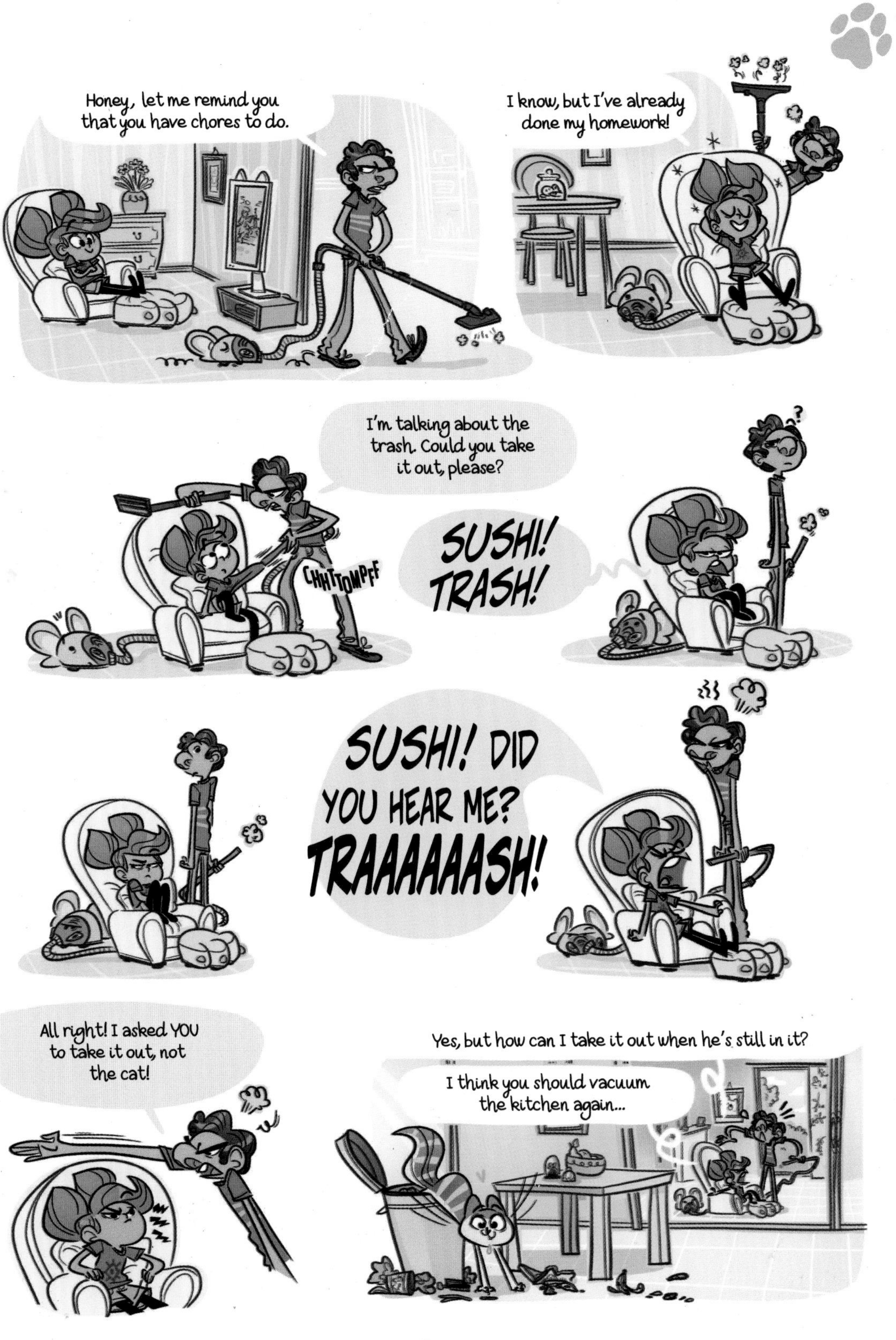

Honey, let me remind you that you have chores to do.
I know, but I've already done my homework!
I'm talking about the trash. Could you take it out, please?
CHHTTOMPFF
SUSHI! TRASH!
SUSHI! DID YOU HEAR ME? TRAAAAAASH!
All right! I asked YOU to take it out, not the cat!
Yes, but how can I take it out when he's still in it?
I think you should vacuum the kitchen again...

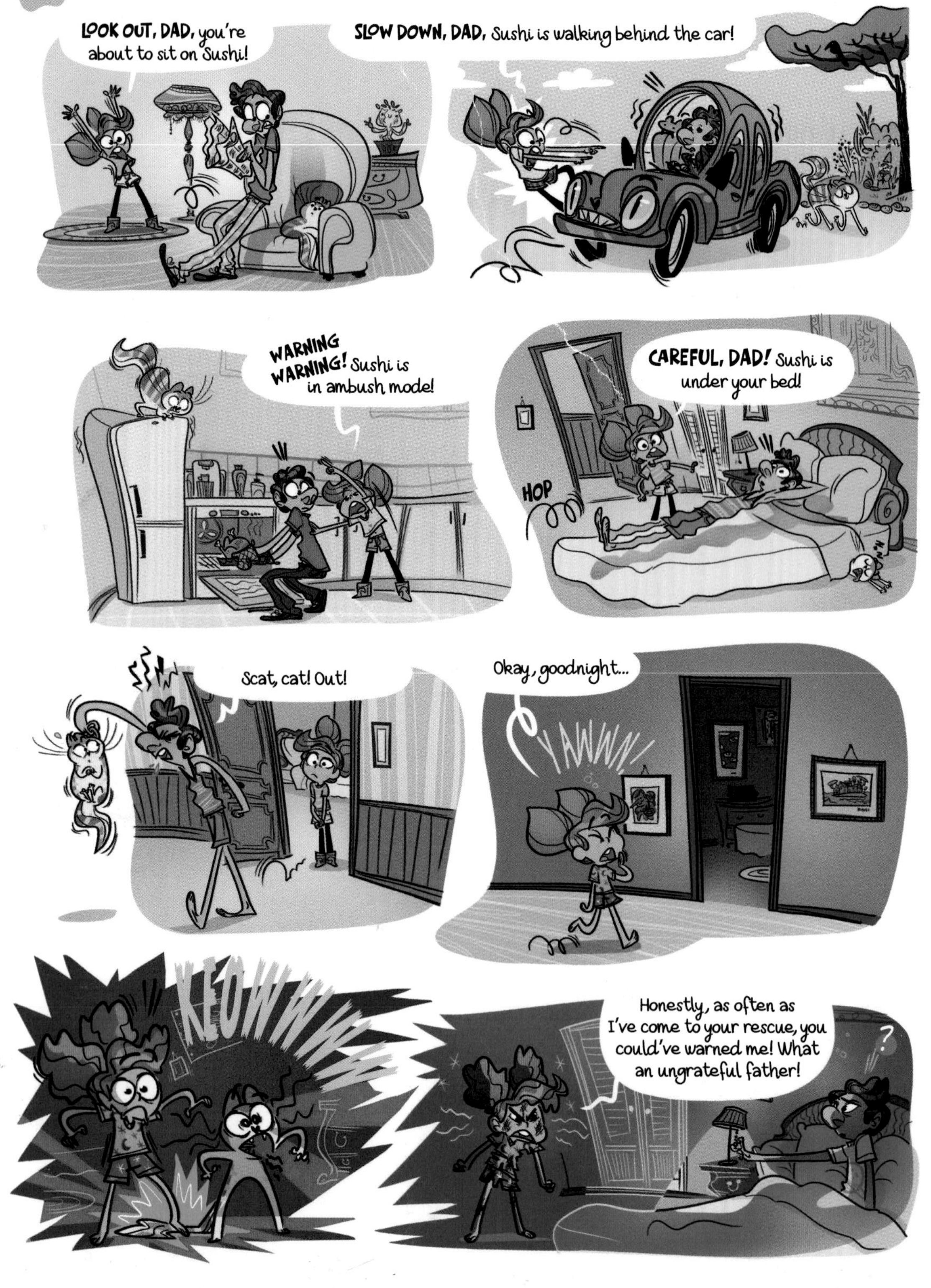
LOOK OUT, DAD, you're about to sit on Sushi!
SLOW DOWN, DAD, Sushi is walking behind the car!
WARNING WARNING! Sushi is in ambush mode!
CAREFUL, DAD! Sushi is under your bed!
HOP
Scat, cat! Out!
Okay, goodnight...
YAWWN!
KEOWWWW
Honestly, as often as I've come to your rescue, you could've warned me! What an ungrateful father!
?

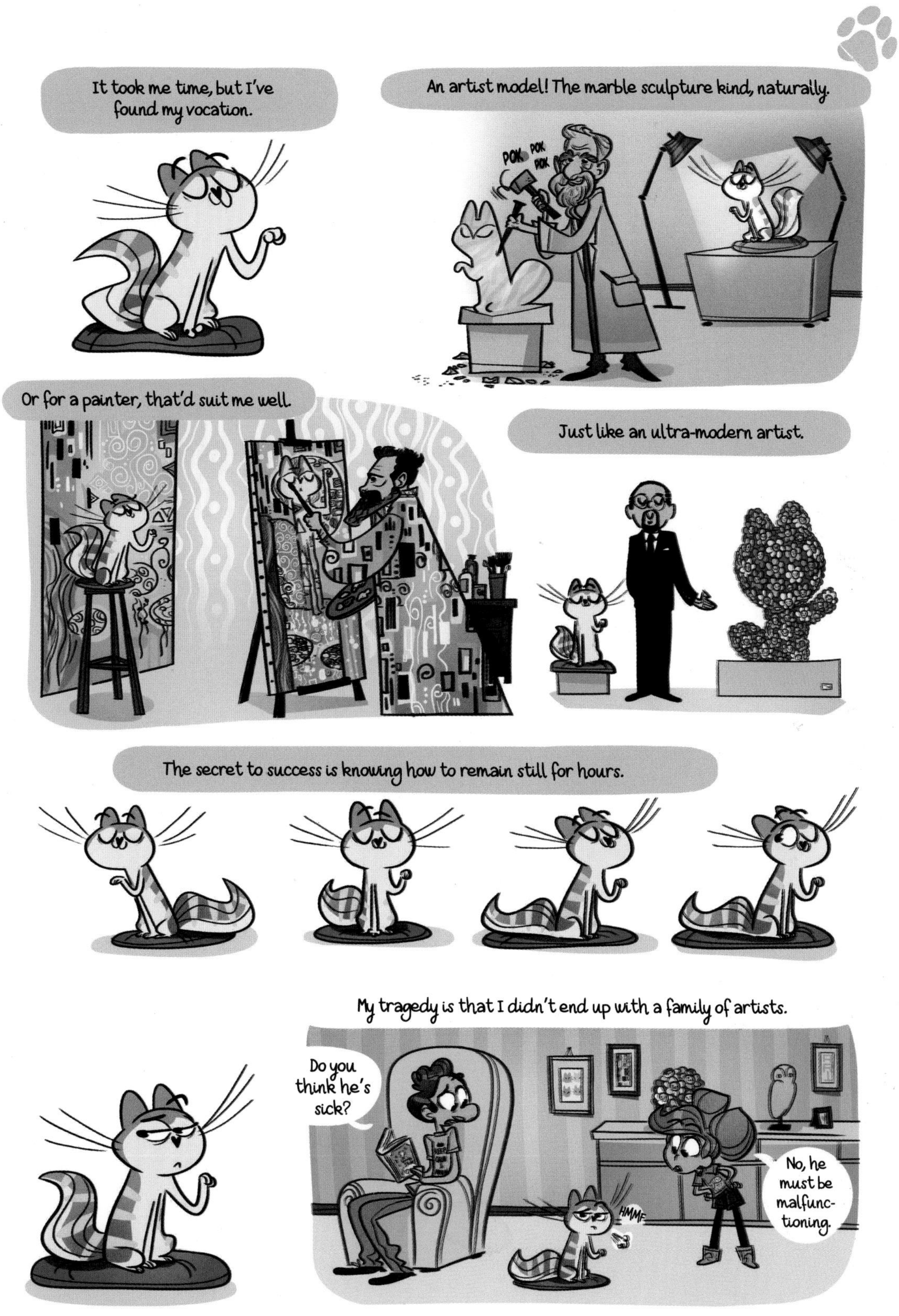
It took me time, but I've found my vocation.
An artist model! The marble sculpture kind, naturally.
POK POK POK
Or for a painter, that'd suit me well.
Just like an ultra-modern artist.
The secret to success is knowing how to remain still for hours.
My tragedy is that I didn't end up with a family of artists.
Do you think he's sick?
HMMF
No, he must be malfunctioning.

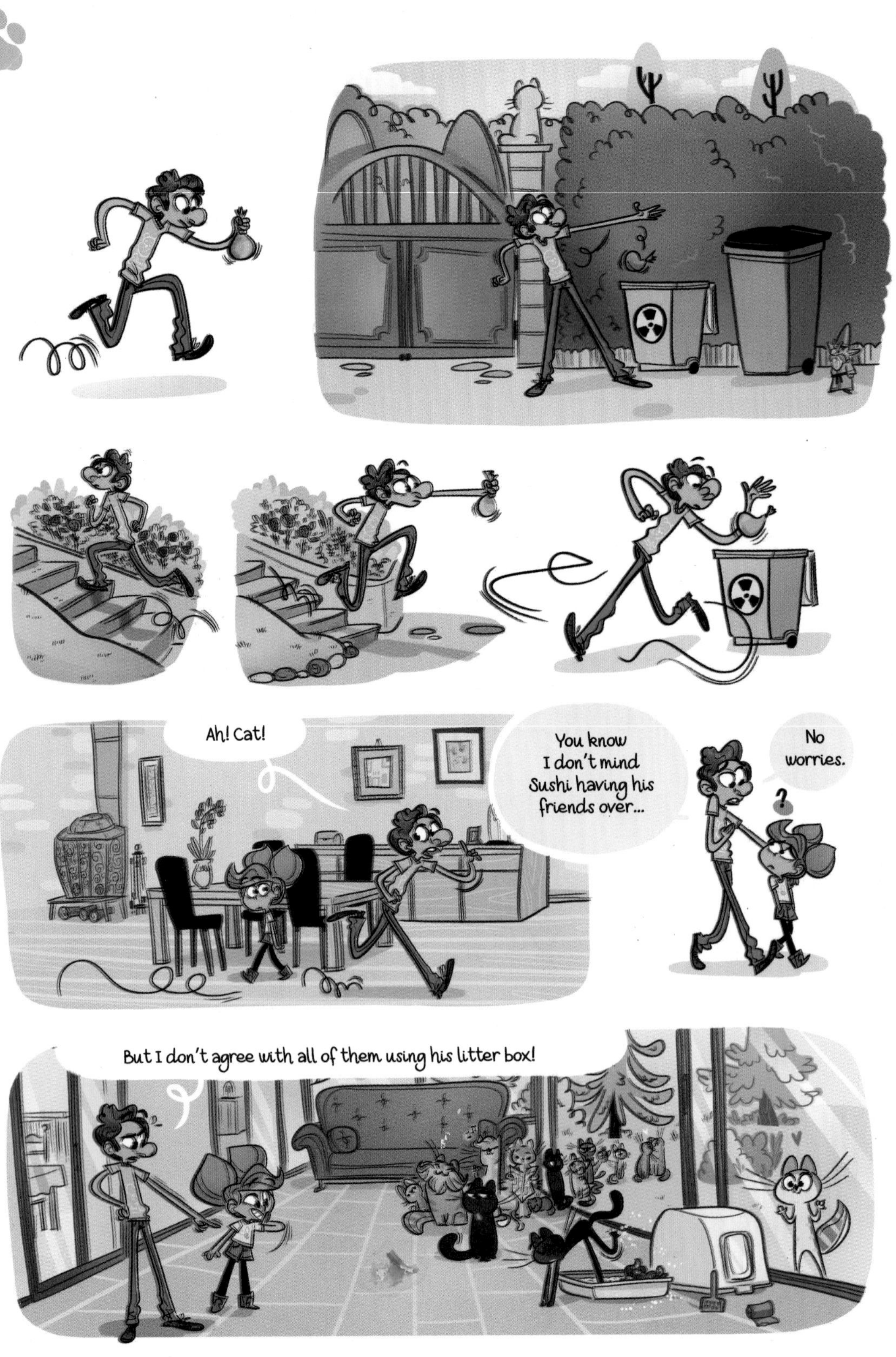
Ah! Cat!
You know I don't mind Sushi having his friends over...
No worries.
?
But I don't agree with all of them using his litter box!

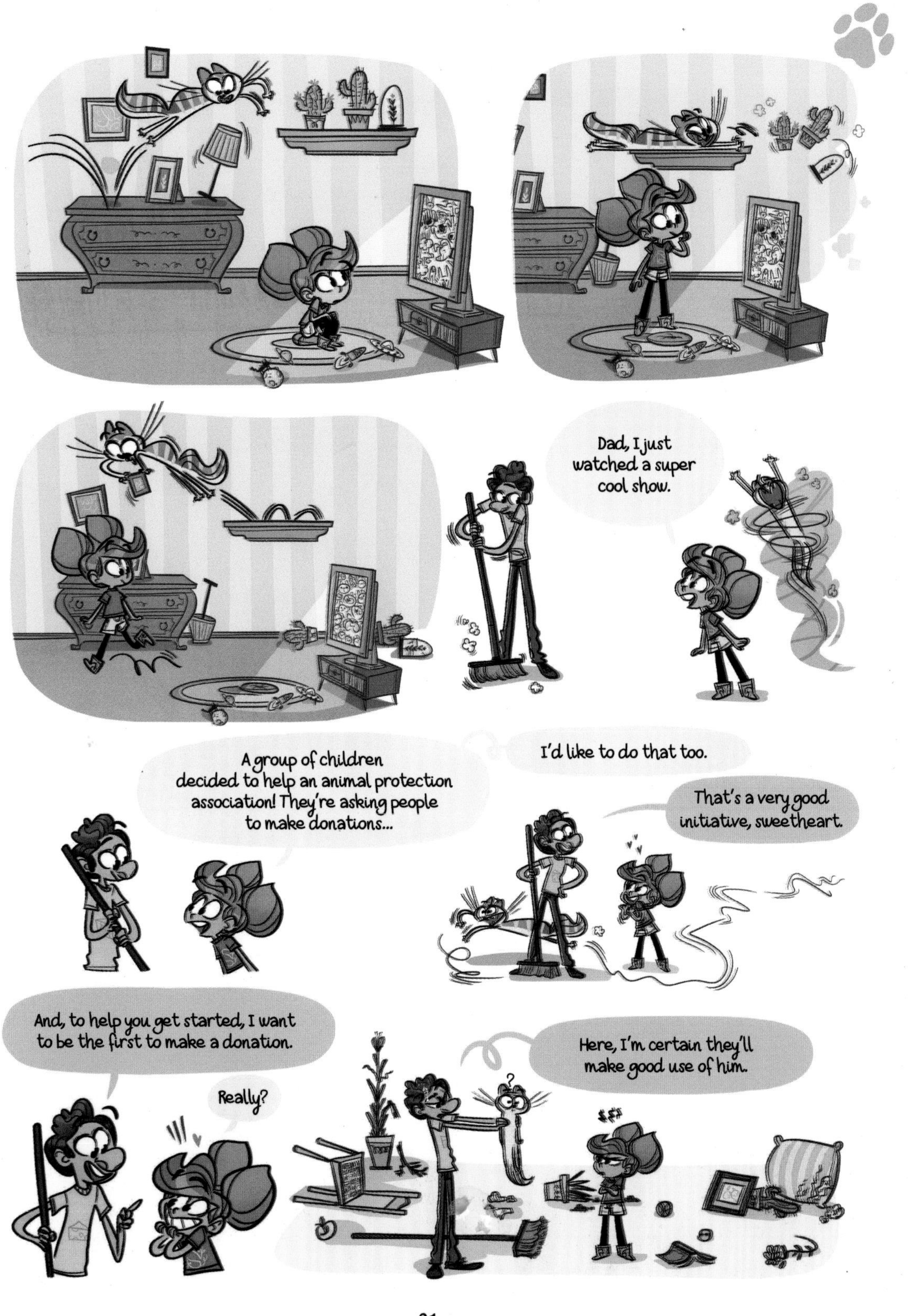
Dad, I just watched a super cool show.
A group of children decided to help an animal protection association! They're asking people to make donations...
I'd like to do that too.
That's a very good initiative, sweetheart.
And, to help you get started, I want to be the first to make a donation.
Really?
Here, I'm certain they'll make good use of him.

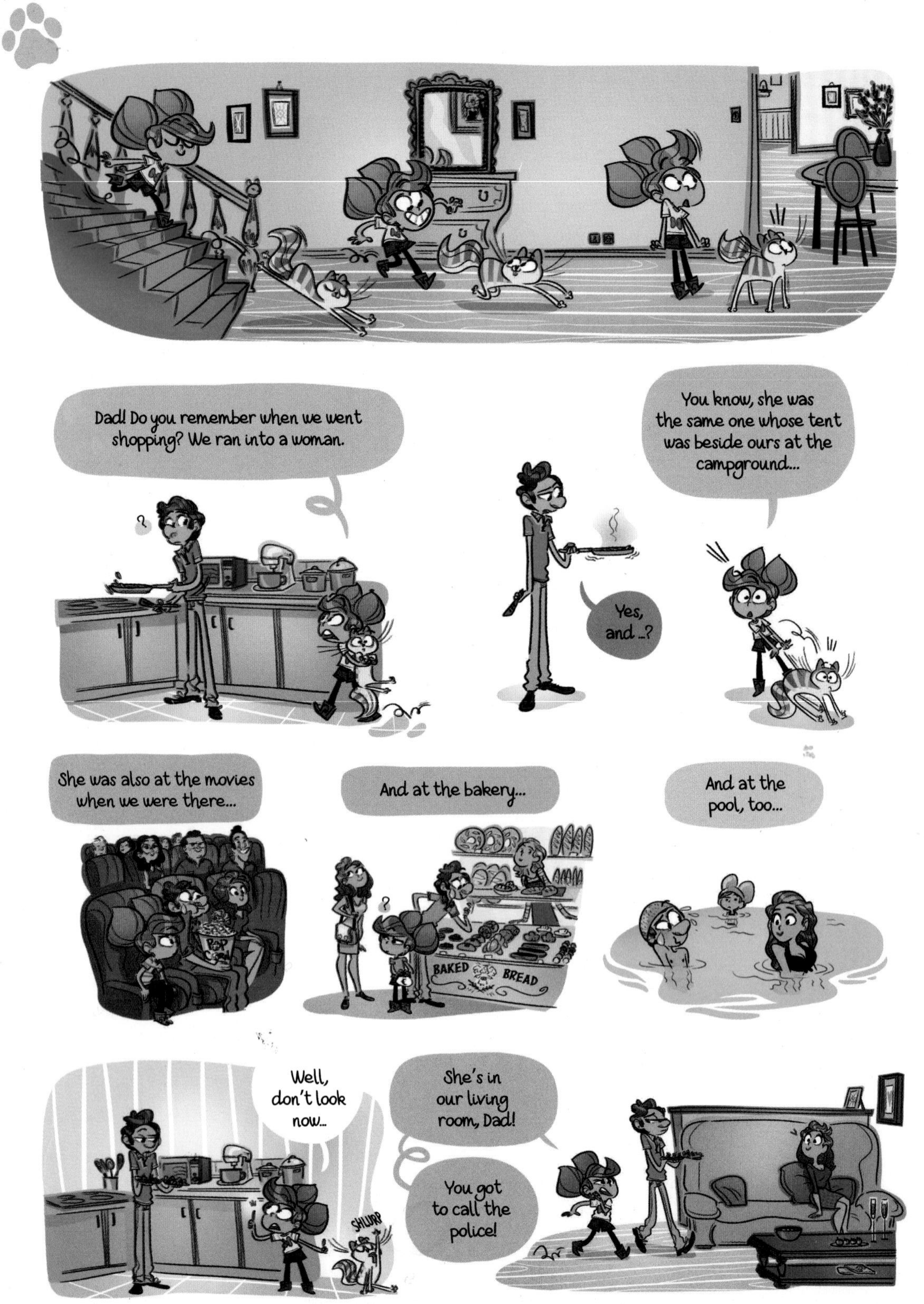

Dad! Do you remember when we went shopping? We ran into a woman.
Yes, and ...?
You know, she was the same one whose tent was beside ours at the campground...
She was also at the movies when we were there...
POP CORN
And at the bakery...
BAKED BREAD
And at the pool, too...
Well, don't look now...
SHLURP
She's in our living room, Dad!
You got to call the police!

So, what do you think of SAMANTHA? Did you notice she's really kind with kids?

She loves music a lot...

...cooks better than a master class top chef...

..has culture that'd make a library turn green... hee hee...

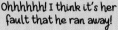

She even helped us find Sushi when he did that hiding at the campground number again!

Ohhhhhh! I think it's her fault that he ran away!

SNIIIFF

From giving him lots of slimy hugs with her sunscreen slathered cheeks.

Ahhhh, you've opened my eyes! It's her fault I almost lost my kitty cat at that campground.

Uhh... well, no... I don't think so...

YUCK!

I hope I never see her again! NE-VER!

Okay, Sam, don't be mad at me, but we'll do the official introductions some other day...

PPRRRRR

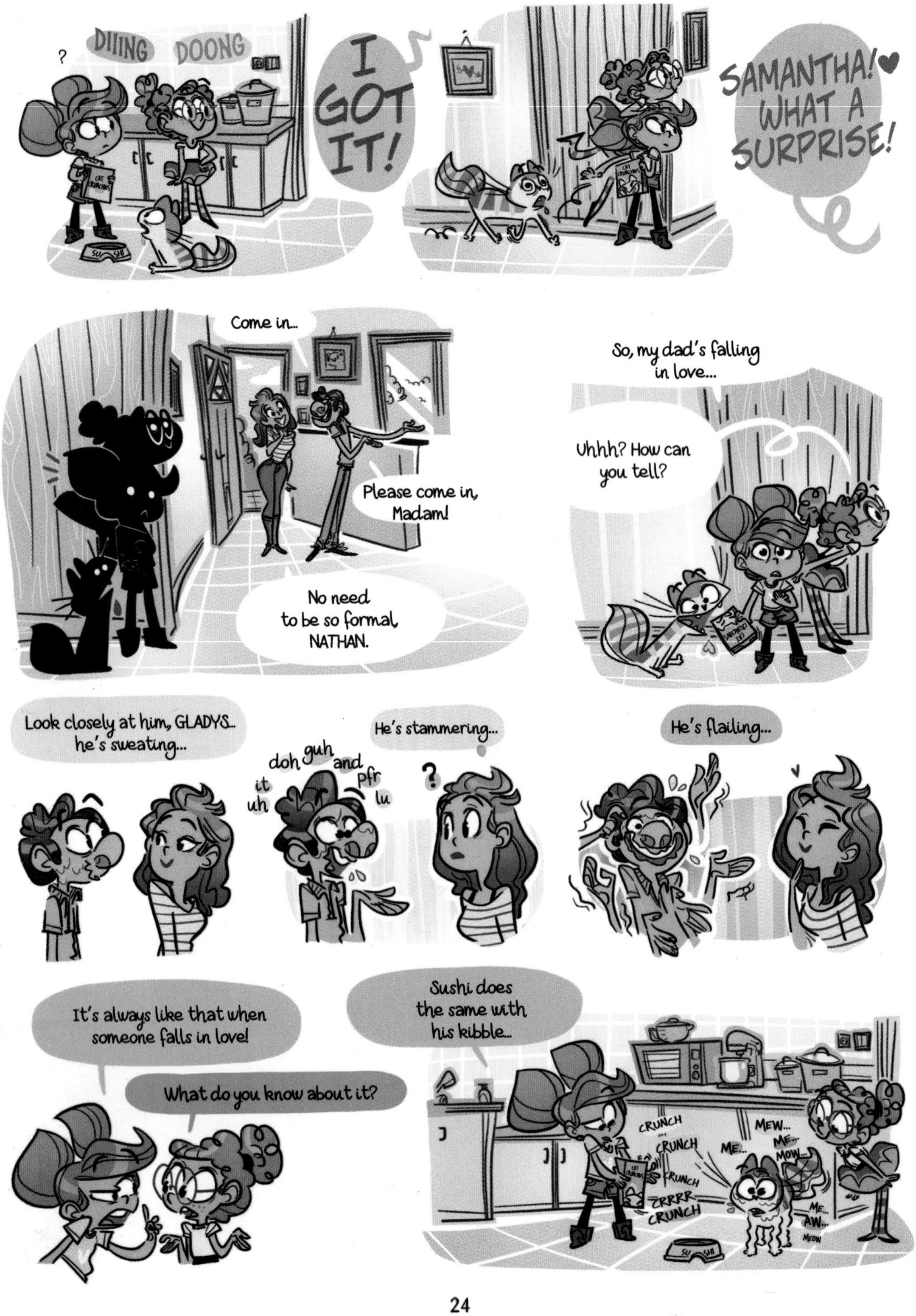
?
DIIING DOONG
CAT CRUNCHIES
SU SHI
I GOT IT!
SAMANTHA! WHAT A SURPRISE!
Come in...
Please come in, Madam!
No need to be so formal, NATHAN.
So, my dad's falling in love...
Uhhh? How can you tell?
Look closely at him, GLADYS... he's sweating...
He's stammering...
it uh doh guh and pfr lu
?
He's flailing...
It's always like that when someone falls in love!
What do you know about it?
Sushi does the same with his kibble...
CRUNCH CRUNCH CRUNCH CRRRR CRUNCH
MEW... ME... MOW... ME... ME... AW... MEOW

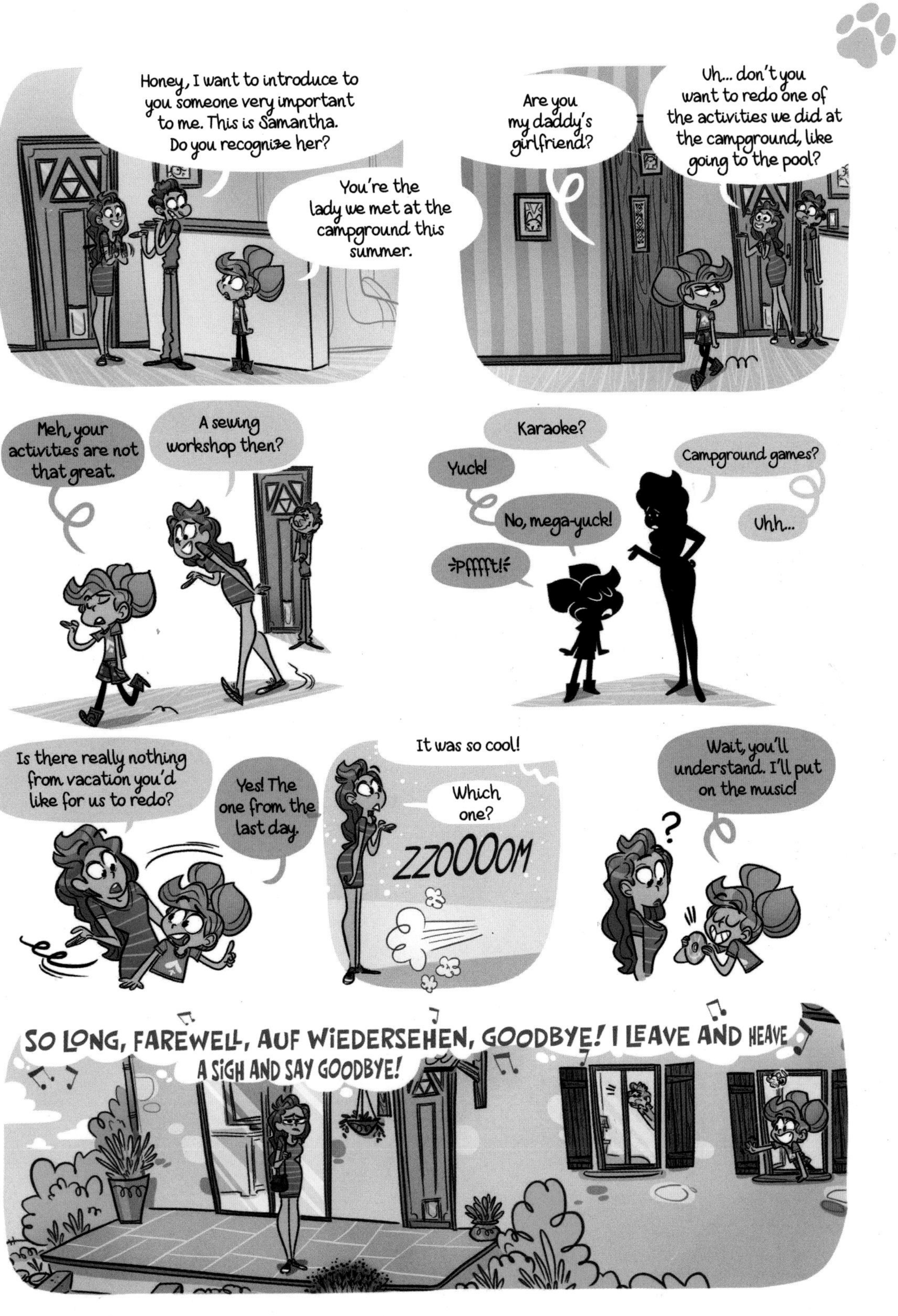
Honey, I want to introduce to you someone very important to me. This is Samantha. Do you recognize her?
You're the lady we met at the campground this summer.
Are you my daddy's girlfriend?
Uh... don't you want to redo one of the activities we did at the campground, like going to the pool?
Meh, your activities are not that great.
A sewing workshop then?
Karaoke?
Yuck!
Campground games?
No, mega-yuck!
Uhh...
Pfffft!
Is there really nothing from vacation you'd like for us to redo?
Yes! The one from the last day.
It was so cool!
Which one?
ZZOOOOM
Wait, you'll understand. I'll put on the music!
?
SO LONG, FAREWELL, AUF WIEDERSEHEN, GOODBYE! I LEAVE AND HEAVE A SIGH AND SAY GOODBYE!

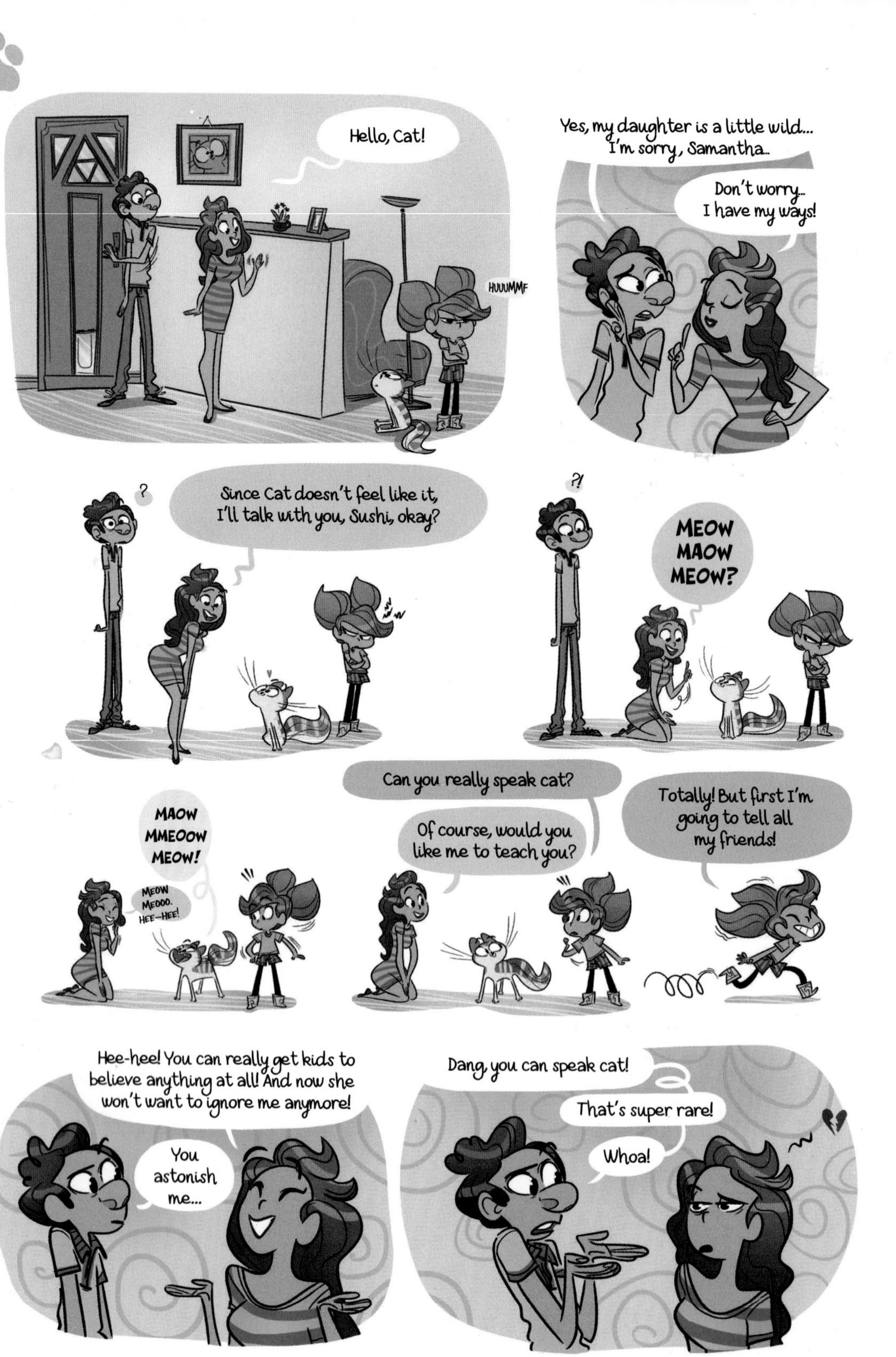
Hello, Cat!
HUUUMMF
Yes, my daughter is a little wild... I'm sorry, Samantha...
Don't worry... I have my ways!
?
Since Cat doesn't feel like it, I'll talk with you, Sushi, okay?
?!
MEOW MAOW MEOW?
MAOW MMEOOW MEOW!
MEOW MEOOO. HEE-HEE!
Can you really speak cat?
Of course, would you like me to teach you?
Totally! But first I'm going to tell all my friends!
Hee-hee! You can really get kids to believe anything at all! And now she won't want to ignore me anymore!
You astonish me...
Dang, you can speak cat!
That's super rare!
Whoa!

Samantha, honey, there's one thing I've got to admit to you...

...so you never have anything to blame me for...

When we looked after the neighbor's birds, it was a nightmare! Sushi had only one desire...

TWEEEEE
PEEEP
TWEEEE
TWEE
PIP
TWEE

...to devour them!

When my coworker DAVID entrusted me with his goldfish, the poor thing almost drowned... Sushi terrorized it so much!

My AUNT PHILOMENA left her hamster with me. I had to lock it in a safe, so Sushi didn't turn it into hash!

KEEE
KWEEEE
KWEEEE
KWEEEE

The neighbor also left his two rabbits with us. Those rodents were a hair from getting gnawed to death.

Frankly, Samantha, this just isn't sensible.

I'd be glad to babysit him for the weekend, but it's at your own risk!

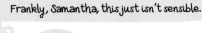

Why don't you simply tell me you don't want to babysit my son rather than invent bogus stories for me?!

27

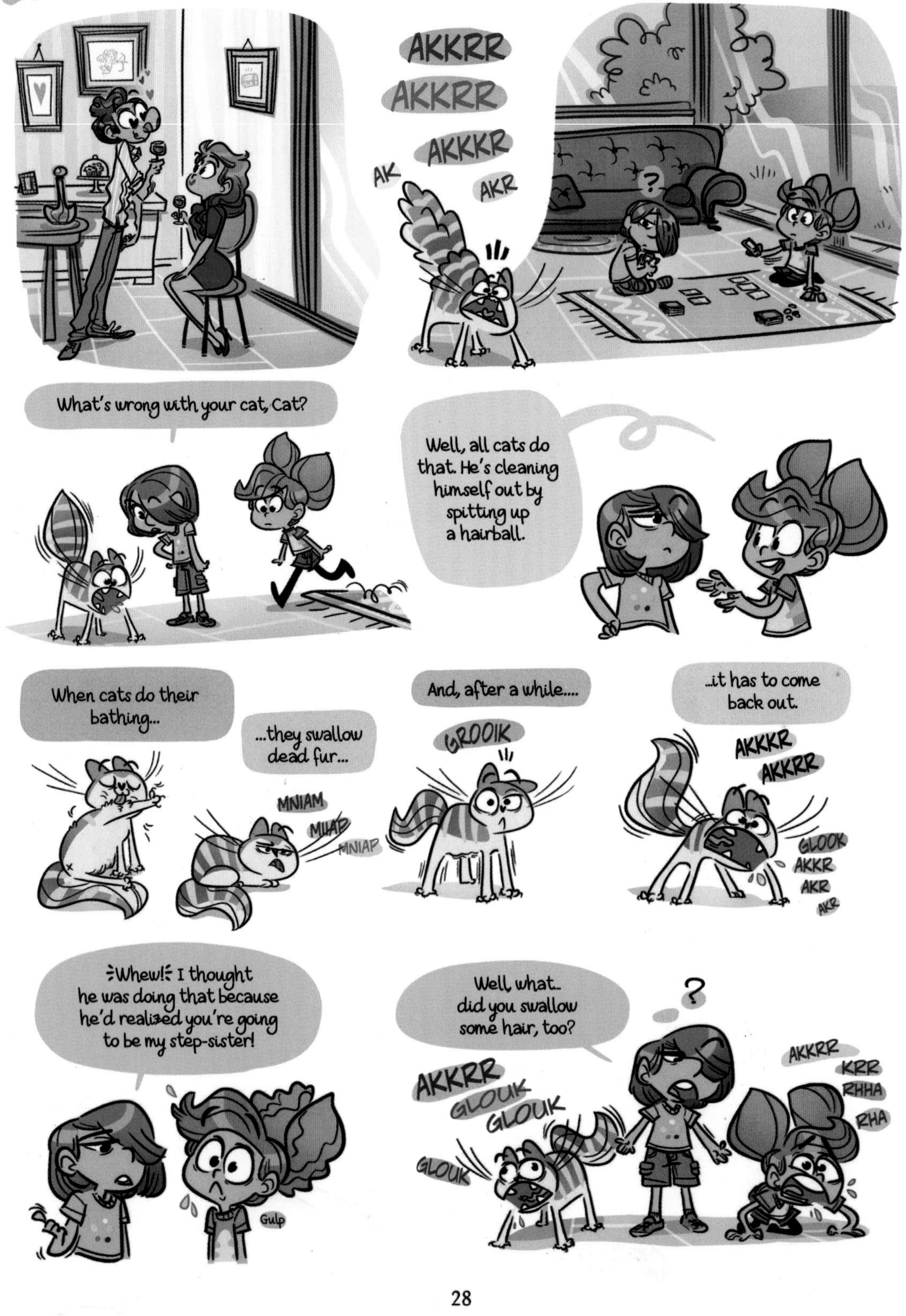
AKKRR
AKKRR
AKKKR
AK
AKR
What's wrong with your cat, Cat?
Well, all cats do that. He's cleaning himself out by spitting up a hairball.
When cats do their bathing...
...they swallow dead fur...
MNIAM
MIIAP
MNIAP
And, after a while....
GROOIK
...it has to come back out.
AKKKR
AKKRR
GLOOK
AKKR
AKR
AKR
Whew! I thought he was doing that because he'd realized you're going to be my step-sister!
Gulp
Well, what... did you swallow some hair, too?
AKKRR
GLOUK
GLOUK
GLOUK
AKKRR
KRR
RHHA
RHA

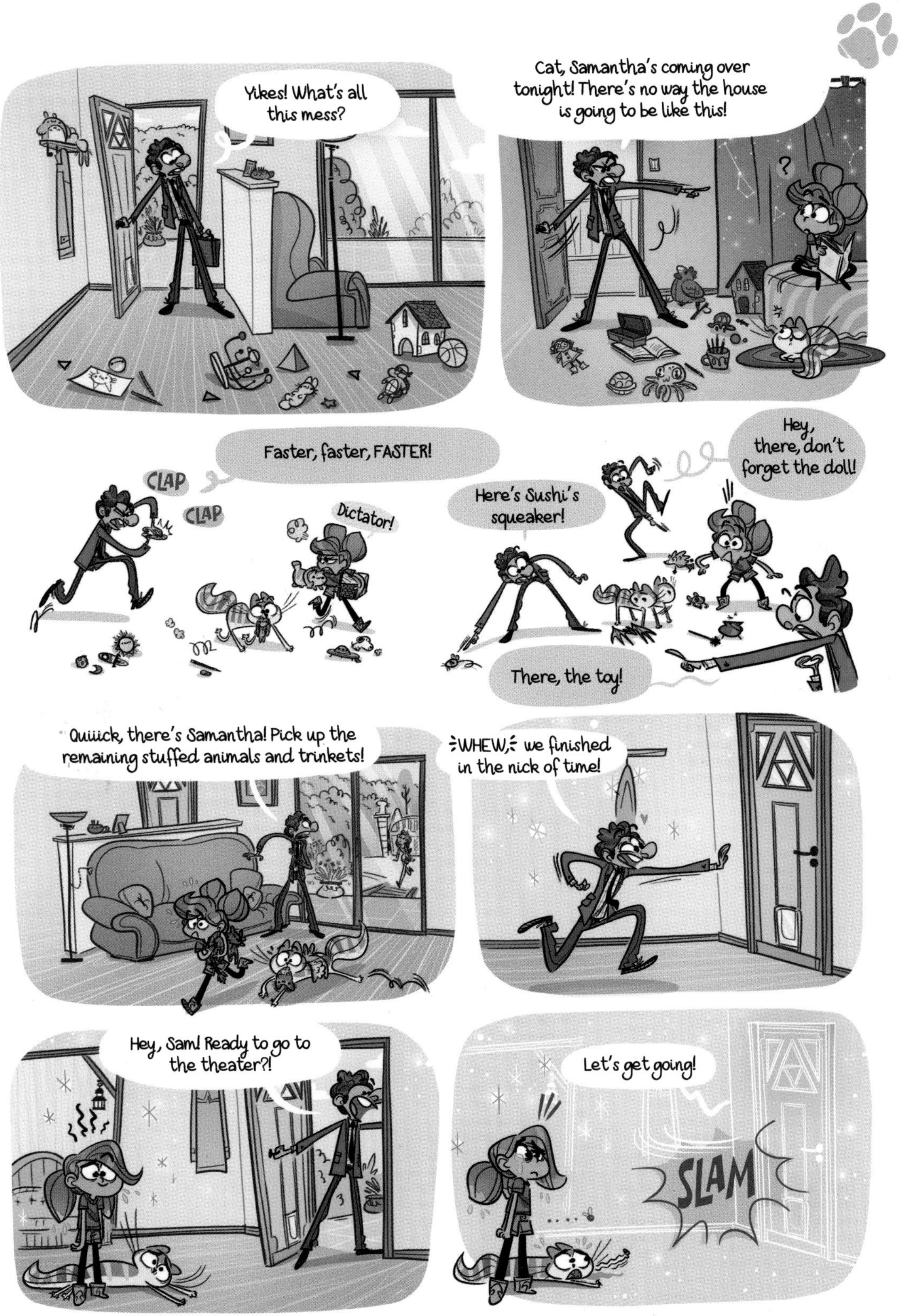

Yikes! What's all this mess?
Cat, Samantha's coming over tonight! There's no way the house is going to be like this!
?
Faster, faster, FASTER!
CLAP
CLAP
Dictator!
Here's Sushi's squeaker!
Hey, there, don't forget the doll!
There, the toy!
Quiiick, there's Samantha! Pick up the remaining stuffed animals and trinkets!
WHEW, we finished in the nick of time!
Hey, Sam! Ready to go to the theater?!
Let's get going!
SLAM

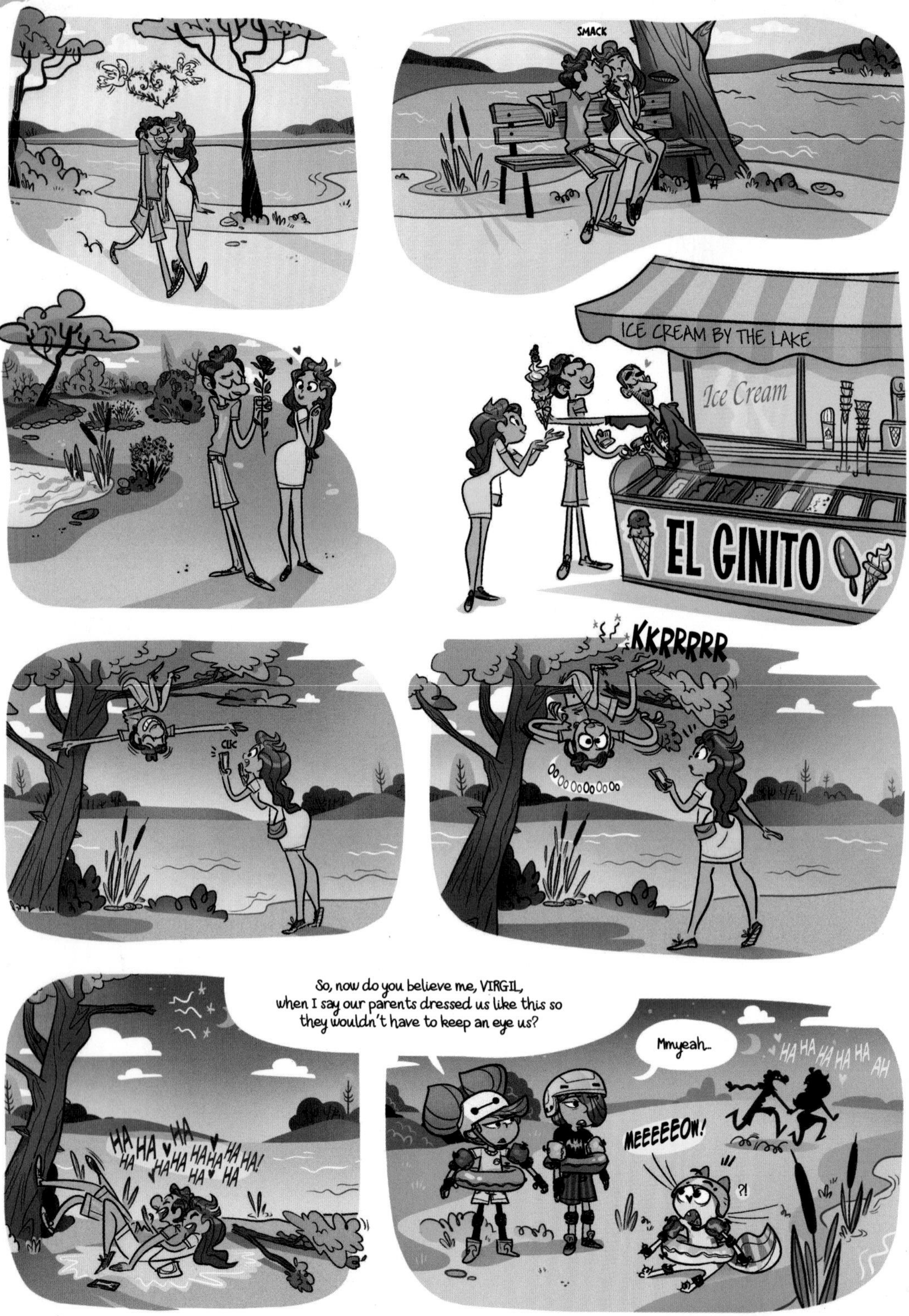
SMACK
ICE CREAM BY THE LAKE
Ice Cream
EL GINITO
CLIC
KKRRRRR
OOOOOOOOOOO
So, now do you believe me, VIRGIL,
when I say our parents dressed us like this so
they wouldn't have to keep an eye us?
HA HA HA HA HAHA HA HA! HA HA HA
Mmyeah...
HA HA HA HA HA HA AH
MEEEEEOW!
?!

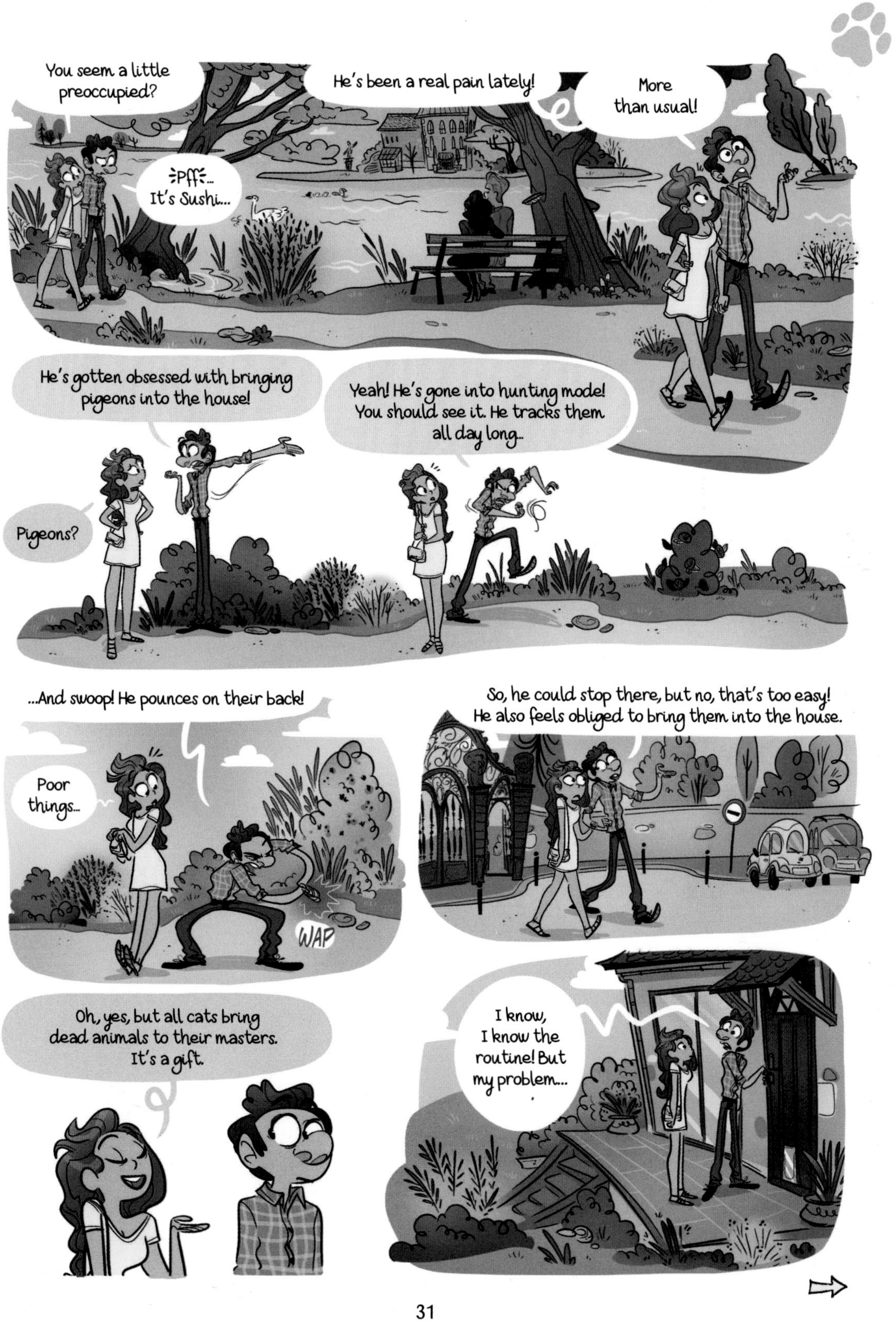

You seem a little preoccupied?
Pff... It's Sushi...
He's been a real pain lately!
More than usual!
He's gotten obsessed with bringing pigeons into the house!
Pigeons?
Yeah! He's gone into hunting mode! You should see it. He tracks them all day long...
...And swoop! He pounces on their back!
Poor things...
WAP
So, he could stop there, but no, that's too easy! He also feels obliged to bring them into the house.
Oh, yes, but all cats bring dead animals to their masters. It's a gift.
I know, I know the routine! But my problem...

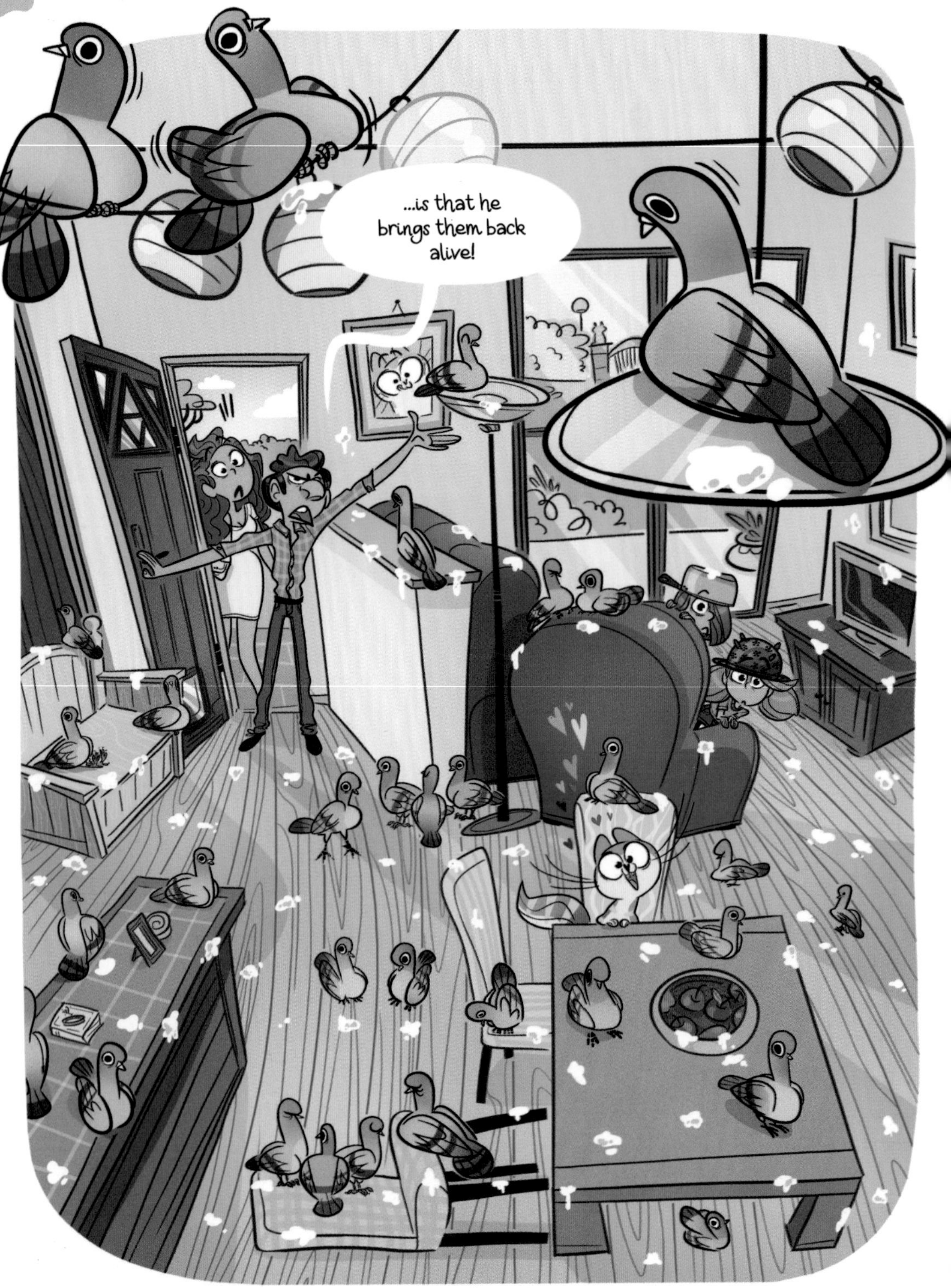
...is that he brings them back alive!

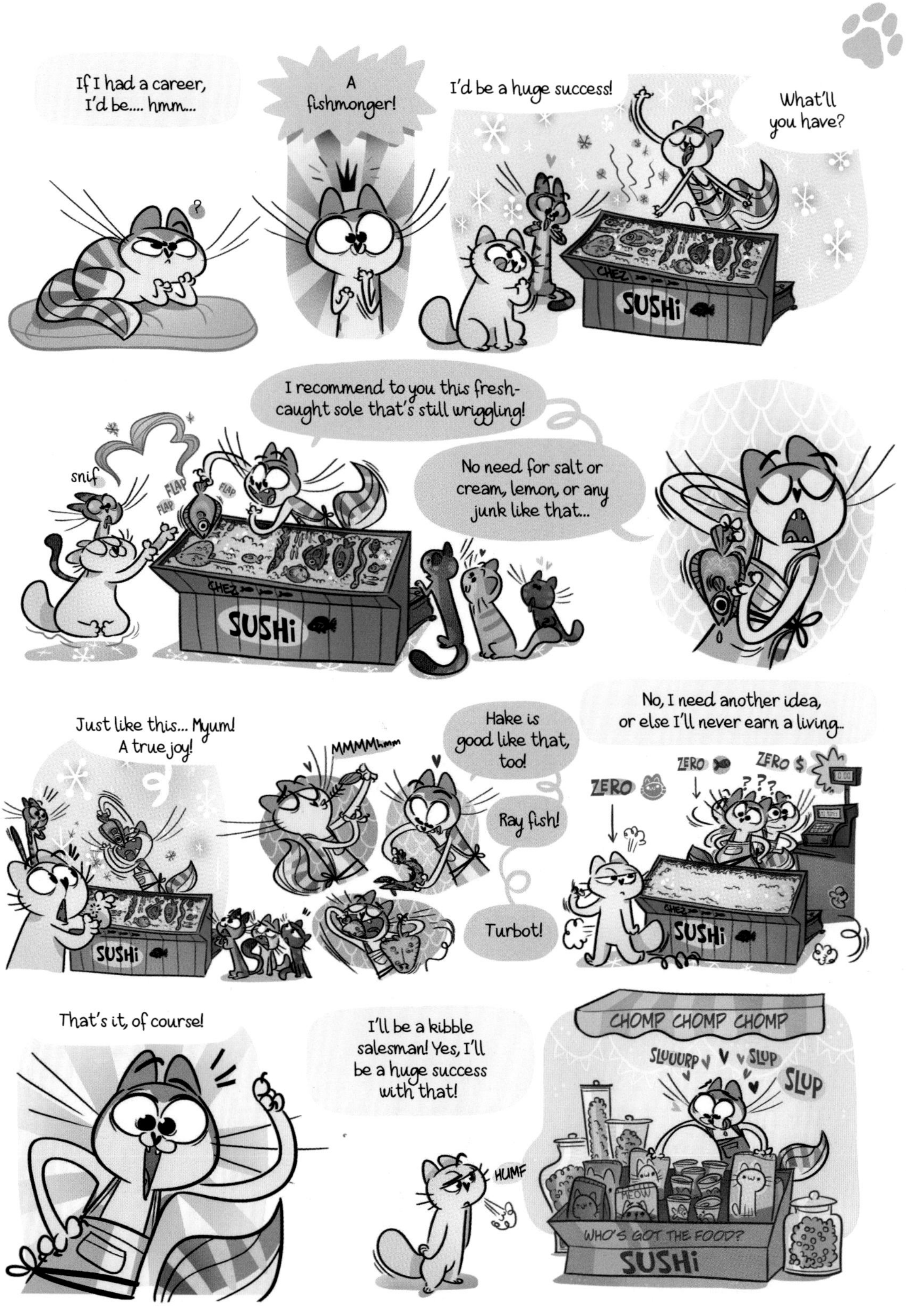
If I had a career,
I'd be.... hmm...
A fishmonger!
I'd be a huge success!
What'll you have?
CHEZ
SUSHi
I recommend to you this fresh-caught sole that's still wriggling!
snif
FLAP
FLAP
FLAP
No need for salt or cream, lemon, or any junk like that...
Just like this... Myum!
A true joy!
MMMMhmm
Hake is good like that, too!
Ray fish!
Turbot!
No, I need another idea,
or else I'll never earn a living..
ZERO
ZERO
ZERO $
? ? ?
That's it, of course!
I'll be a kibble salesman! Yes, I'll be a huge success with that!
CHOMP CHOMP CHOMP
SLUUURP
SLUP
SLUP
HUMF
MEOW
WHO'S GOT THE FOOD?
SUSHi

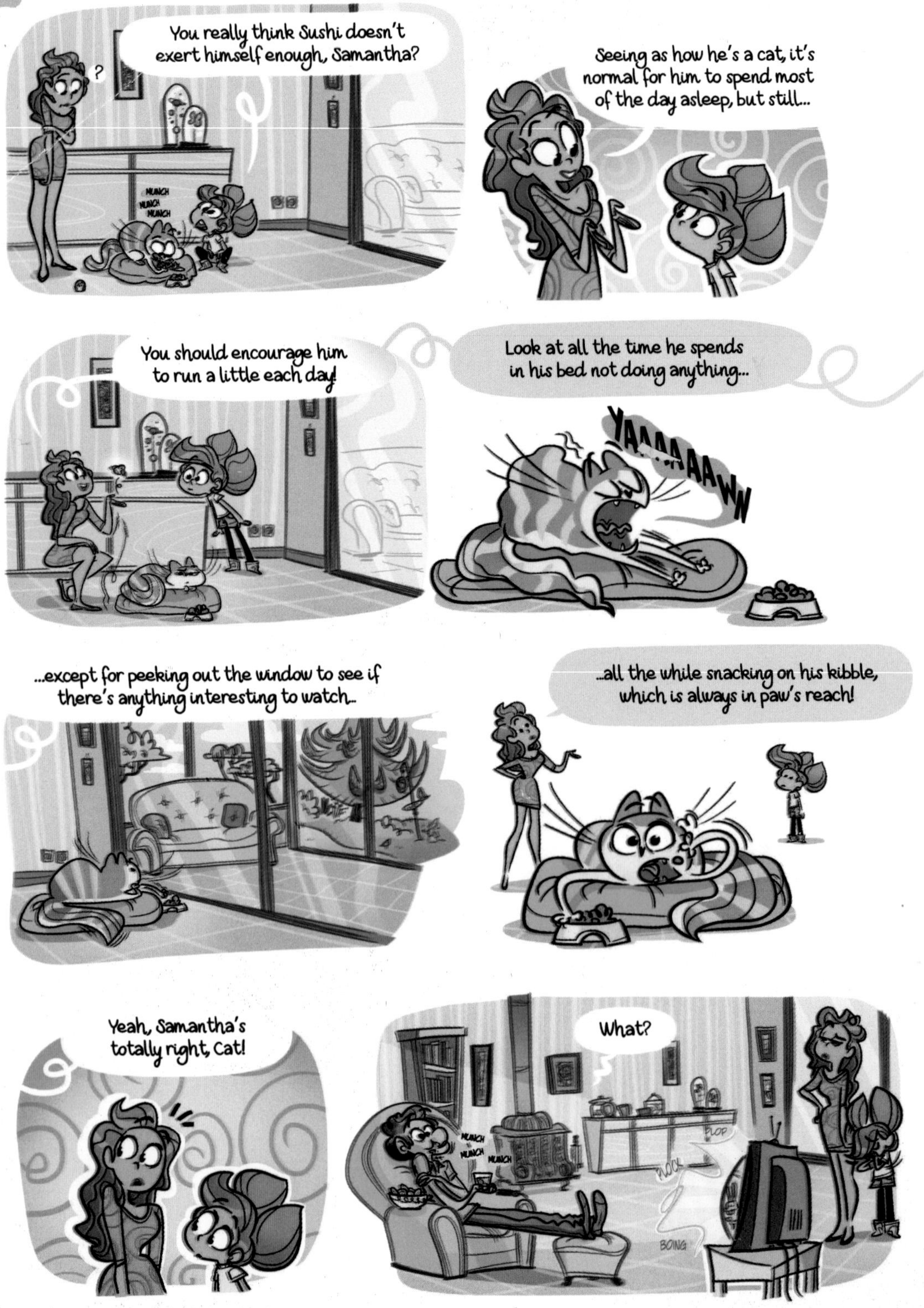
You really think Sushi doesn't exert himself enough, Samantha?
?
MUNCH
MUNCH
MUNCH
Seeing as how he's a cat, it's normal for him to spend most of the day asleep, but still...
You should encourage him to run a little each day!
Look at all the time he spends in his bed not doing anything...
YAAAAAAAWN
...except for peeking out the window to see if there's anything interesting to watch...
...all the while snacking on his kibble, which is always in paw's reach!
Yeah, Samantha's totally right, Cat!
What?
MUNCH
MUNCH
MUNCH
FLOP
PLOCK
BOING

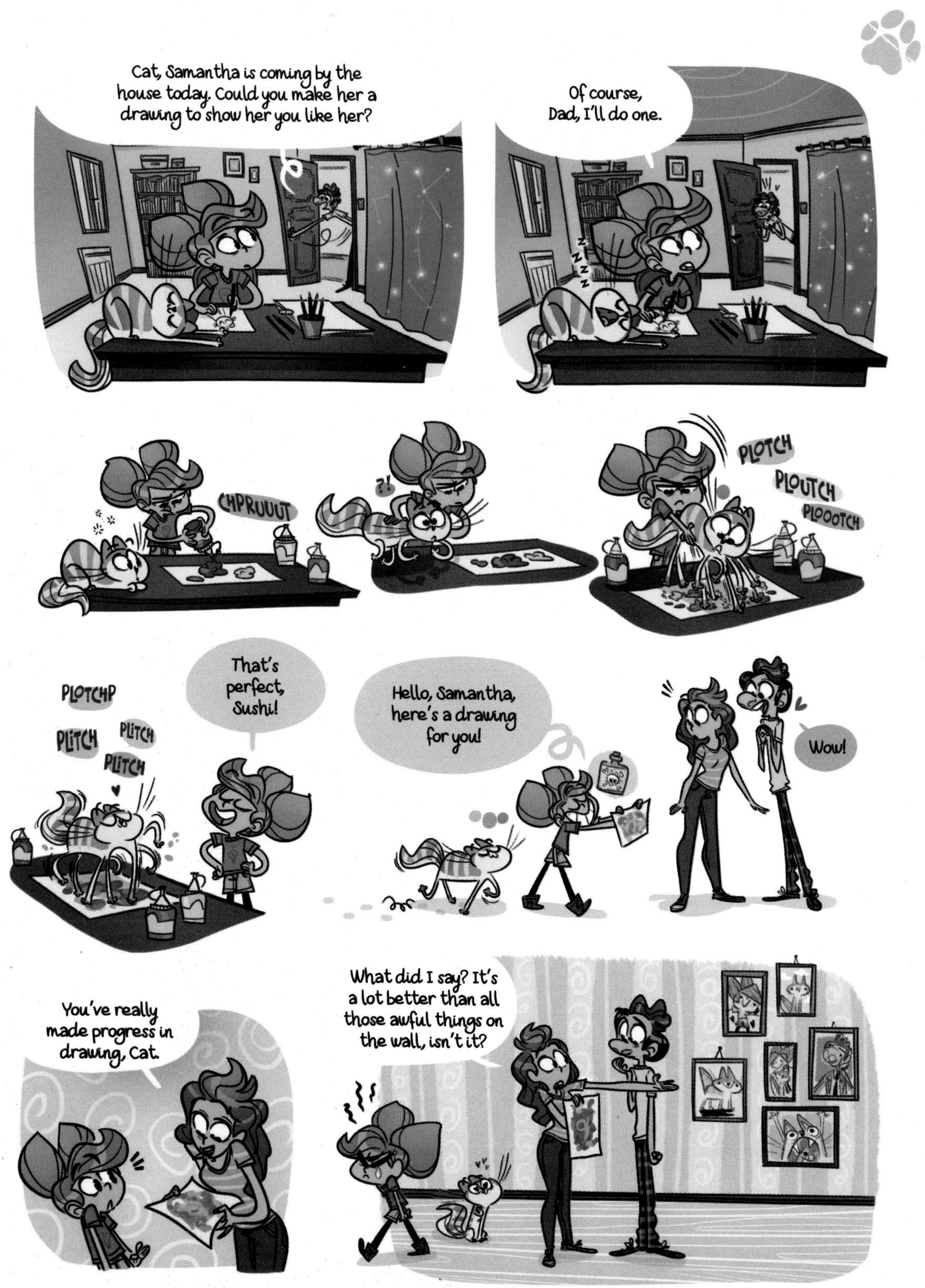
Cat, Samantha is coming by the house today. Could you make her a drawing to show her you like her?
Of course, Dad, I'll do one.
ZZZZ
CHPRUUUT
?!
PLOTCH
PLOUTCH
PLOOOTCH
PLOTCHP
PLITCH
PLITCH
PLITCH
That's perfect, Sushi!
Hello, Samantha, here's a drawing for you!
Wow!
You've really made progress in drawing, Cat.
What did I say? It's a lot better than all those awful things on the wall, isn't it?

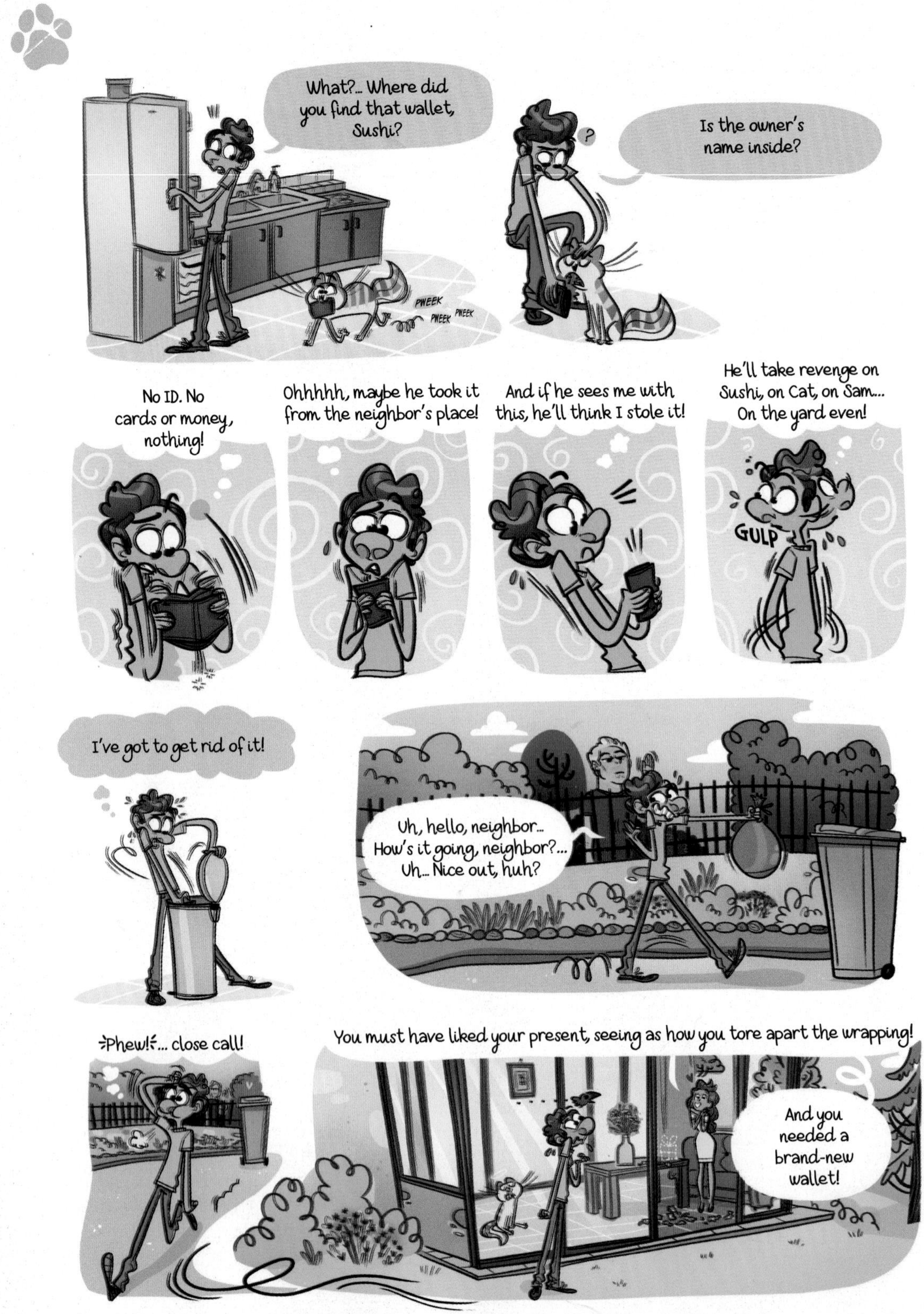
What?... Where did you find that wallet, Sushi?
PWEEK
PWEEK
PWEEK
Is the owner's name inside?
No ID. No cards or money, nothing!
Ohhhhh, maybe he took it from the neighbor's place!
And if he sees me with this, he'll think I stole it!
He'll take revenge on Sushi, on Cat, on Sam... On the yard even!
GULP
I've got to get rid of it!
Uh, hello, neighbor... How's it going, neighbor?... Uh... Nice out, huh?
Phew!... close call!
You must have liked your present, seeing as how you tore apart the wrapping!
And you needed a brand-new wallet!

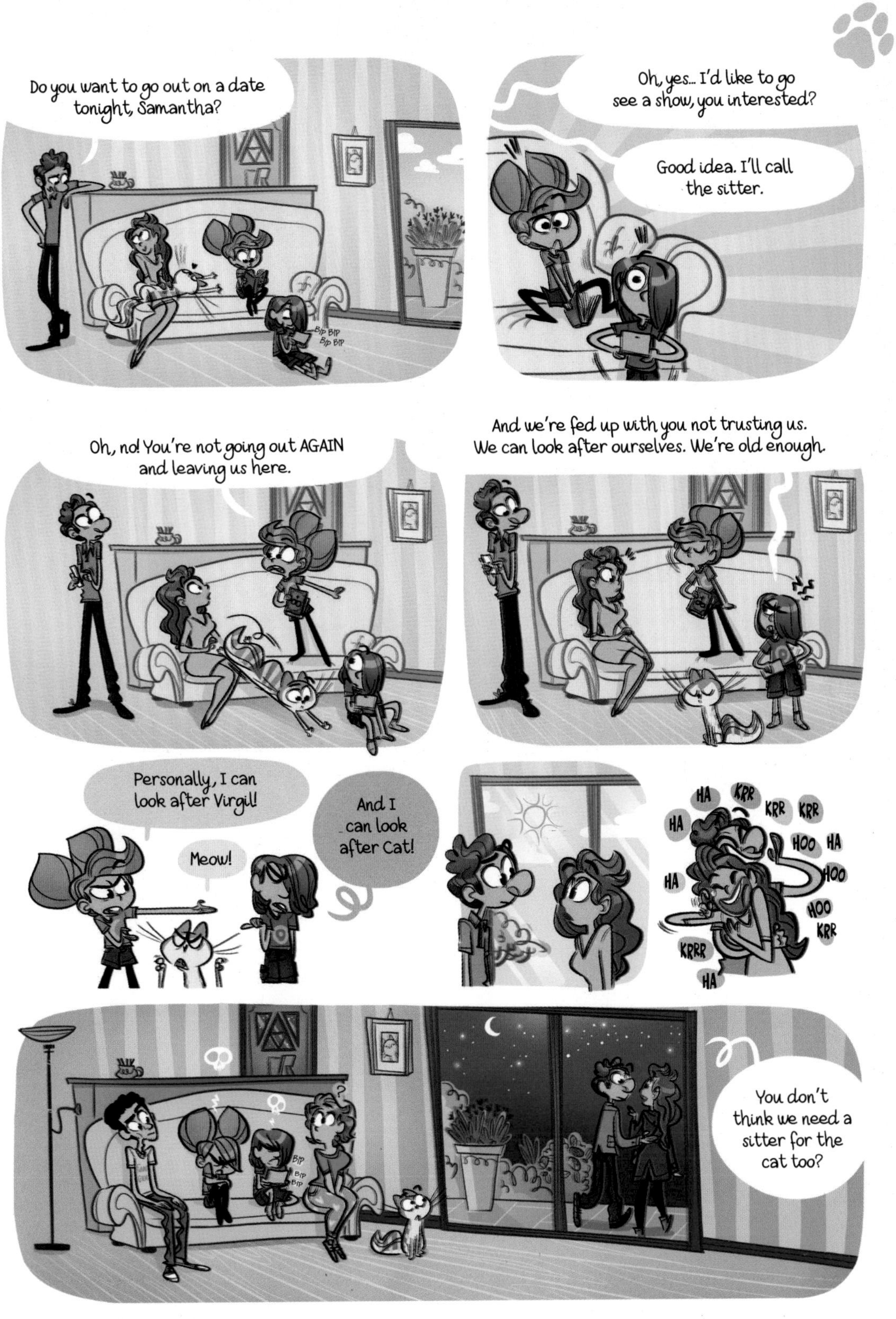

Do you want to go out on a date tonight, Samantha?
BIP BIP BIP BIP
Oh, yes... I'd like to go see a show, you interested?
Good idea. I'll call the sitter.
Oh, no! You're not going out AGAIN and leaving us here.
And we're fed up with you not trusting us. We can look after ourselves. We're old enough.
Personally, I can look after Virgil!
Meow!
And I can look after Cat!
HA KRR KRR KRR HA HOO HA HA HOO HOO KRR KRRR HA
BIP BIP BIP
You don't think we need a sitter for the cat too?

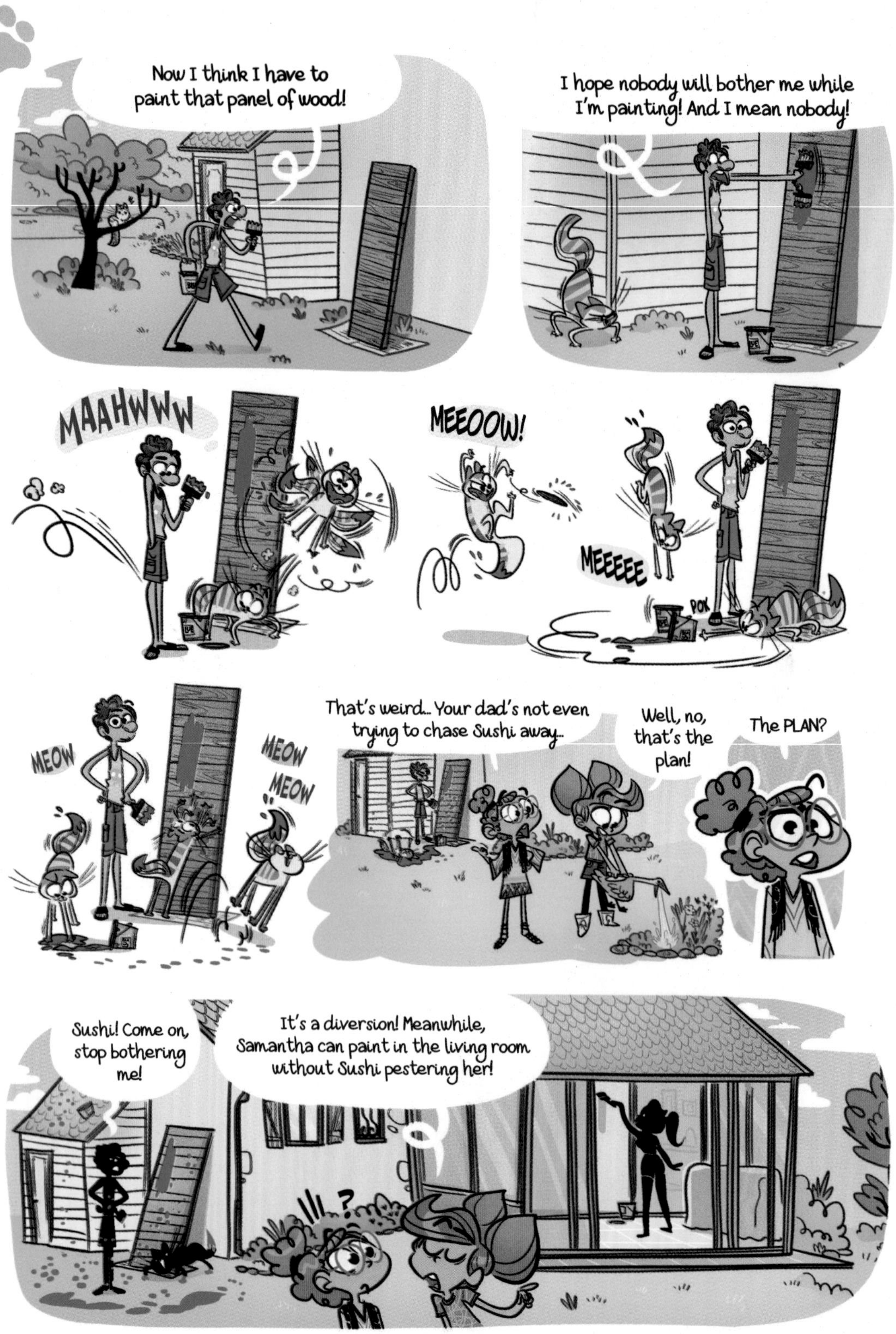
Now I think I have to paint that panel of wood!
I hope nobody will bother me while I'm painting! And I mean nobody!
MAAHWWW
MEEOOW!
MEEEEE
POK
MEOW
MEOW
MEOW
That's weird... Your dad's not even trying to chase Sushi away...
Well, no, that's the plan!
The PLAN?
Sushi! Come on, stop bothering me!
It's a diversion! Meanwhile, Samantha can paint in the living room without Sushi pestering her!

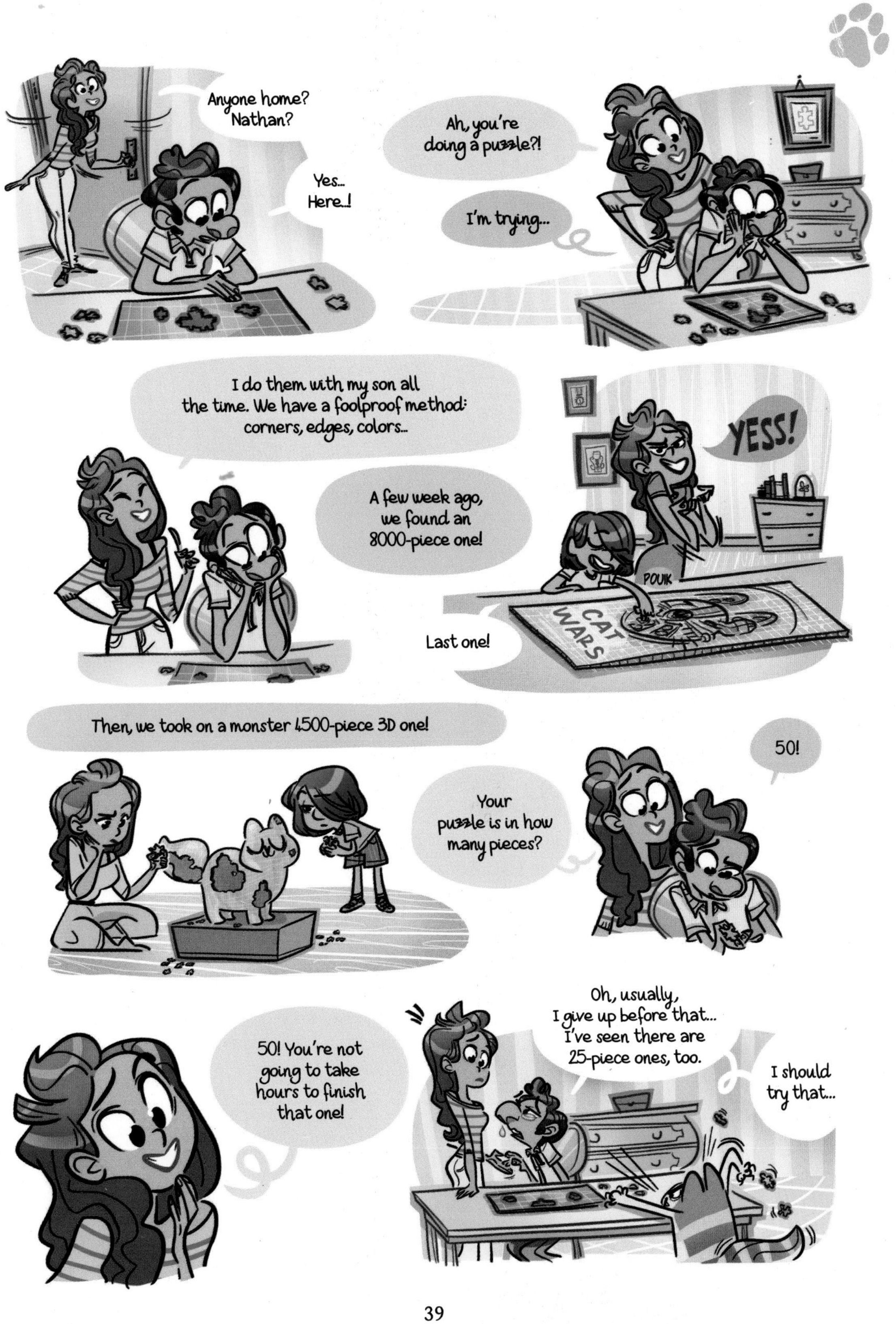
Anyone home? Nathan?
Yes... Here..!
Ah, you're doing a puzzle?!
I'm trying...
I do them with my son all the time. We have a foolproof method: corners, edges, colors...
A few week ago, we found an 8000-piece one!
YESS!
POUIK
CAT WARS
Last one!
Then, we took on a monster 4500-piece 3D one!
Your puzzle is in how many pieces?
50!
50! You're not going to take hours to finish that one!
Oh, usually, I give up before that... I've seen there are 25-piece ones, too.
I should try that...

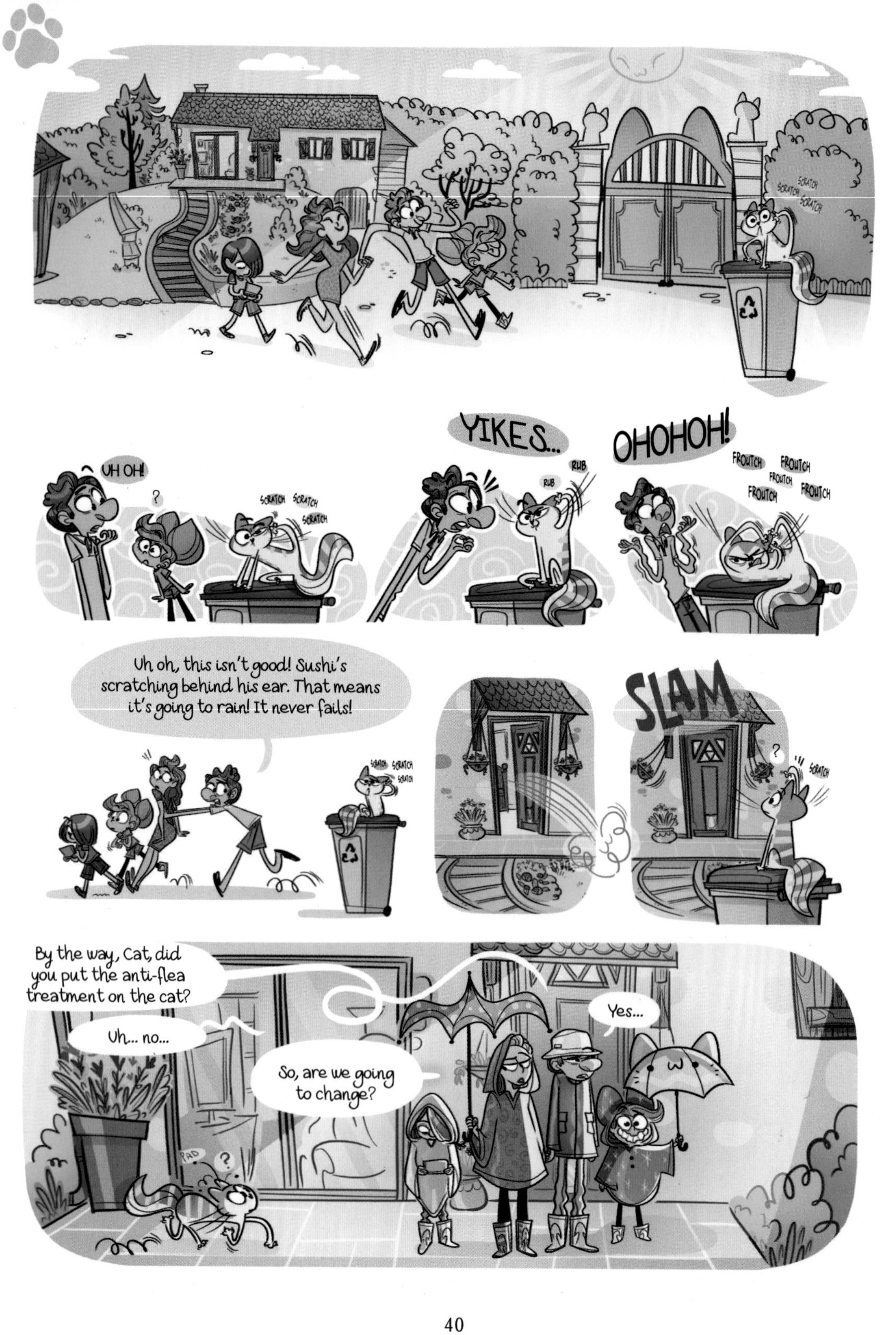
SCRATCH SCRATCH SCRATCH
UH OH!
?
SCRATCH SCRATCH SCRATCH
YIKES...
RUB RUB
OHOHOH!
FROUTCH FROUTCH FROUTCH FROUTCH FROUTCH
Uh oh, this isn't good! Sushi's scratching behind his ear. That means it's going to rain! It never fails!
SCRATCH SCRATCH SCRATCH
SLAM
?
SCRATCH
By the way, Cat, did you put the anti-flea treatment on the cat?
Uh... no...
Yes...
So, are we going to change?
PAD
?

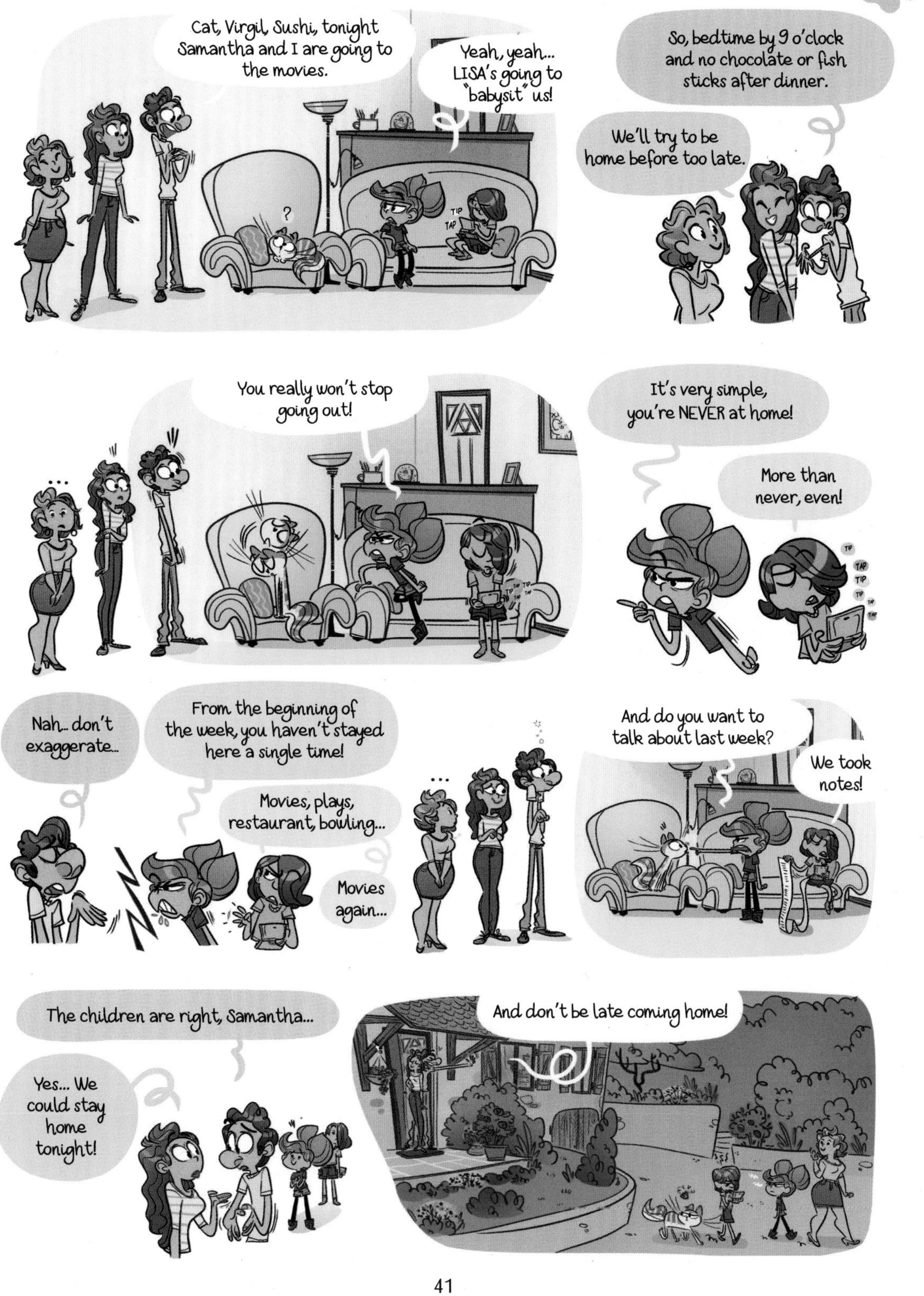

Cat, Virgil, Sushi, tonight Samantha and I are going to the movies.
Yeah, yeah... LISA's going to "babysit" us!
TIP
TAP
So, bedtime by 9 o'clock and no chocolate or fish sticks after dinner.
We'll try to be home before too late.
You really won't stop going out!
It's very simple, you're NEVER at home!
More than never, even!
TIP
TAP
TIP
TIP
TAP
TAP
Nah... don't exaggerate...
From the beginning of the week, you haven't stayed here a single time!
Movies, plays, restaurant, bowling...
Movies again...
And do you want to talk about last week?
We took notes!
The children are right, Samantha...
Yes... We could stay home tonight!
And don't be late coming home!

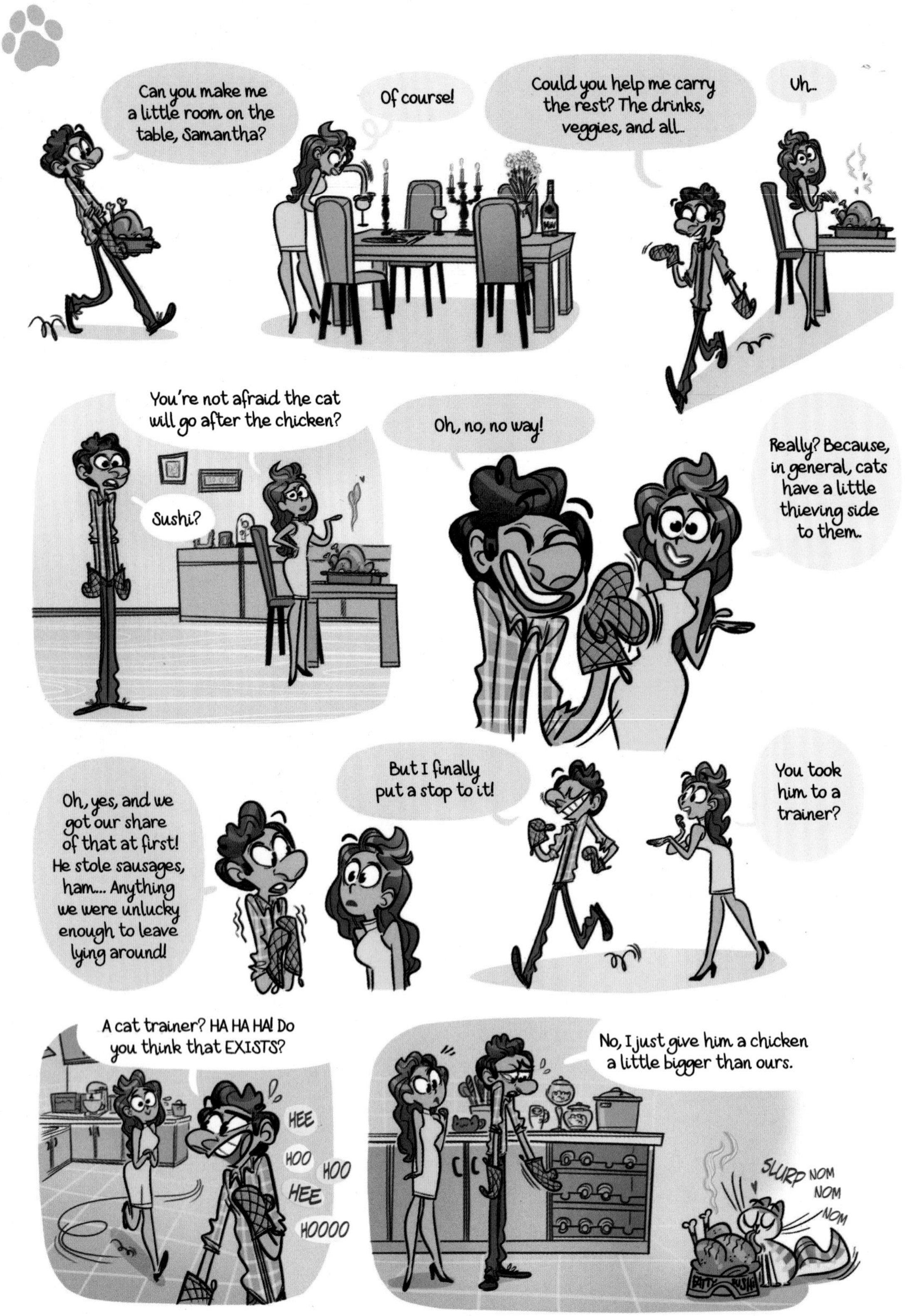

Can you make me a little room on the table, Samantha?
Of course!
Could you help me carry the rest? The drinks, veggies, and all...
Uh...
You're not afraid the cat will go after the chicken?
Sushi?
Oh, no, no way!
Really? Because, in general, cats have a little thieving side to them.
Oh, yes, and we got our share of that at first! He stole sausages, ham... Anything we were unlucky enough to leave lying around!
But I finally put a stop to it!
You took him to a trainer?
A cat trainer? HA HA HA! Do you think that EXISTS?
HEE
HOO
HOO
HEE
HOOOO
No, I just give him a chicken a little bigger than ours.
SLURP
NOM
NOM
NOM

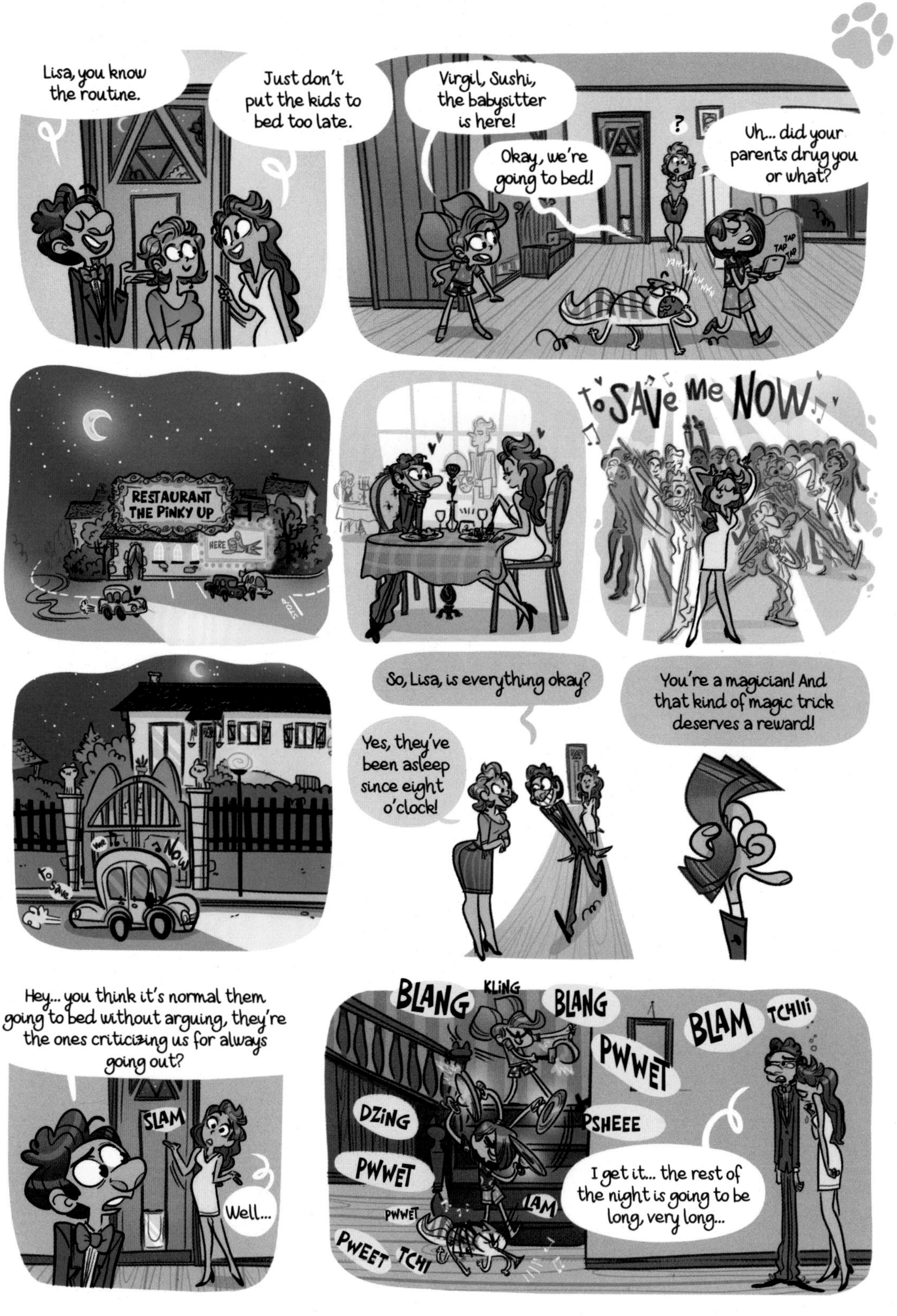

Lisa, you know the routine.
Just don't put the kids to bed too late.
Virgil, Sushi, the babysitter is here!
Okay, we're going to bed!
?
Uh... did your parents drug you or what?
TAP TAP TAP
RESTAURANT THE PINKY UP
HERE
TO SAVE ME NOW
So, Lisa, is everything okay?
Yes, they've been asleep since eight o'clock!
You're a magician! And that kind of magic trick deserves a reward!
Hey... you think it's normal them going to bed without arguing, they're the ones criticizing us for always going out?
SLAM
Well...
BLANG
KLING
BLANG
BLAM
TCHLII
PWWET
DZING
PSHEEE
PWWET
I get it... the rest of the night is going to be long, very long...
PWWET
LAM
PWEET
TCHI

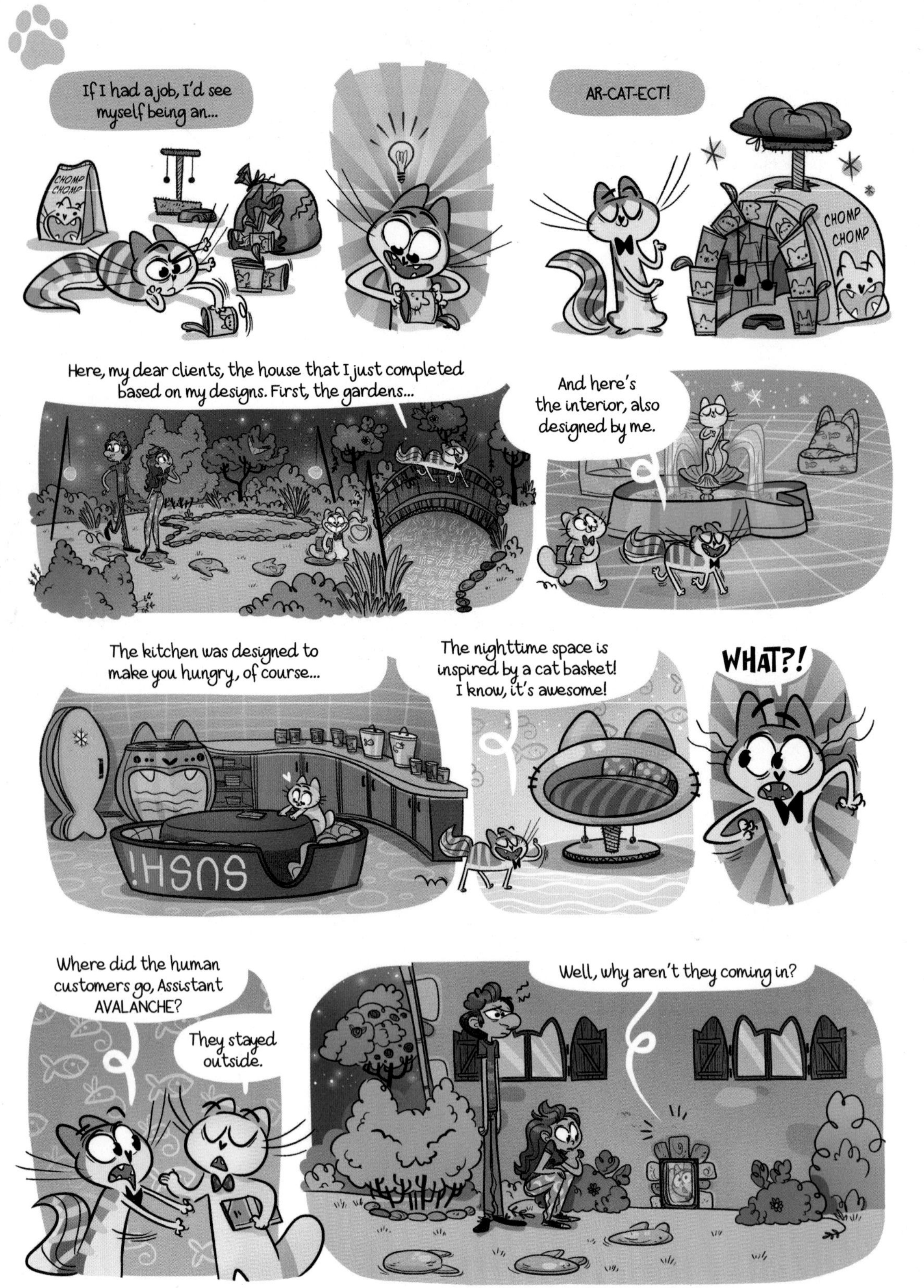

If I had a job, I'd see myself being an...
CHOMP CHOMP
AR-CAT-ECT!
CHOMP CHOMP
Here, my dear clients, the house that I just completed based on my designs. First, the gardens...
And here's the interior, also designed by me.
The kitchen was designed to make you hungry, of course...
The nighttime space is inspired by a cat basket! I know, it's awesome!
WHAT?!
Where did the human customers go, Assistant AVALANCHE?
They stayed outside.
Well, why aren't they coming in?

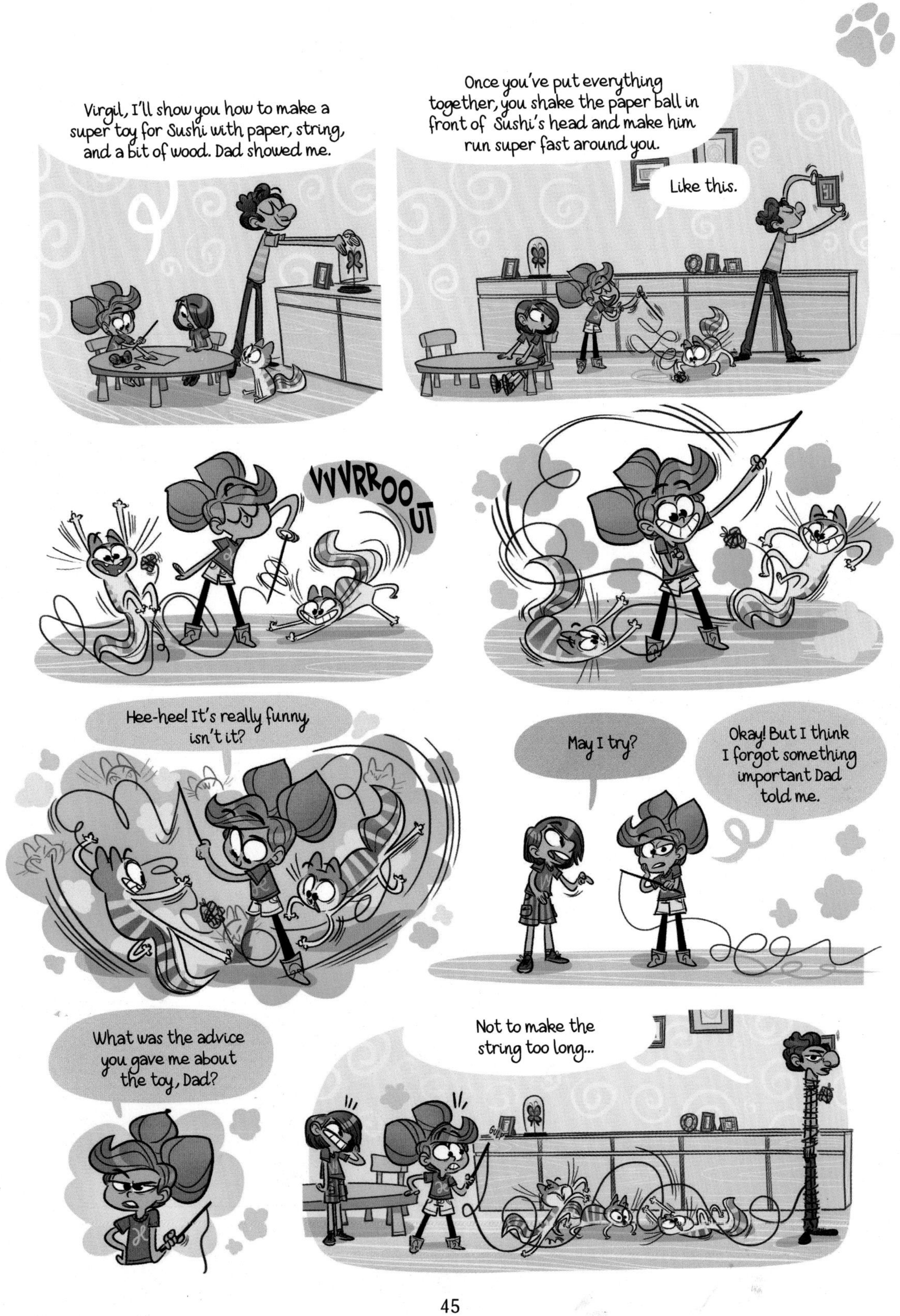

Virgil, I'll show you how to make a super toy for Sushi with paper, string, and a bit of wood. Dad showed me.
Once you've put everything together, you shake the paper ball in front of Sushi's head and make him run super fast around you.
Like this.
VVVRROOOUT
Hee-hee! It's really funny isn't it?
May I try?
Okay! But I think I forgot something important Dad told me.
What was the advice you gave me about the toy, Dad?
Not to make the string too long...

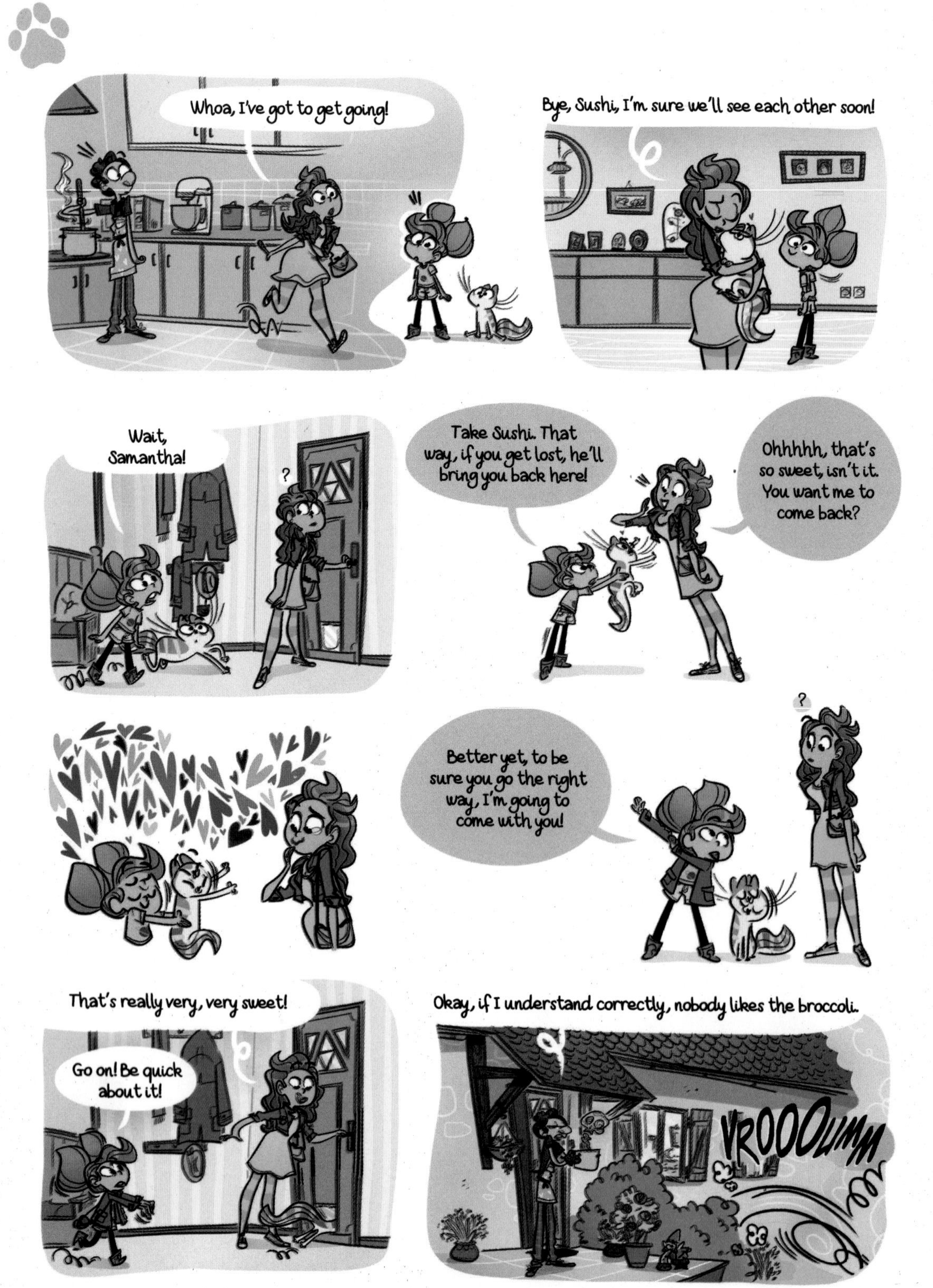
Whoa, I've got to get going!
Bye, Sushi, I'm sure we'll see each other soon!
Wait, Samantha!
?
Take Sushi. That way, if you get lost, he'll bring you back here!
Ohhhhh, that's so sweet, isn't it. You want me to come back?
Better yet, to be sure you go the right way, I'm going to come with you!
?
That's really very, very sweet!
Go on! Be quick about it!
Okay, if I understand correctly, nobody likes the broccoli.
VROOOUMM

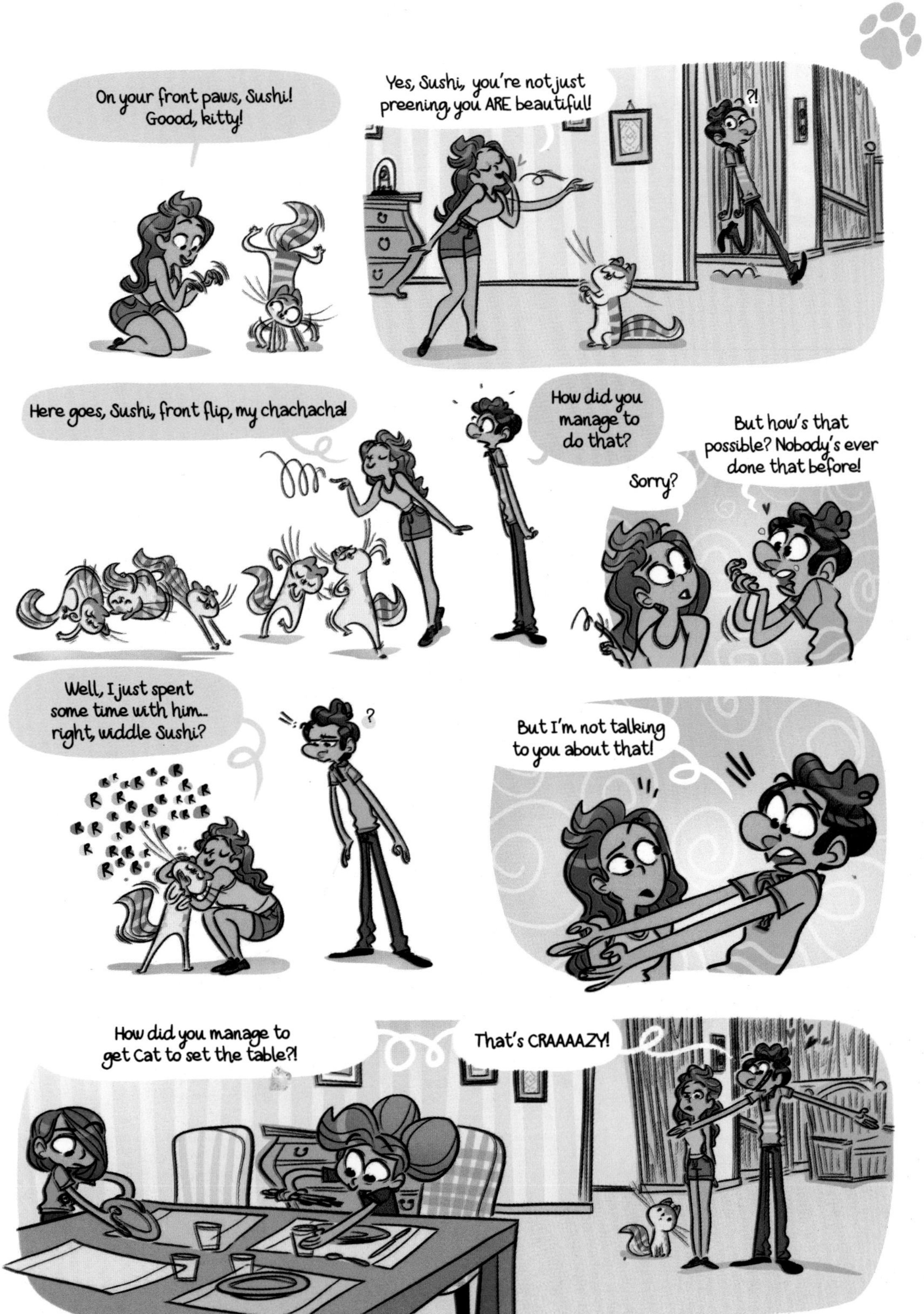
On your front paws, Sushi! Goood, kitty!
Yes, Sushi, you're not just preening, you ARE beautiful!
?!
Here goes, Sushi, front flip, my chachacha!
How did you manage to do that?
Sorry?
But how's that possible? Nobody's ever done that before!
Well, I just spent some time with him... right, widdle Sushi?
?
But I'm not talking to you about that!
How did you manage to get Cat to set the table?!
That's CRAAAAZY!

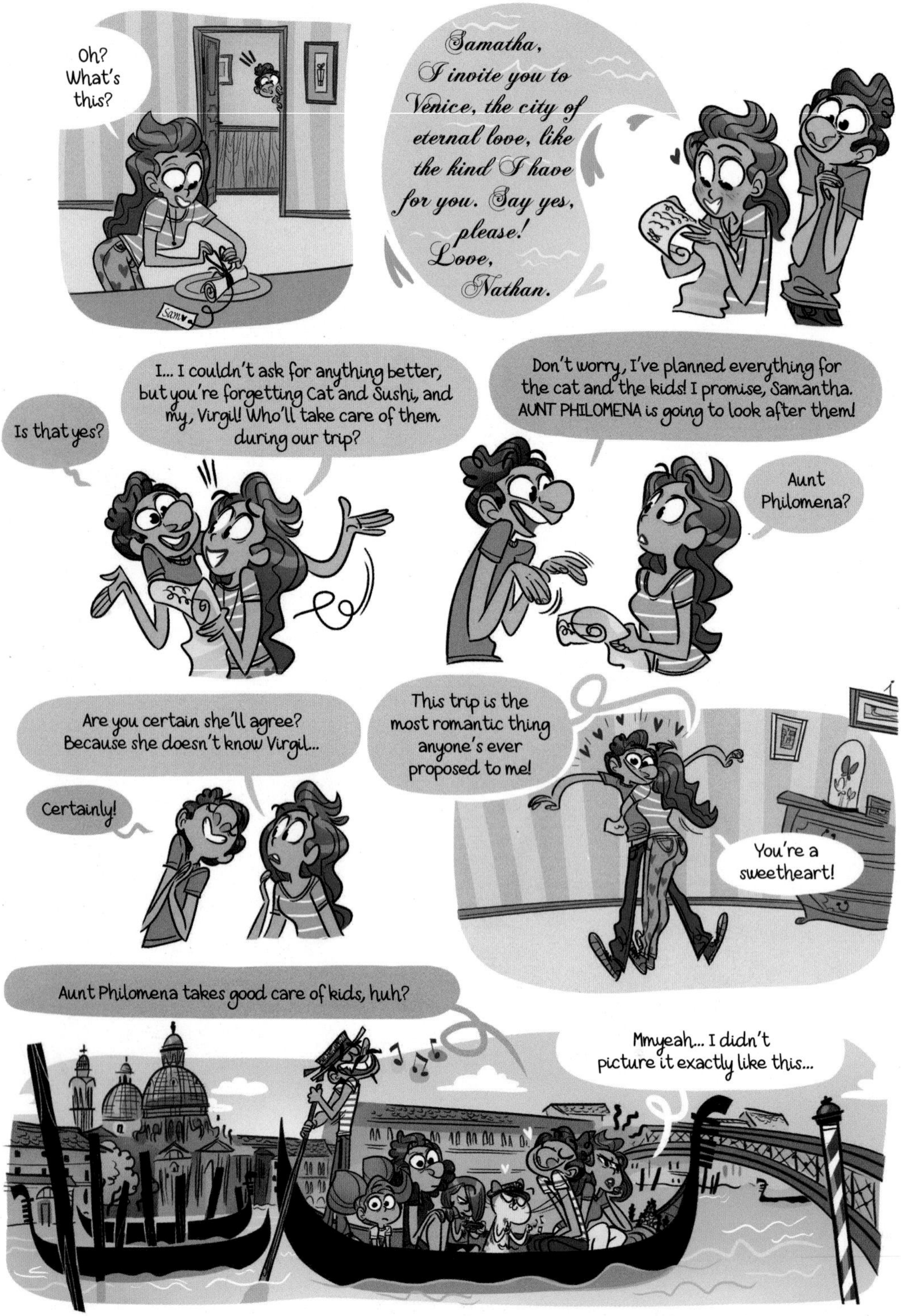
Oh? What's this?
Sam♥
Samatha, I invite you to Venice, the city of eternal love, like the kind I have for you. Say yes, please! Love, Nathan.
Is that yes?
I... I couldn't ask for anything better, but you're forgetting Cat and Sushi, and my, Virgil! Who'll take care of them during our trip?
Don't worry, I've planned everything for the cat and the kids! I promise, Samantha. AUNT PHILOMENA is going to look after them!
Aunt Philomena?
Are you certain she'll agree? Because she doesn't know Virgil...
Certainly!
This trip is the most romantic thing anyone's ever proposed to me!
You're a sweetheart!
Aunt Philomena takes good care of kids, huh?
Mmyeah... I didn't picture it exactly like this...

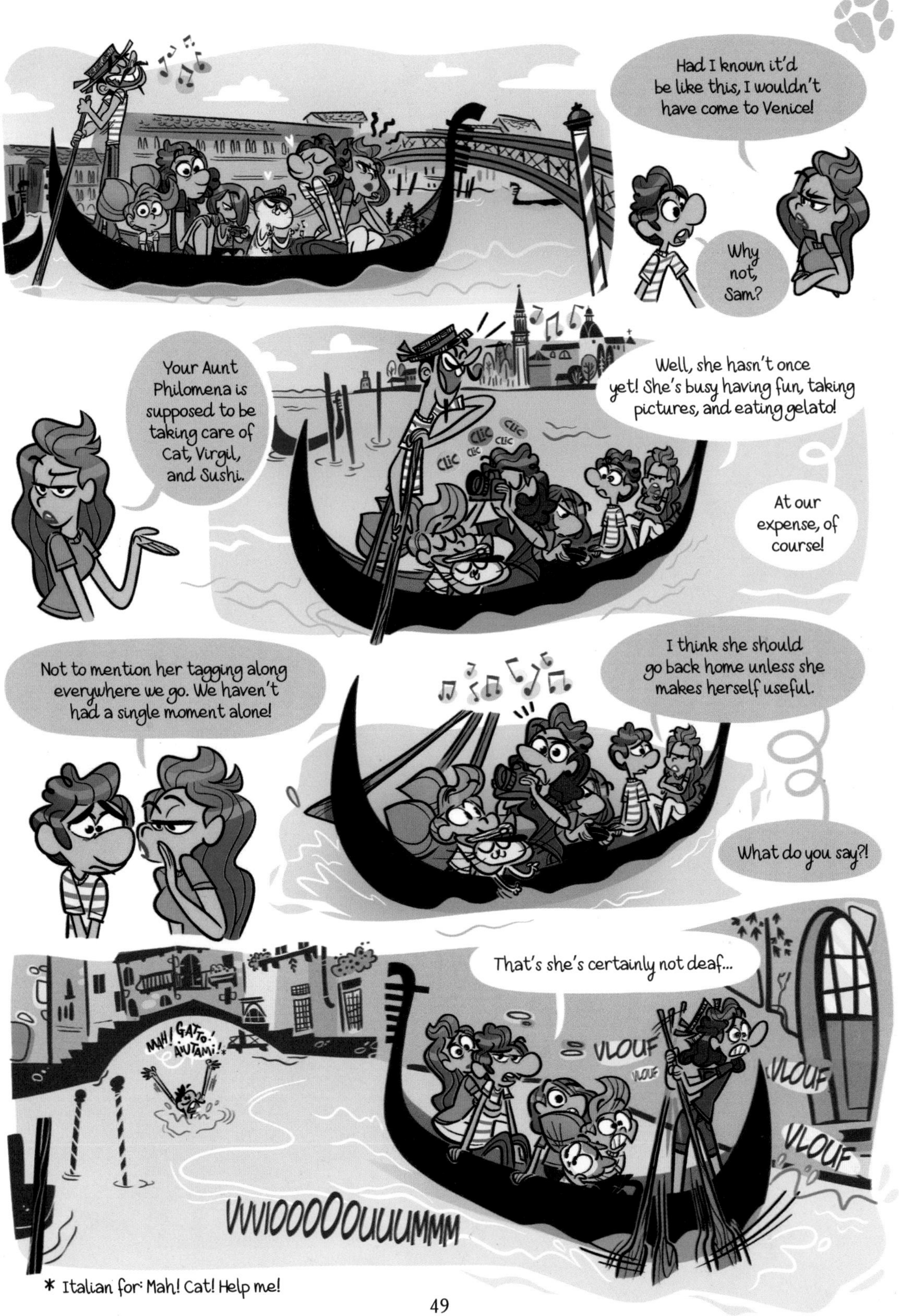
Had I known it'd be like this, I wouldn't have come to Venice!
Why not, Sam?
Your Aunt Philomena is supposed to be taking care of Cat, Virgil, and Sushi.
CLIC CLIC CLIC CLIC CLIC
Well, she hasn't once yet! She's busy having fun, taking pictures, and eating gelato!
At our expense, of course!
Not to mention her tagging along everywhere we go. We haven't had a single moment alone!
I think she should go back home unless she makes herself useful.
What do you say?!
That's she's certainly not deaf...
MAH! GATTO! AIUTAMI!*
VLOUF
VLOUF
VLOUF
VLOUF
VVIOOOOOUUUMMM

* Italian for: Mah! Cat! Help me!

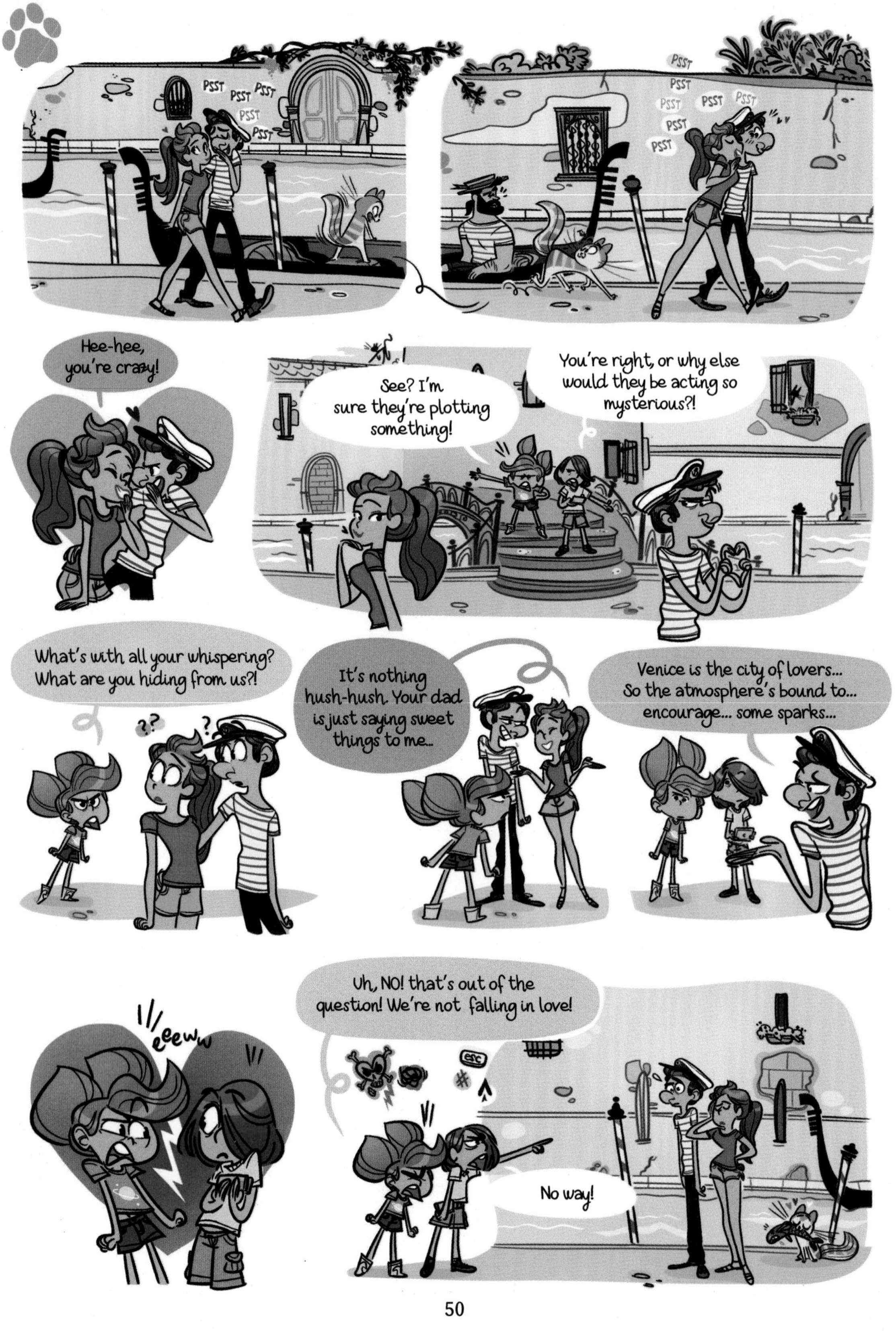
PSST PSST PSST PSST PSST
PSST PSST PSST PSST PSST PSST PSST
Hee-hee, you're crazy!
See? I'm sure they're plotting something!
You're right, or why else would they be acting so mysterious?!
What's with all your whispering? What are you hiding from us?!
It's nothing hush-hush. Your dad is just saying sweet things to me...
Venice is the city of lovers... So the atmosphere's bound to... encourage... some sparks...
eeeww
Uh, NO! that's out of the question! We're not falling in love!
No way!

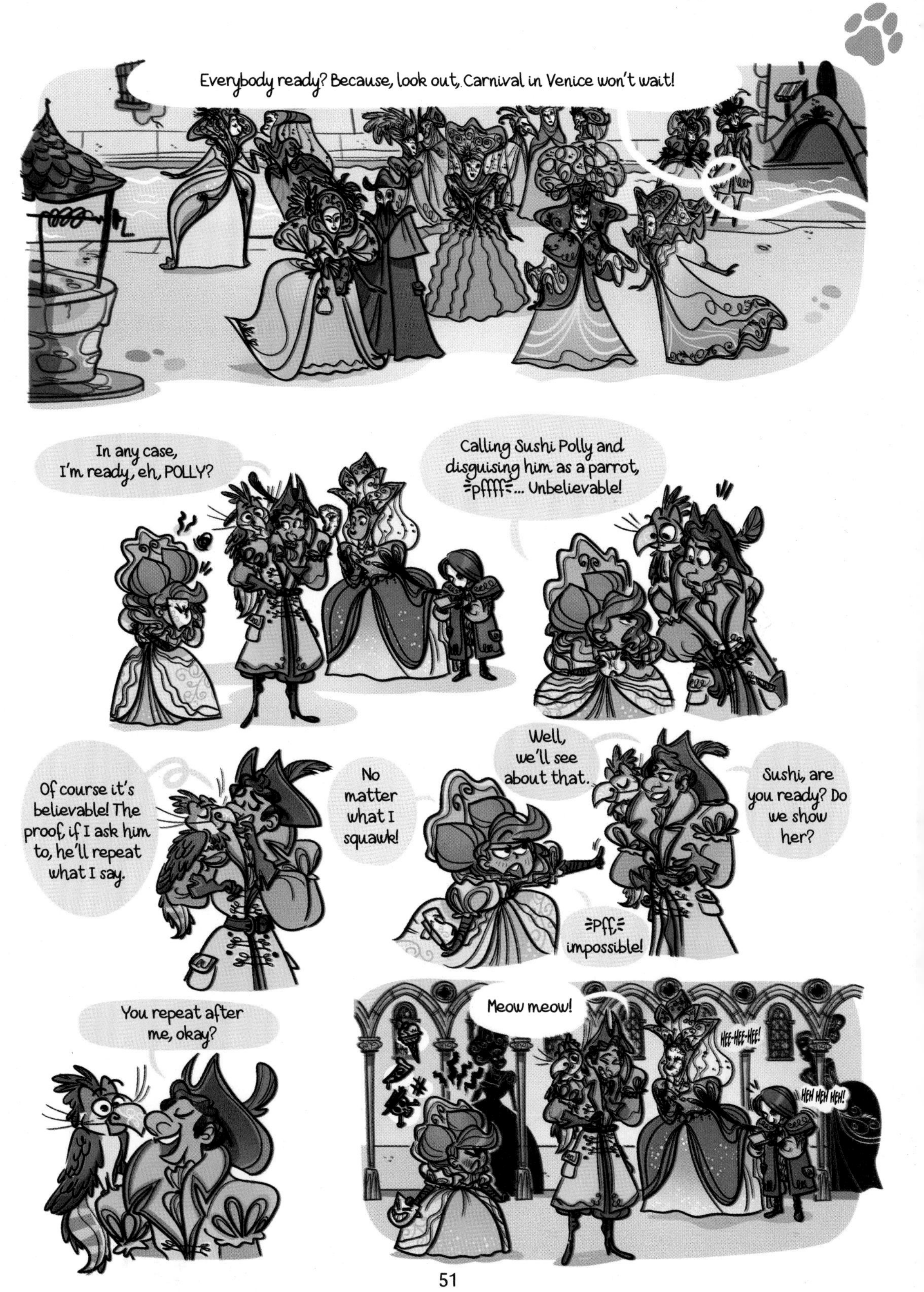
Everybody ready? Because, look out, Carnival in Venice won't wait!
In any case, I'm ready, eh, POLLY?
Calling Sushi Polly and disguising him as a parrot, pffff... Unbelievable!
Of course it's believable! The proof, if I ask him to, he'll repeat what I say.
No matter what I squawk!
Well, we'll see about that.
Sushi, are you ready? Do we show her?
Pff, impossible!
You repeat after me, okay?
Meow meow!
HEE-HEE-HEE!
HEH HEH HEH!

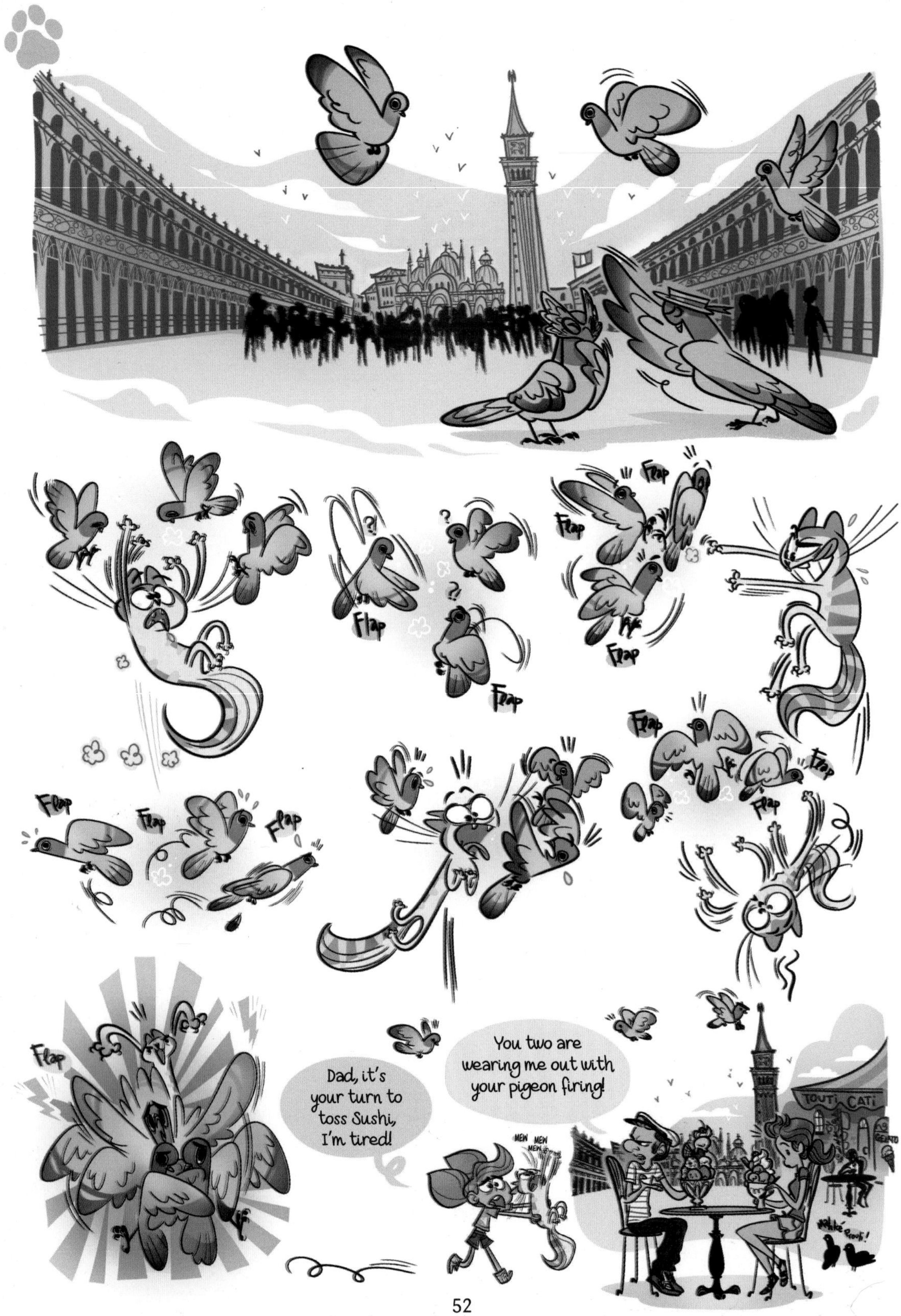
Flap
Flap
Flap
Flap
Flap
Flap
Flap
Flap
Flap
Flap
Flap
Dad, it's your turn to toss Sushi, I'm tired!
You two are wearing me out with your pigeon firing!
MEW MEW MEW
TOUTI CATI

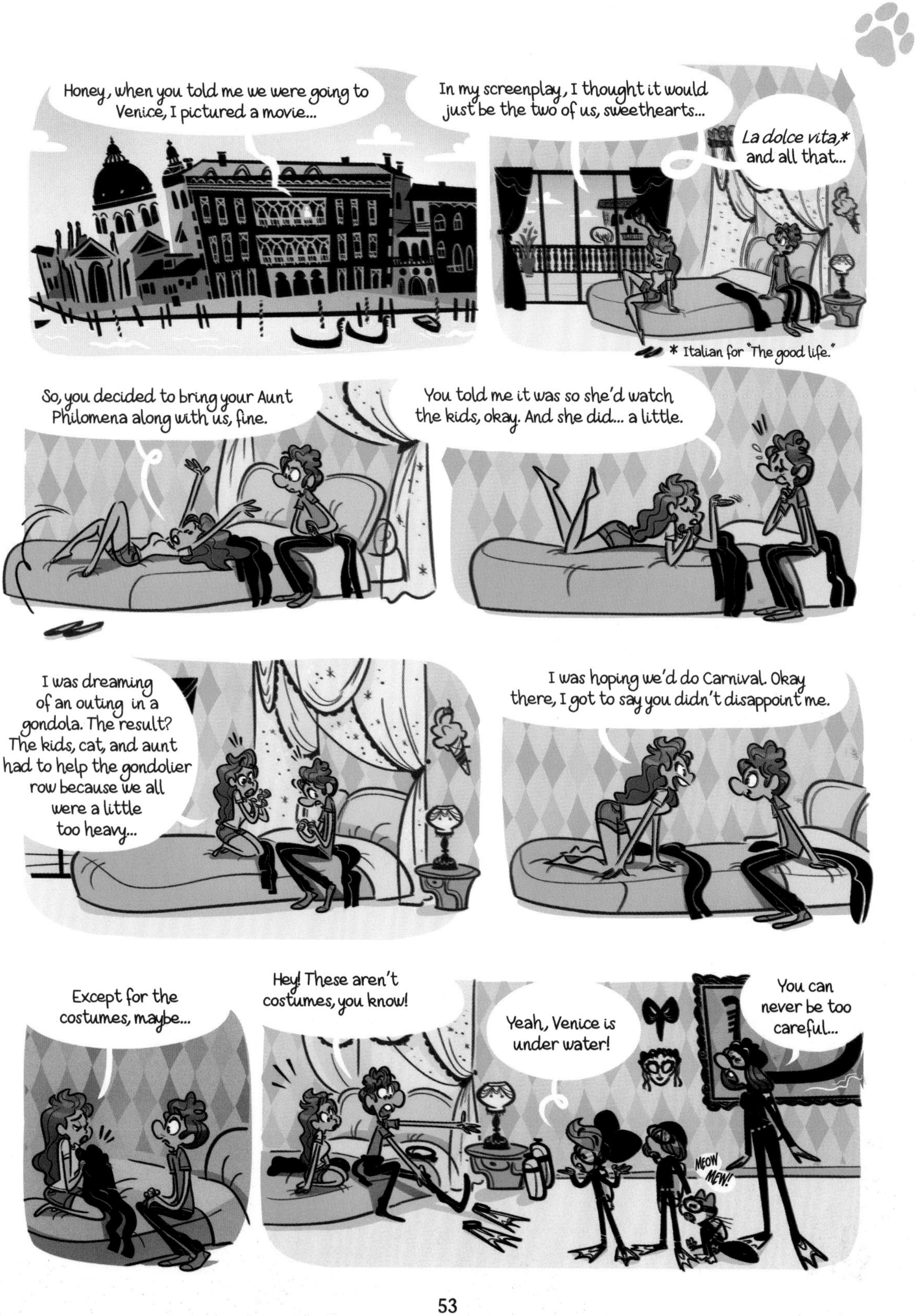
Honey, when you told me we were going to Venice, I pictured a movie...
In my screenplay, I thought it would just be the two of us, sweethearts...
*La dolce vita,** and all that...
* Italian for "The good life."
So, you decided to bring your Aunt Philomena along with us, fine.
You told me it was so she'd watch the kids, okay. And she did... a little.
I was dreaming of an outing in a gondola. The result? The kids, cat, and aunt had to help the gondolier row because we all were a little too heavy...
I was hoping we'd do Carnival. Okay there, I got to say you didn't disappoint me.
Except for the costumes, maybe...
Hey! These aren't costumes, you know!
Yeah, Venice is under water!
You can never be too careful...
MEOW
MEW!

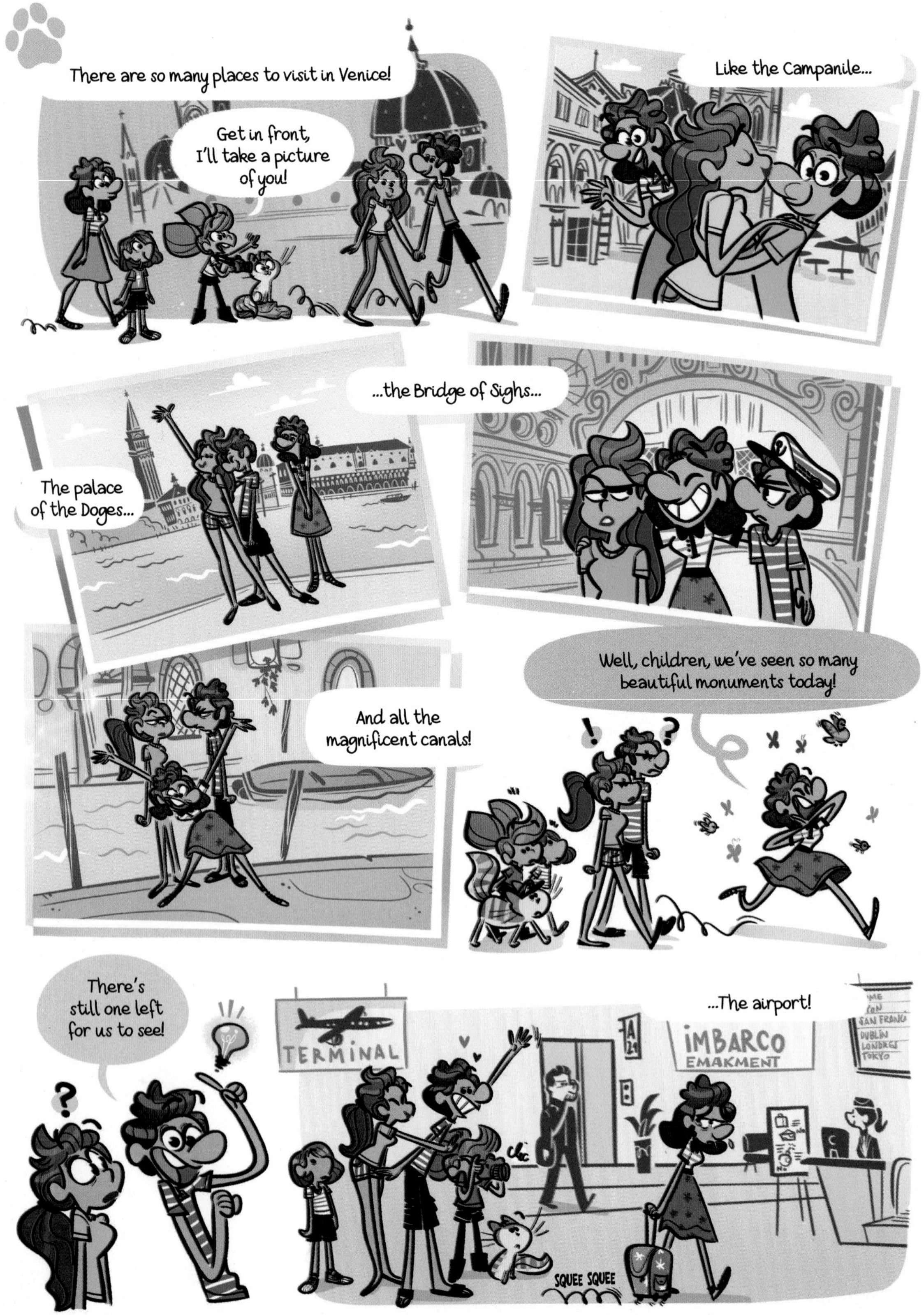
There are so many places to visit in Venice!
Get in front, I'll take a picture of you!
Like the Campanile...
The palace of the Doges...
...the Bridge of Sighs...
And all the magnificent canals!
Well, children, we've seen so many beautiful monuments today!
There's still one left for us to see!
TERMINAL
...The airport!
iMBARCO
EMAKMENT
DUBLIN
TOKYO
SQUEE SQUEE

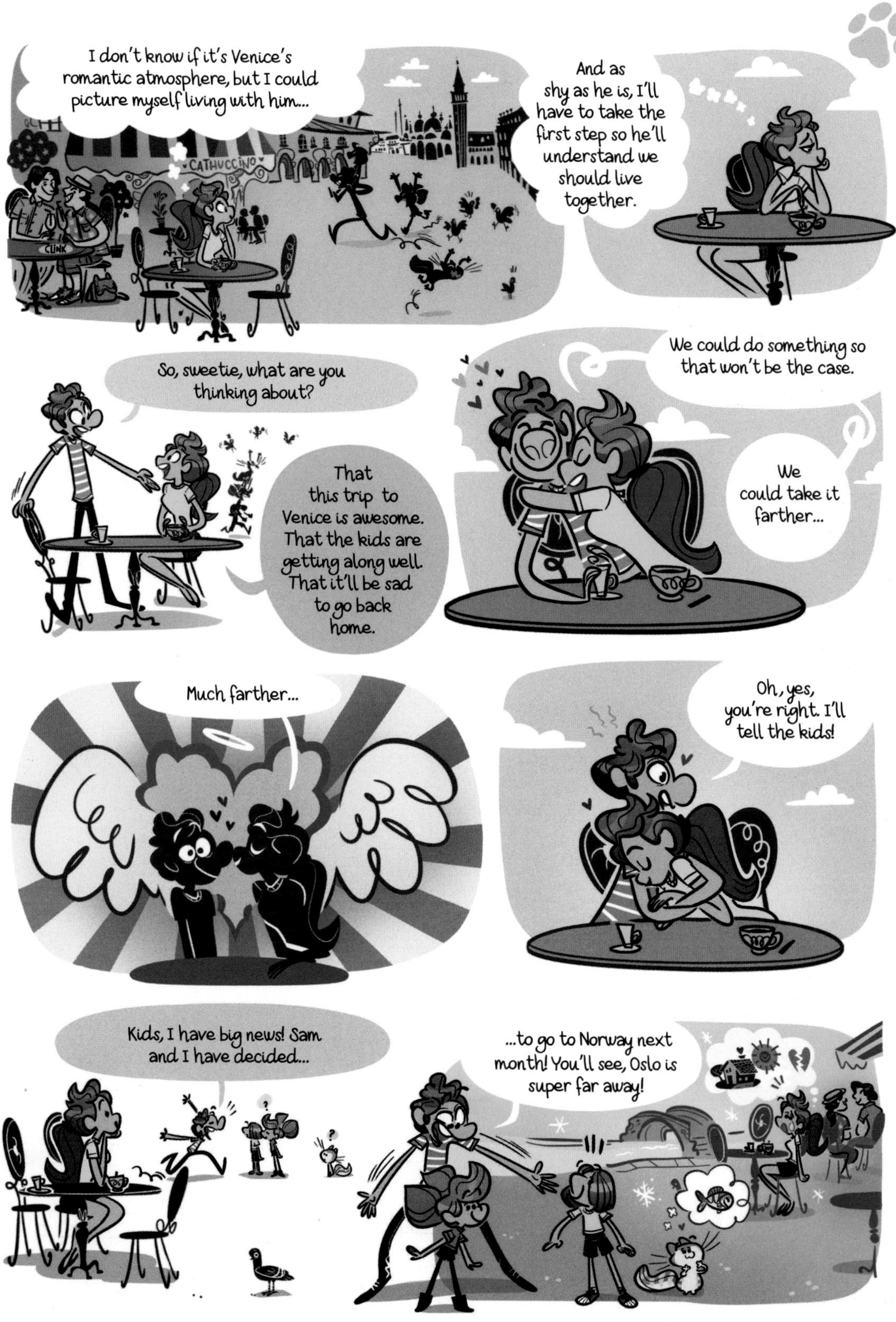
I don't know if it's Venice's romantic atmosphere, but I could picture myself living with him...
CATHUCCINO
CLINK
And as shy as he is, I'll have to take the first step so he'll understand we should live together.
So, sweetie, what are you thinking about?
That this trip to Venice is awesome. That the kids are getting along well. That it'll be sad to go back home.
We could do something so that won't be the case.
We could take it farther...
Much farther...
Oh, yes, you're right. I'll tell the kids!
Kids, I have big news! Sam and I have decided...
...to go to Norway next month! You'll see, Oslo is super far away!

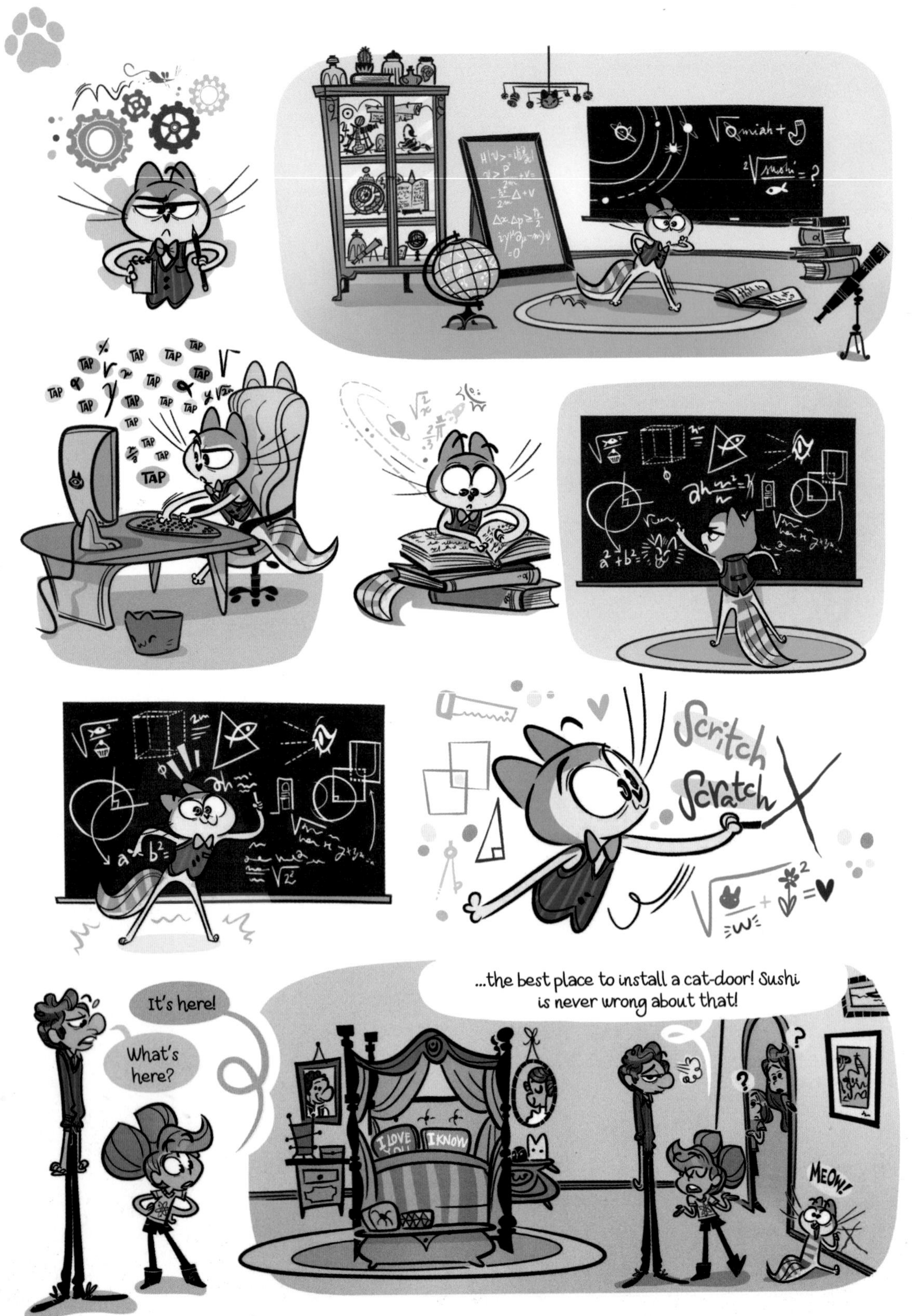
TAP TAP TAP TAP TAP TAP TAP TAP TAP TAP TAP TAP TAP
Scritch
Scratch
It's here!
What's here?
...the best place to install a cat-door! Sushi is never wrong about that!
I LOVE YOU
I KNOW
MEOW!

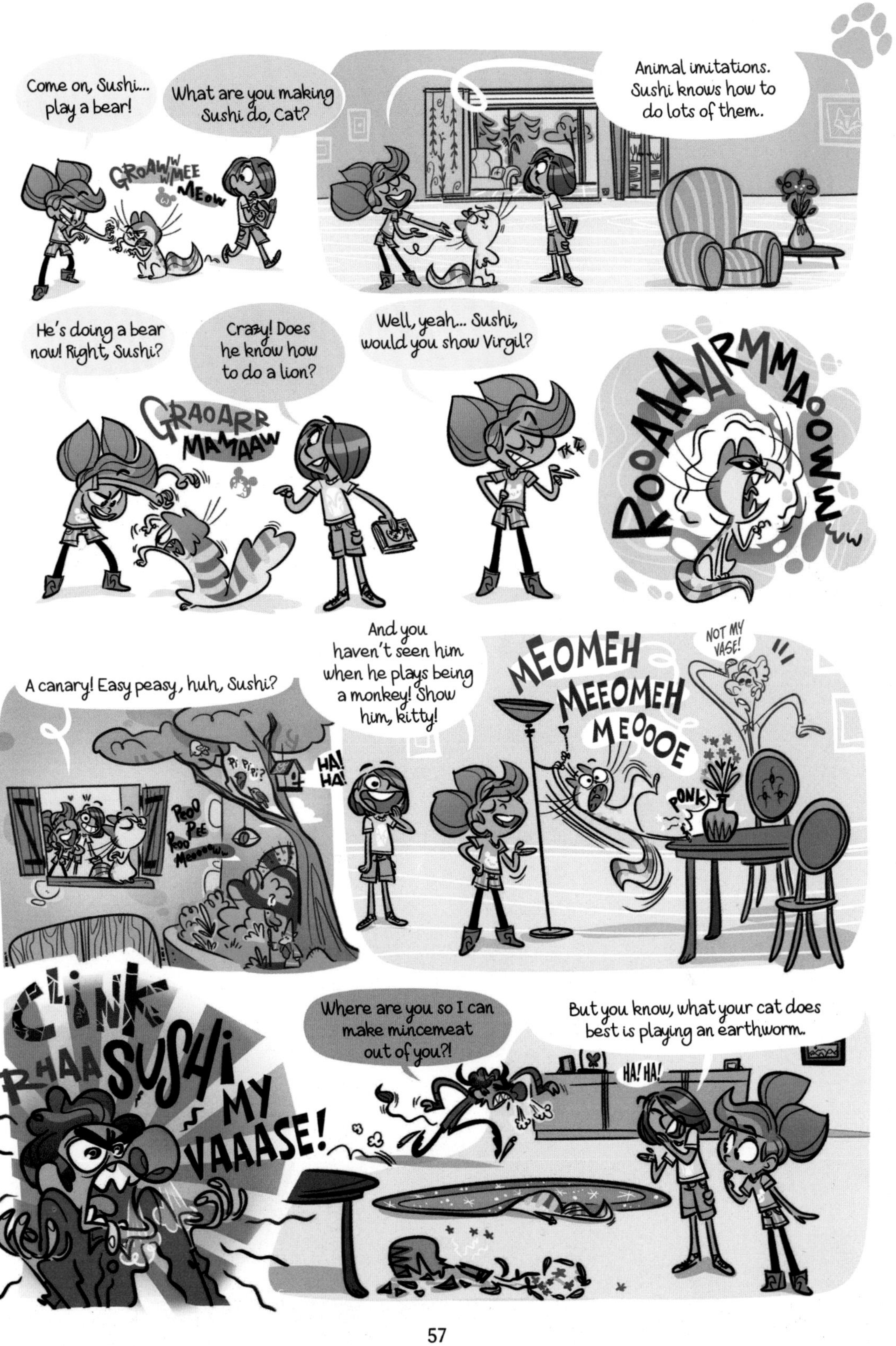

Come on, Sushi... play a bear!
What are you making Sushi do, Cat?
GROAWWMEE MEOW
Animal imitations. Sushi knows how to do lots of them.
He's doing a bear now! Right, Sushi?
Crazy! Does he know how to do a lion?
GRAOARR MAMAAW
Well, yeah... Sushi, would you show Virgil?
ROOAAAARMMAOOWWWWW
A canary! Easy peasy, huh, Sushi?
PI PIPI?
HA! HA!
PEOO PEE PEOO MEOOOOW
And you haven't seen him when he plays being a monkey! Show him, kitty!
MEOMEH MEEOMEH MEOOOE
NOT MY VASE!
PONK
CLINK
RHAA SUSHI MY VAAASE!
Where are you so I can make mincemeat out of you?!
HA! HA!
But you know, what your cat does best is playing an earthworm.

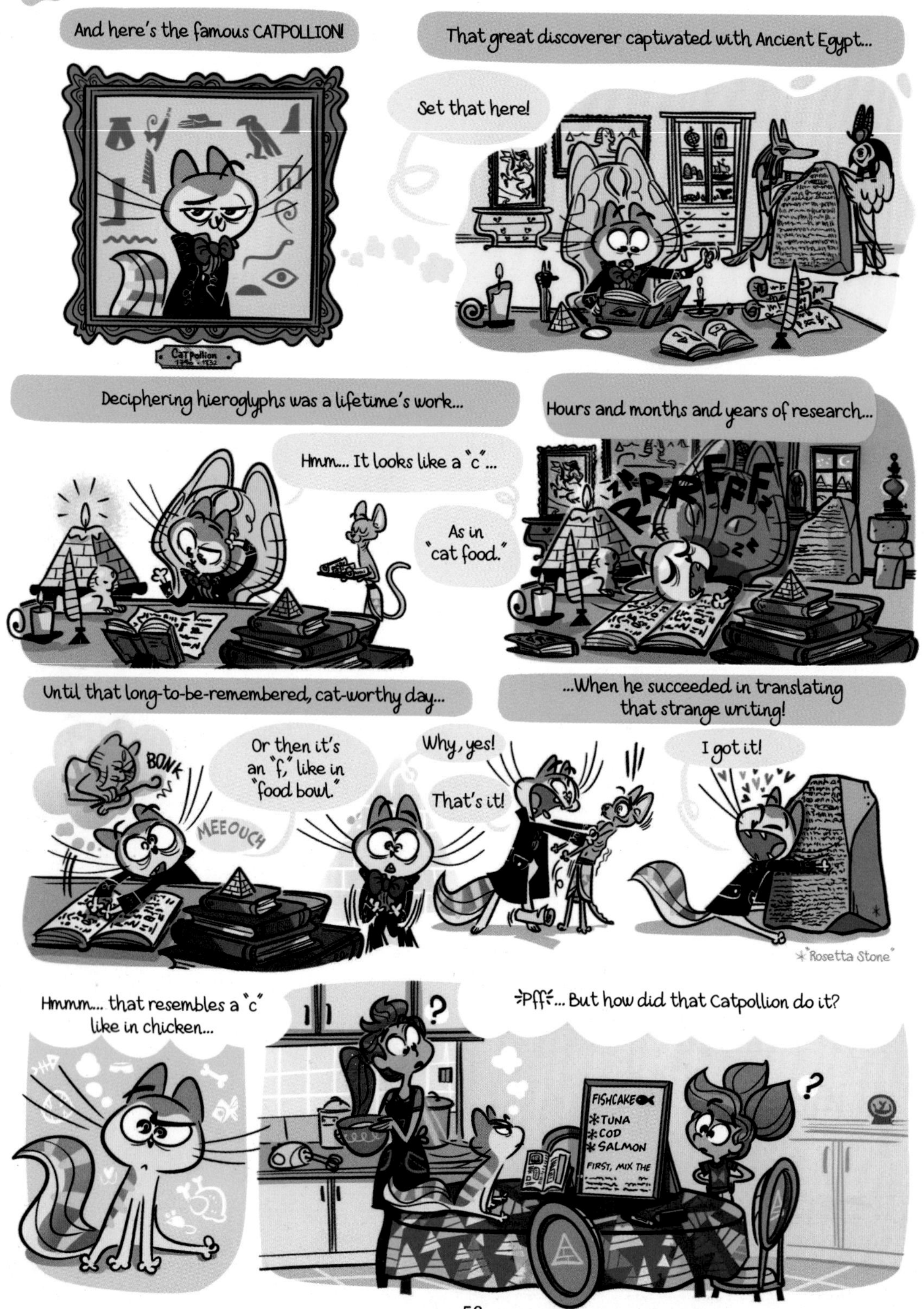
And here's the famous CATPOLLION!
Catpollion
That great discoverer captivated with Ancient Egypt...
Set that here!
Deciphering hieroglyphs was a lifetime's work...
Hmm... It looks like a "c"...
As in "cat food."
Hours and months and years of research...
Until that long-to-be-remembered, cat-worthy day...
BONK
MEEOUCH
Or then it's an "f," like in "food bowl."
...When he succeeded in translating that strange writing!
Why, yes!
That's it!
I got it!
*"Rosetta Stone"
Hmmm... that resembles a "c" like in chicken...
?
Pff... But how did that Catpollion do it?
FISHCAKE
*TUNA
*COD
*SALMON
FIRST, MIX THE
?

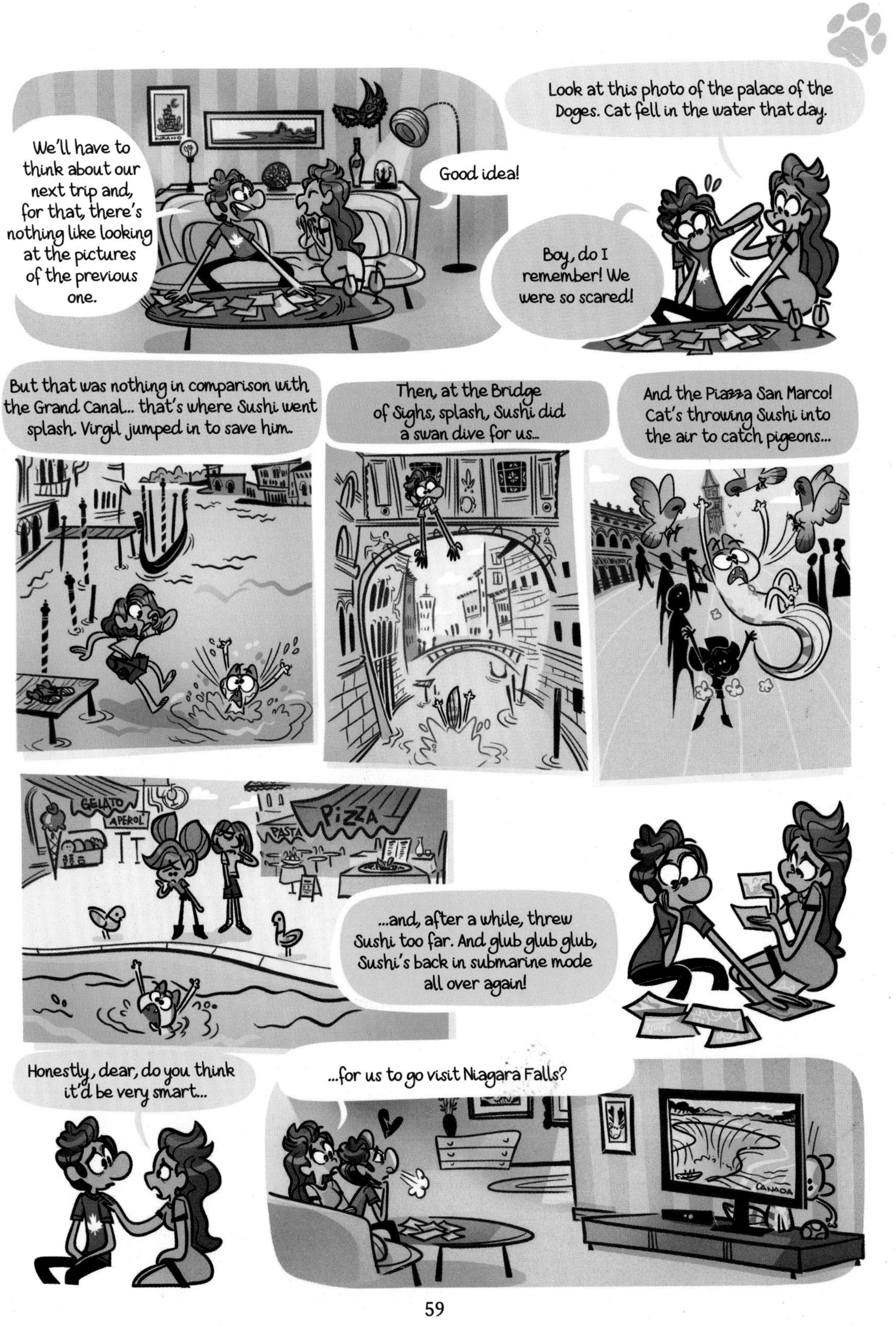
We'll have to think about our next trip and, for that, there's nothing like looking at the pictures of the previous one.
Good idea!
Look at this photo of the palace of the Doges. Cat fell in the water that day.
Boy, do I remember! We were so scared!
But that was nothing in comparison with the Grand Canal... that's where Sushi went splash. Virgil jumped in to save him.
Then, at the Bridge of Sighs, splash, Sushi did a swan dive for us...
And the Piazza San Marco! Cat's throwing Sushi into the air to catch pigeons...
GELATO
APEROL
PASTA
PIZZA
...and, after a while, threw Sushi too far. And glub glub glub, Sushi's back in submarine mode all over again!
Honestly, dear, do you think it'd be very smart...
...for us to go visit Niagara Falls?
CANADA

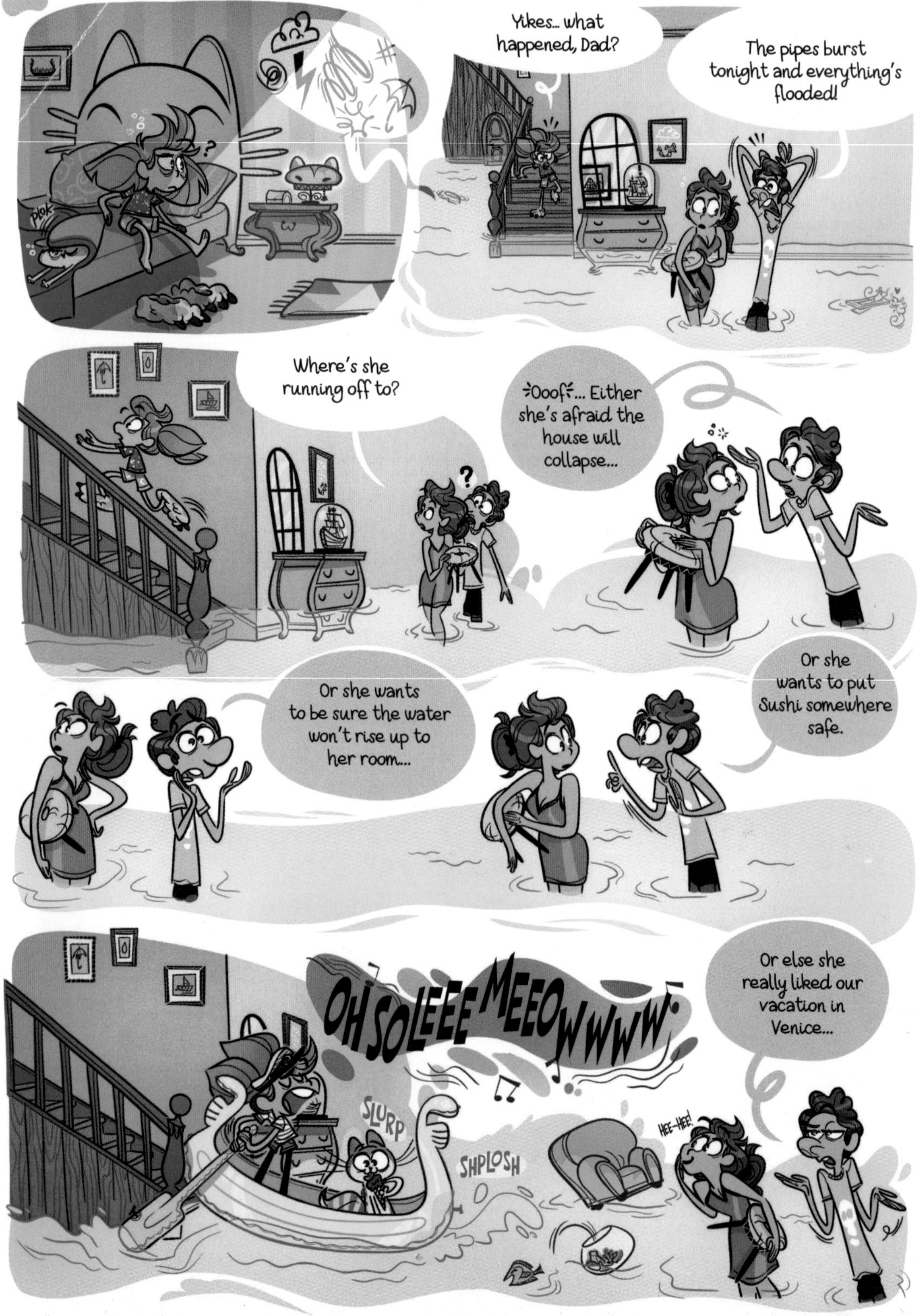
PLOK
Yikes... what happened, Dad?
The pipes burst tonight and everything's flooded!
Where's she running off to?
Ooof... Either she's afraid the house will collapse...
Or she wants to be sure the water won't rise up to her room...
Or she wants to put Sushi somewhere safe.
OH SOLEEE MEEOWWWW
Or else she really liked our vacation in Venice...
SLURP
SHPLOSH
HEE-HEE!

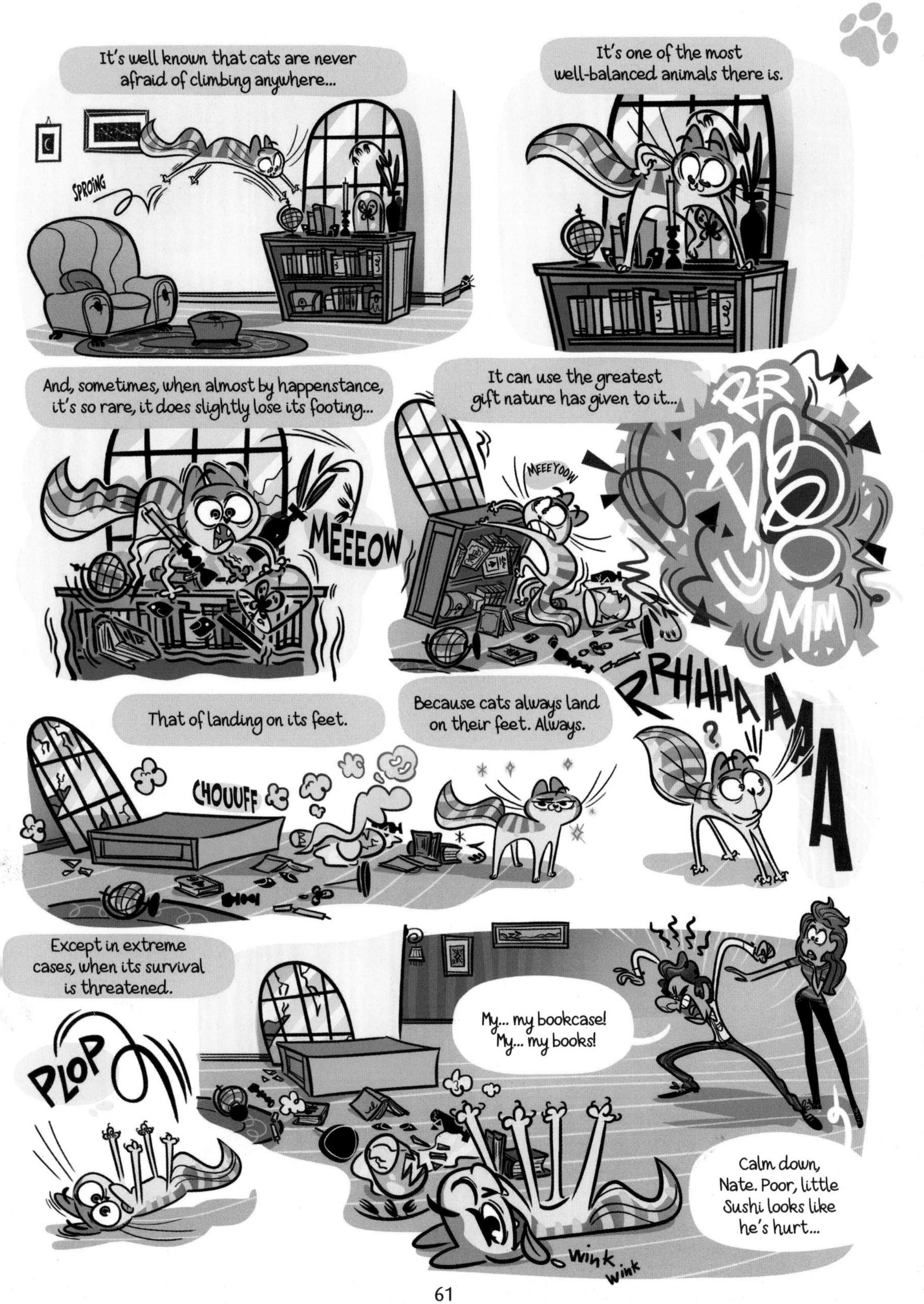
It's well known that cats are never afraid of climbing anywhere...
SPROING
It's one of the most well-balanced animals there is.
And, sometimes, when almost by happenstance, it's so rare, it does slightly lose its footing...
MEEEOW
It can use the greatest gift nature has given to it...
MEEEYOOW
RRBBOOMM
RRHHHAAAAA
That of landing on its feet.
Because cats always land on their feet. Always.
CHOUUFF
Except in extreme cases, when its survival is threatened.
PLOP
My... my bookcase! My... my books!
Calm down, Nate. Poor, little Sushi looks like he's hurt...
wink wink

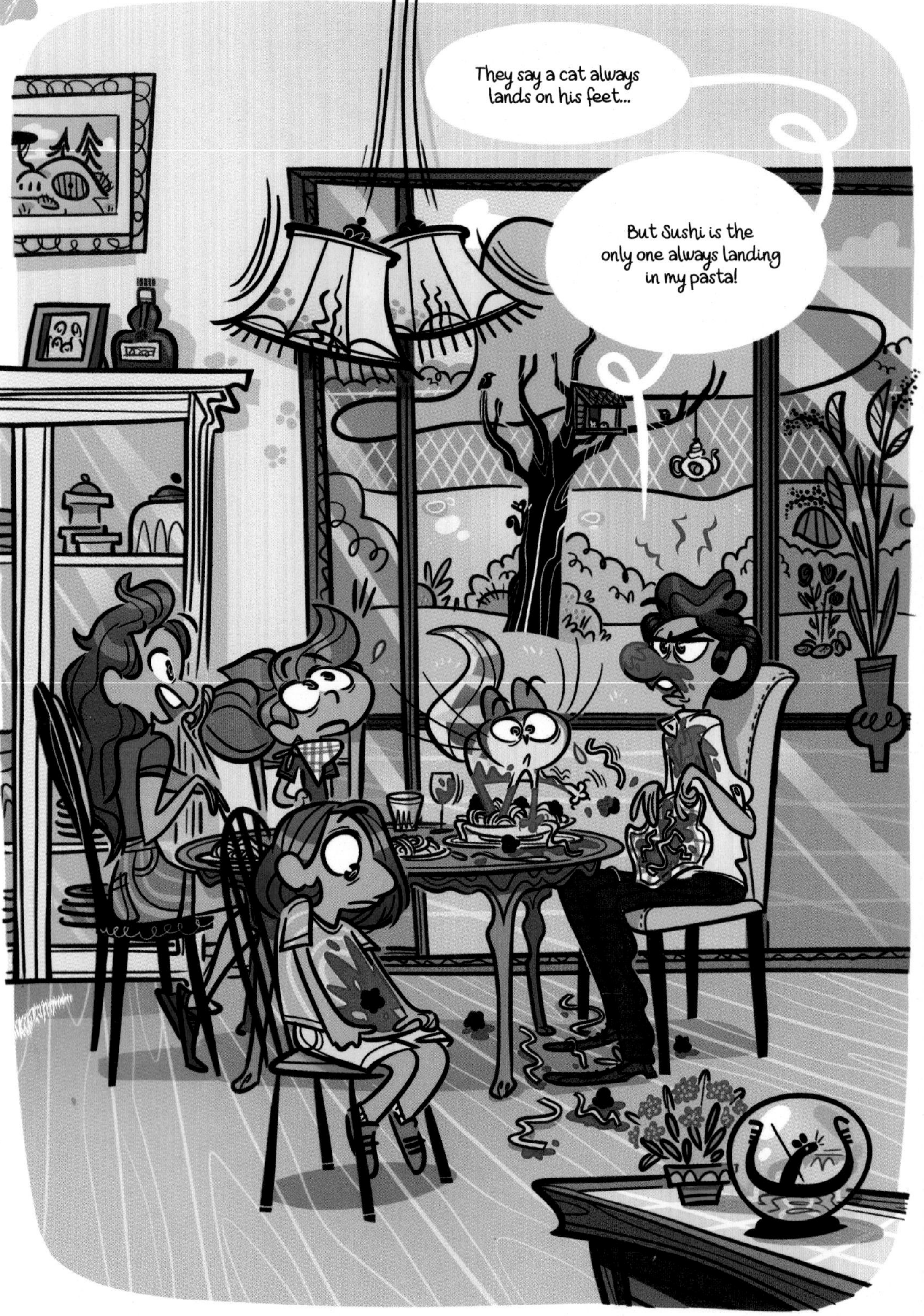
They say a cat always lands on his feet...
But Sushi is the only one always landing in my pasta!

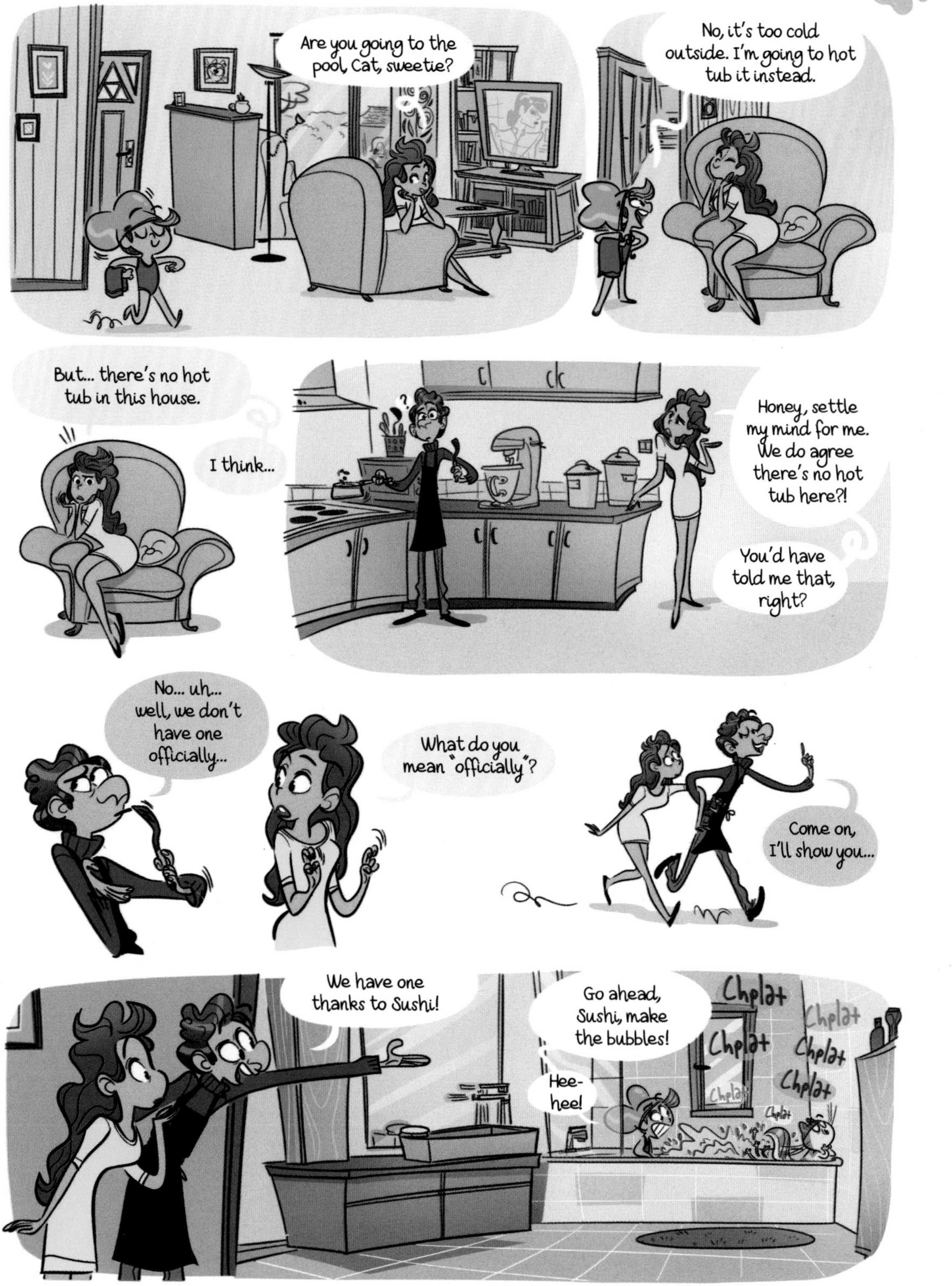
Are you going to the pool, Cat, sweetie?
No, it's too cold outside. I'm going to hot tub it instead.
But... there's no hot tub in this house.
I think...
Honey, settle my mind for me. We do agree there's no hot tub here?!
You'd have told me that, right?
No... uh... well, we don't have one officially...
What do you mean "officially"?
Come on, I'll show you...
We have one thanks to Sushi!
Go ahead, Sushi, make the bubbles!
Hee-hee!
Chplat
Chplat
Chplat
Chplat
Chplat

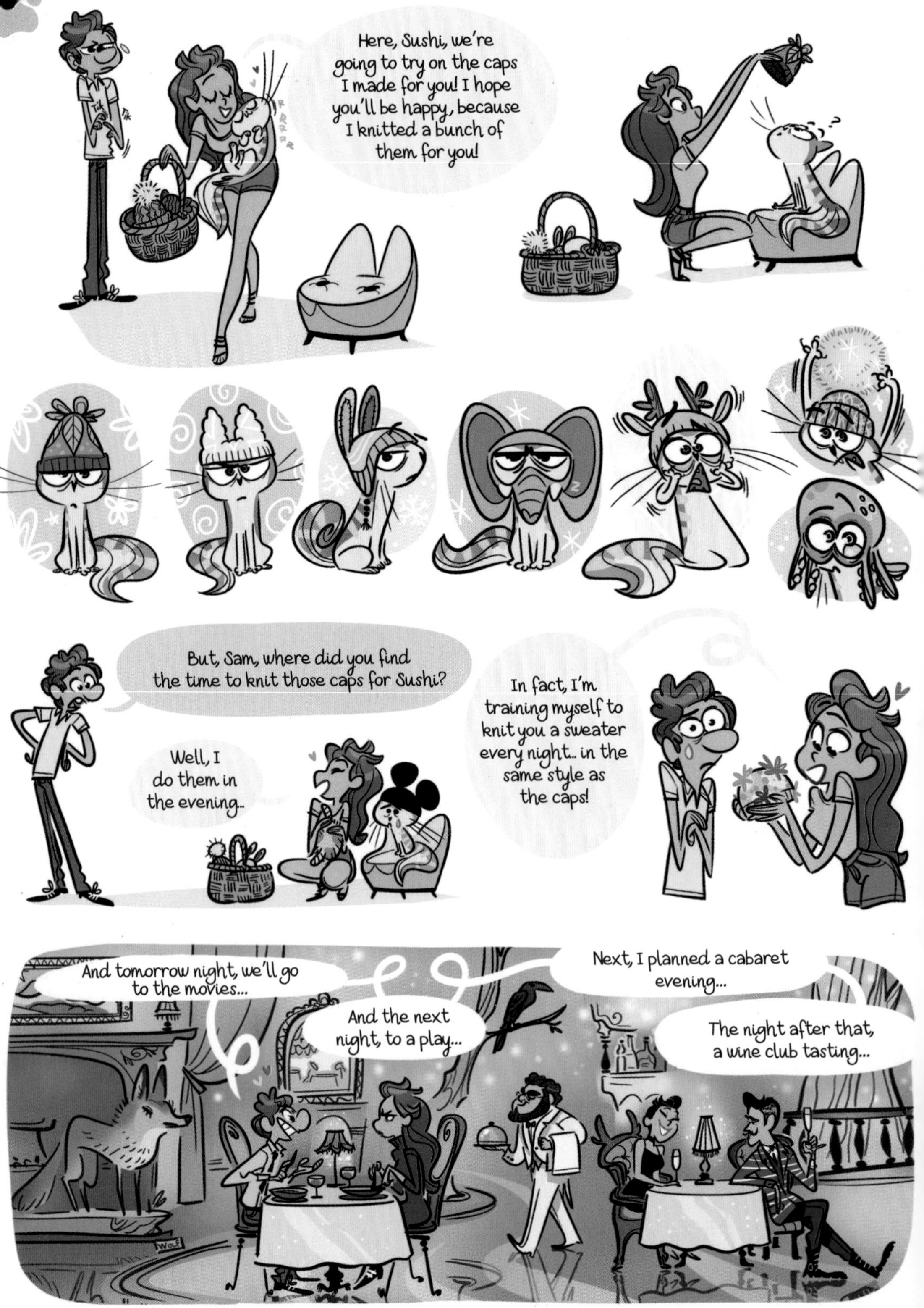
Here, Sushi, we're going to try on the caps I made for you! I hope you'll be happy, because I knitted a bunch of them for you!
But, Sam, where did you find the time to knit those caps for Sushi?
Well, I do them in the evening..
In fact, I'm training myself to knit you a sweater every night.. in the same style as the caps!
And tomorrow night, we'll go to the movies...
And the next night, to a play...
Next, I planned a cabaret evening...
The night after that, a wine club tasting...

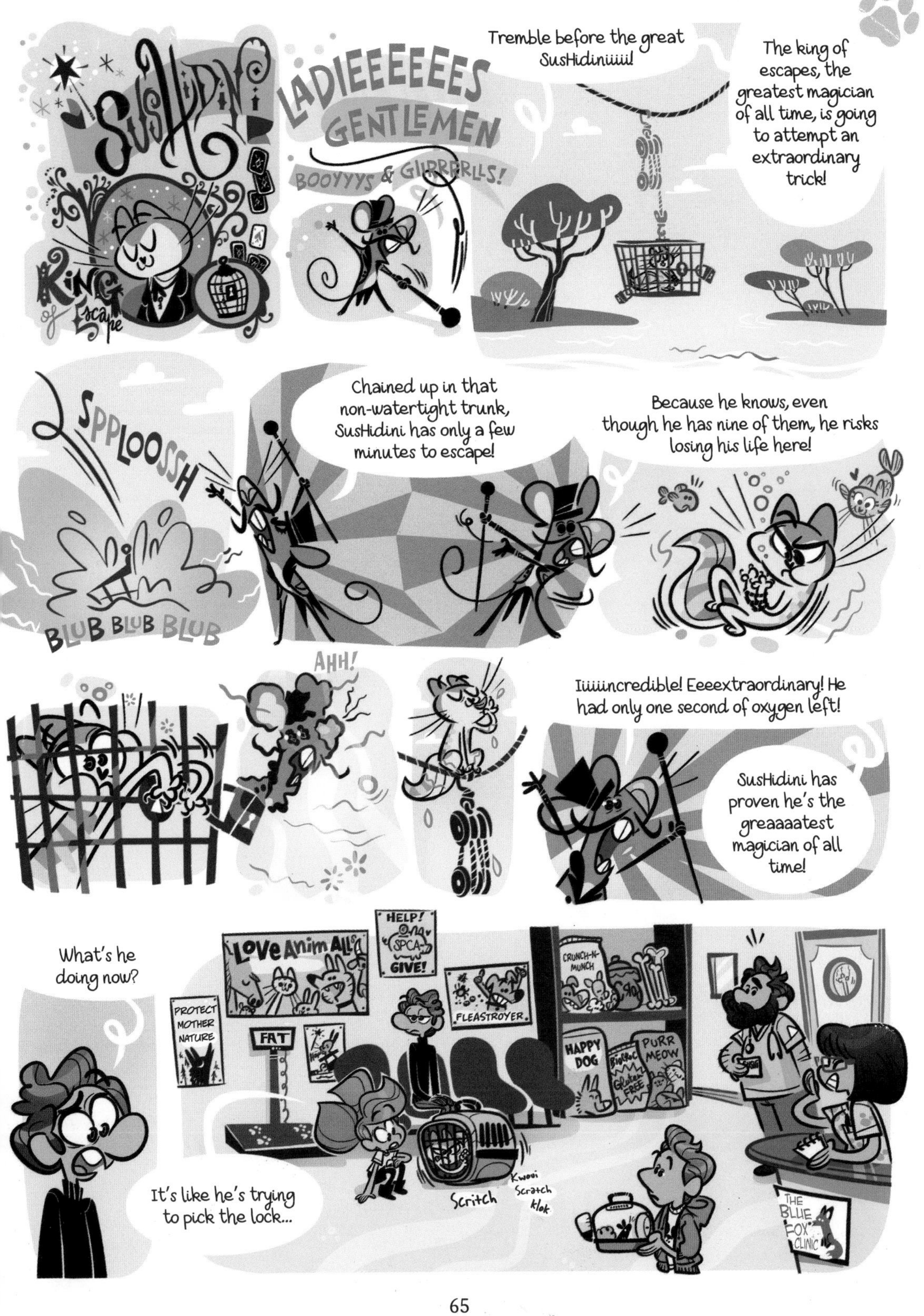
SusHidini
King of Escape
LADIEEEEEES GENTLEMEN
BOOYYYS & GIRRRRRLLS!
Tremble before the great SusHidiniiiii!
The king of escapes, the greatest magician of all time, is going to attempt an extraordinary trick!
SPPLOOSSH
BLUB BLUB BLUB
Chained up in that non-watertight trunk, SusHidini has only a few minutes to escape!
Because he knows, even though he has nine of them, he risks losing his life here!
AHH!
Iiiiiincredible! Eeeextraordinary! He had only one second of oxygen left!
SusHidini has proven he's the greaaaatest magician of all time!
What's he doing now?
LOVE AnimALLS
HELP! SPCA GIVE!
PROTECT MOTHER NATURE
FAT
FLEASTROYER
CRUNCH-N-MUNCH
HAPPY DOG
BioRoc Gluten FREE
PURR MEOW
It's like he's trying to pick the lock...
Scritch
Kwoui Scratch klok
THE BLUE FOX CLINIC

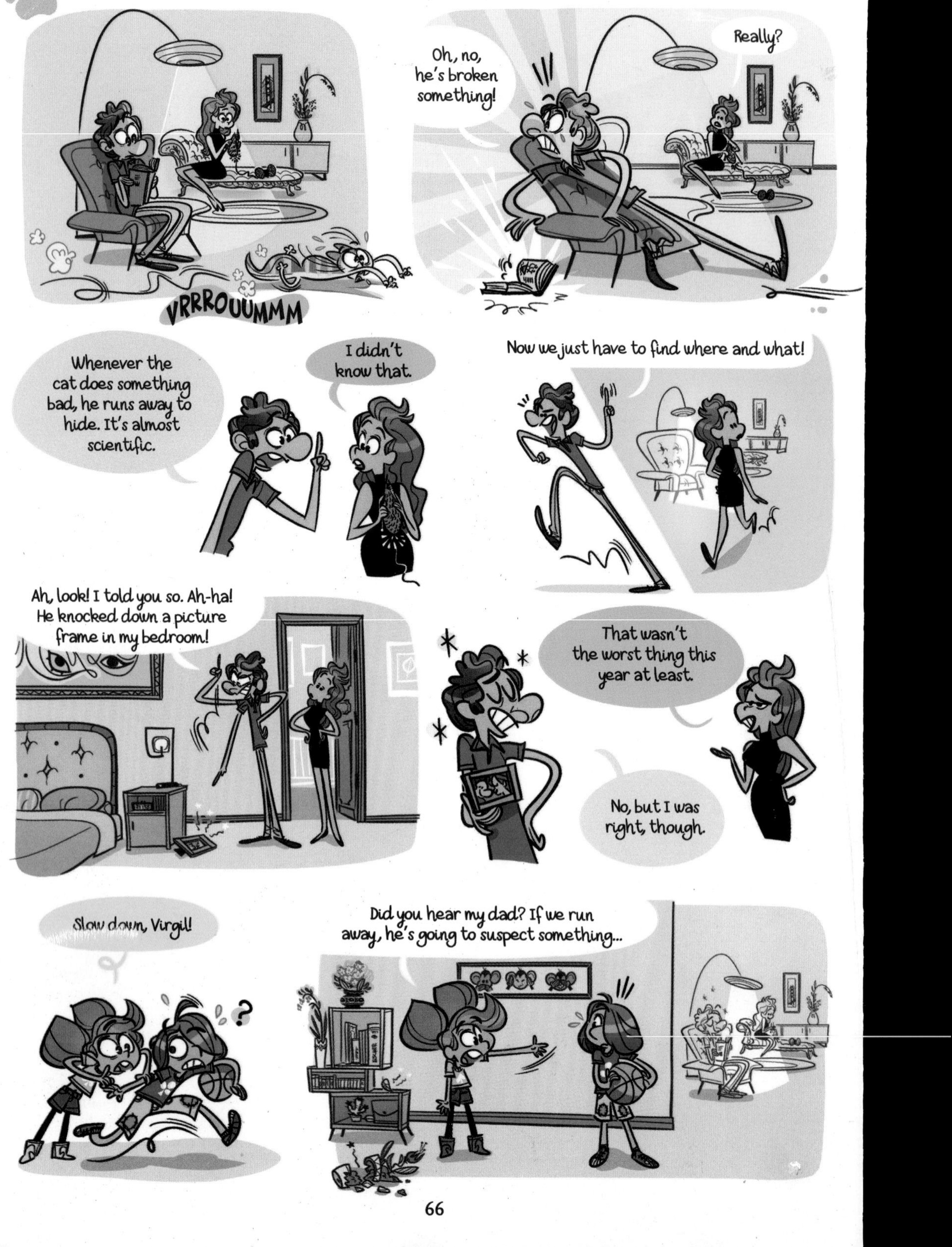
VRRROUUMMM
Oh, no, he's broken something!
Really?
Whenever the cat does something bad, he runs away to hide. It's almost scientific.
I didn't know that.
Now we just have to find where and what!
Ah, look! I told you so. Ah-ha! He knocked down a picture frame in my bedroom!
That wasn't the worst thing this year at least.
No, but I was right, though.
Slow down, Virgil!
Did you hear my dad? If we run away, he's going to suspect something...

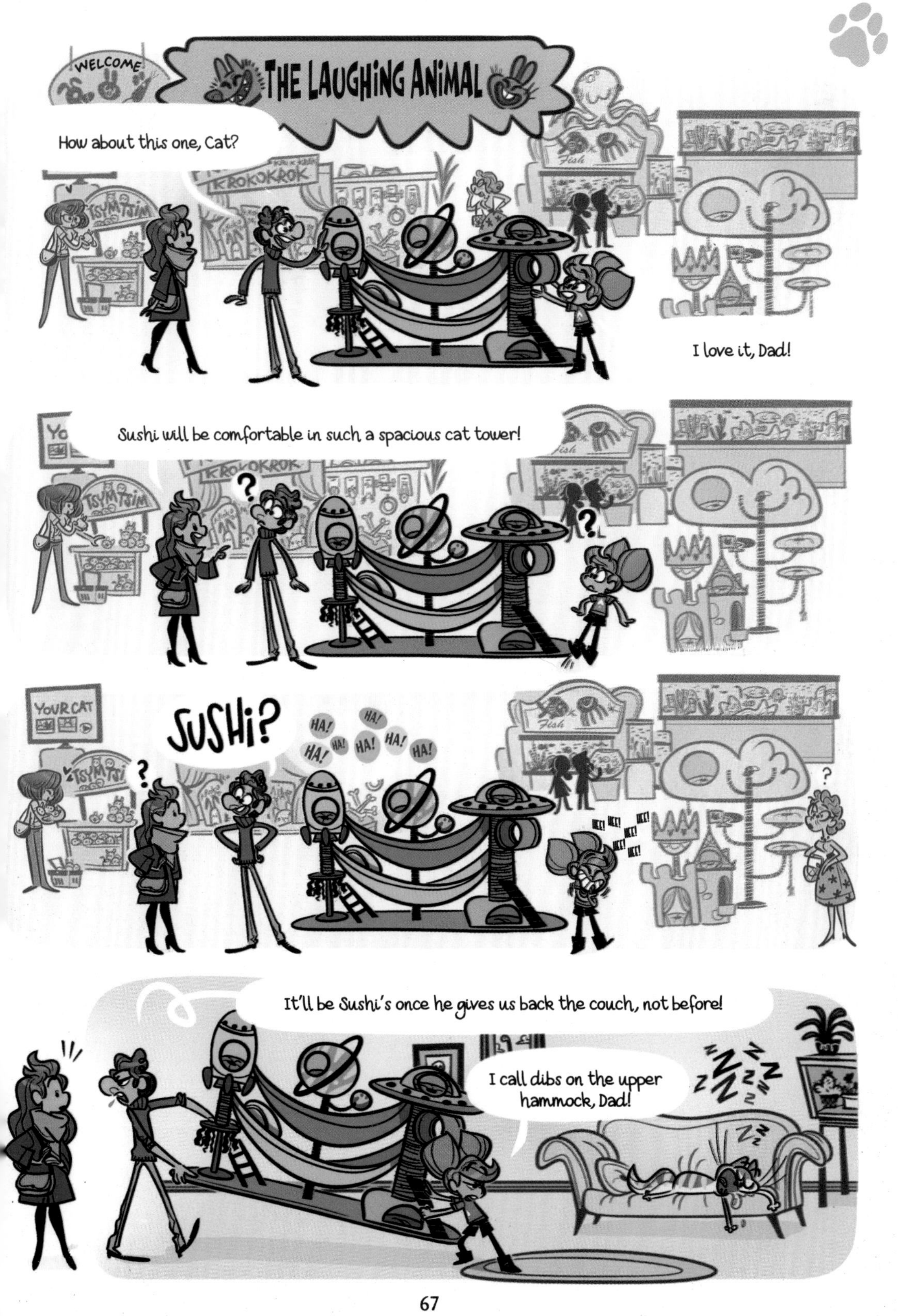
WELCOME
THE LAUGHING ANIMAL
How about this one, Cat?
KROKOKROK
TSYMTSIM
Fish
I love it, Dad!
Sushi will be comfortable in such a spacious cat tower!
YOUR CAT
SUSHI?
HA! HA! HA! HA! HA! HA!
HEE! HEE! HEE! HEE! HEE! HEE!
It'll be Sushi's once he gives us back the couch, not before!
I call dibs on the upper hammock, Dad!
ZZZ

Sam! Why are you on these magazines?!

Oh, did Virgil show you that? Well, that was my old job. When I was younger, I was a model.

You were a MODEL? CRA-ZY!

So cool! How do you become a model? Tell me. Come on, tell me!

First, you have to make a "book"!

A book is a portfolio of photos of you in a variety of poses that you show at castings.

Cats-things?

YOUNG BEAUTY

That's a meeting where, if they like your book, you're chosen for advertising shoots in magazines.

You have to give it your all!

Only a few are selected. There were 50 young women at the casting for that cover.

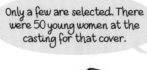

Got it! I'm on it!

If you're interested, Cat, I can--

Forget it, Sam!

It's not "really" for her!

Quick, Sushi! We'll do your book-folio-thingy and hurry to the cats-things!

CHKRK

CLICK CLIC

clic

BRRR

Give it your all!

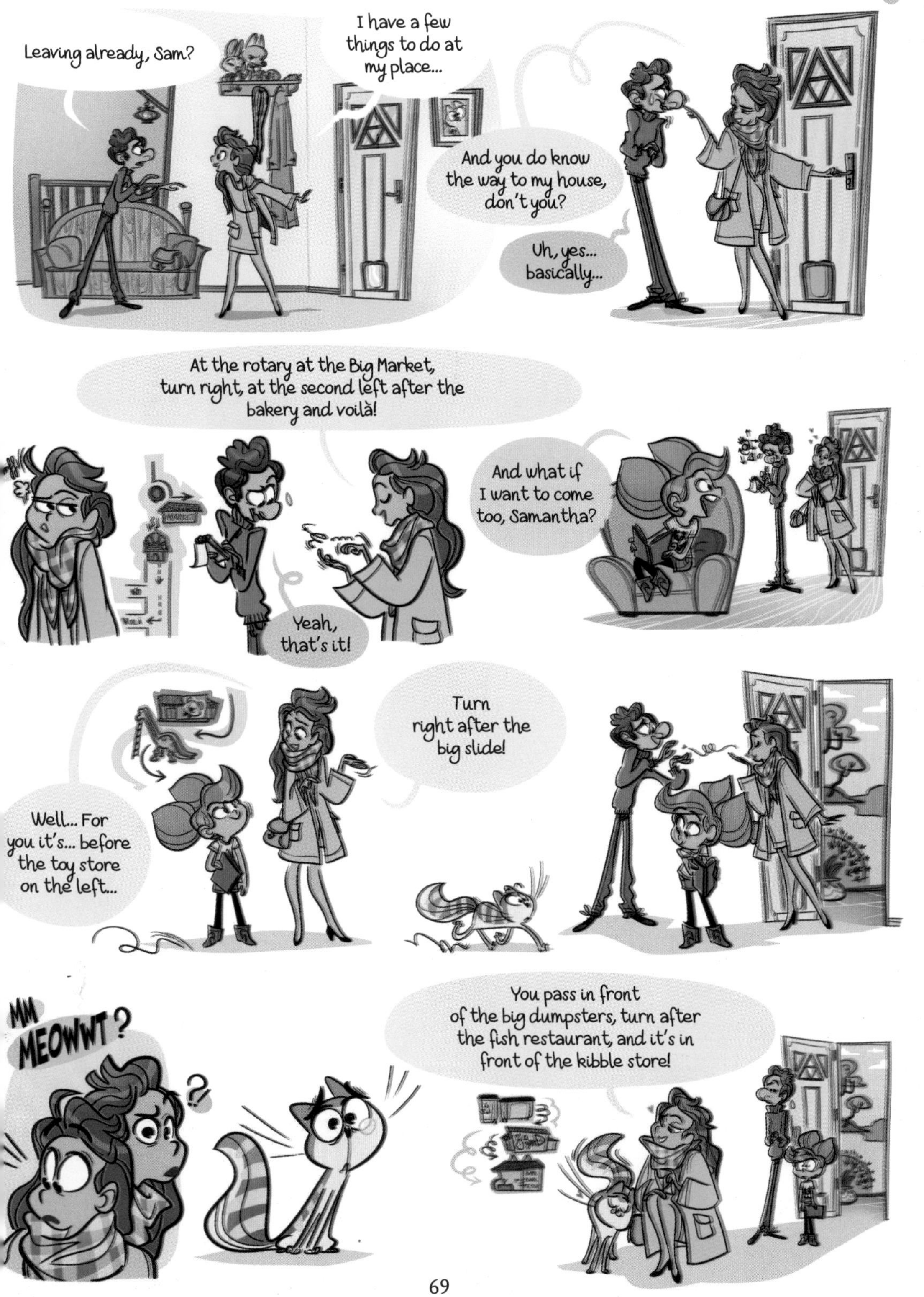
Leaving already, Sam?
I have a few things to do at my place...
And you do know the way to my house, don't you?
Uh, yes... basically...
At the rotary at the Big Market, turn right, at the second left after the bakery and voilà!
Yeah, that's it!
And what if I want to come too, Samantha?
Well... For you it's... before the toy store on the left...
Turn right after the big slide!
MM MEOWWT?
You pass in front of the big dumpsters, turn after the fish restaurant, and it's in front of the kibble store!

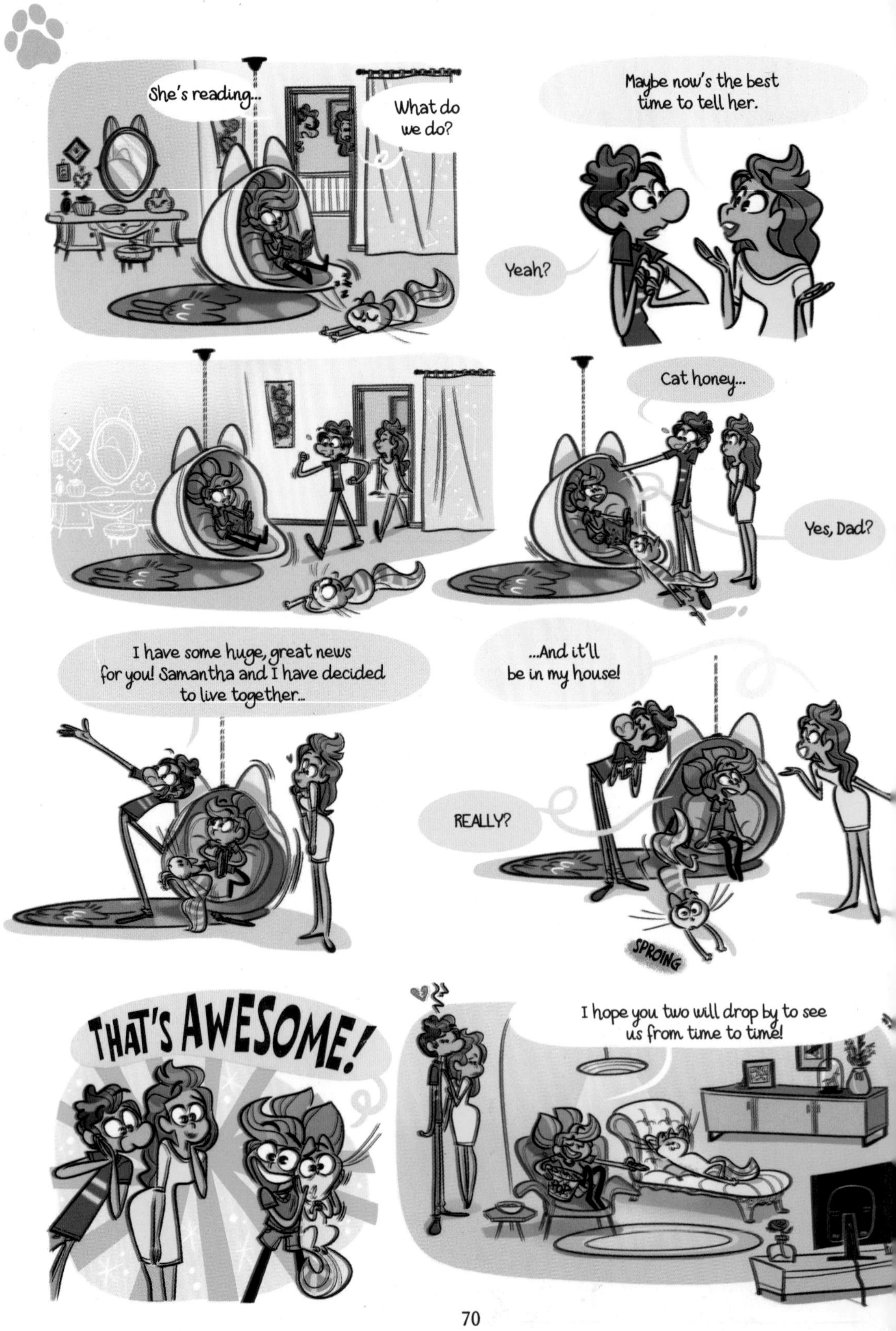
She's reading...
What do we do?
Maybe now's the best time to tell her.
Yeah?
Cat honey...
Yes, Dad?
I have some huge, great news for you! Samantha and I have decided to live together...
...And it'll be in my house!
REALLY?
SPROING
THAT'S AWESOME!
I hope you two will drop by to see us from time to time!

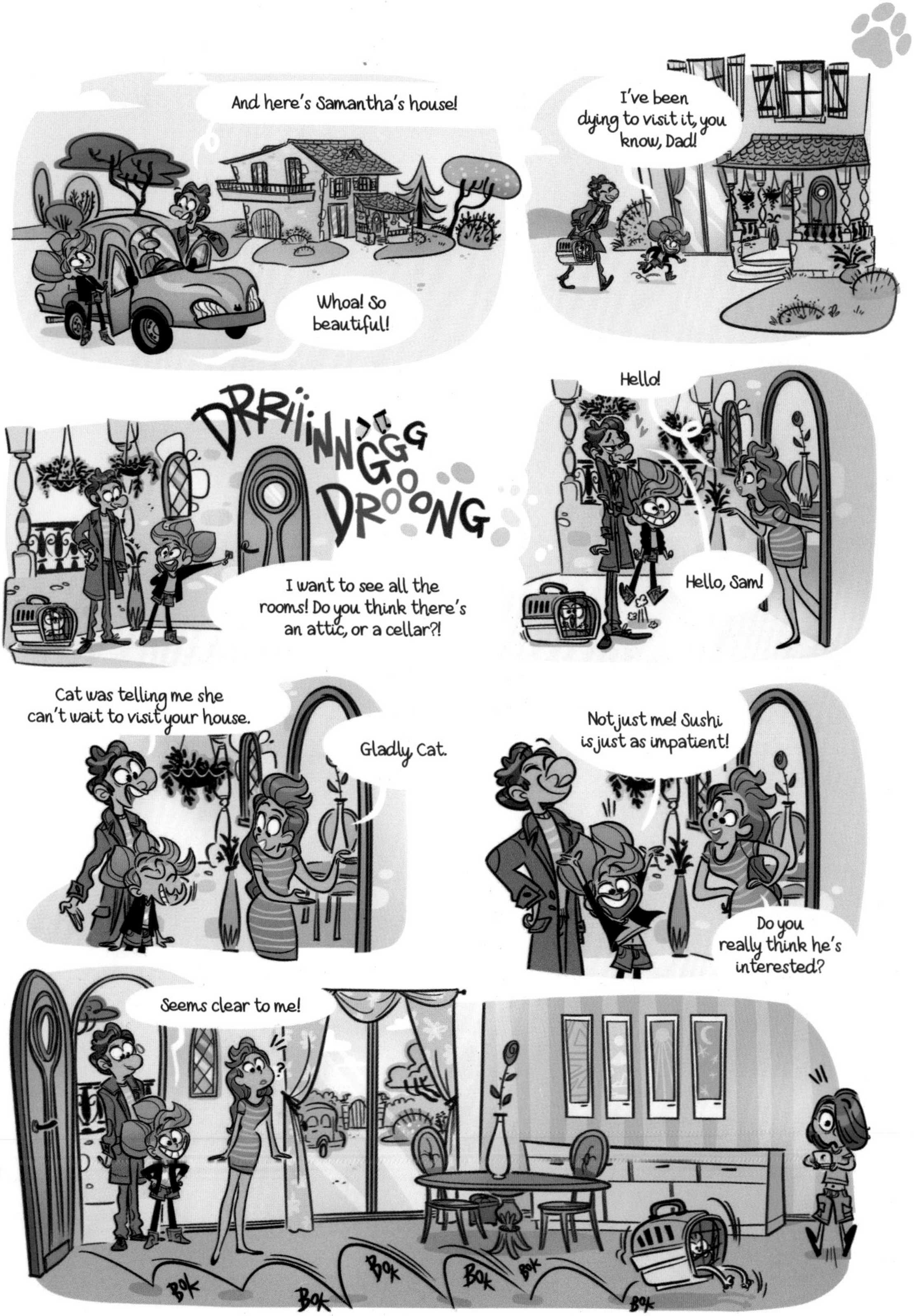
And here's Samantha's house!
Whoa! So beautiful!
I've been dying to visit it, you know, Dad!
DRRIIINNGGG DROOONG
I want to see all the rooms! Do you think there's an attic, or a cellar?!
Hello!
Hello, Sam!
Cat was telling me she can't wait to visit your house.
Gladly, Cat.
Not just me! Sushi is just as impatient!
Do you really think he's interested?
Seems clear to me!
BOK
BOK
BOK
BOK
BOK
BOK

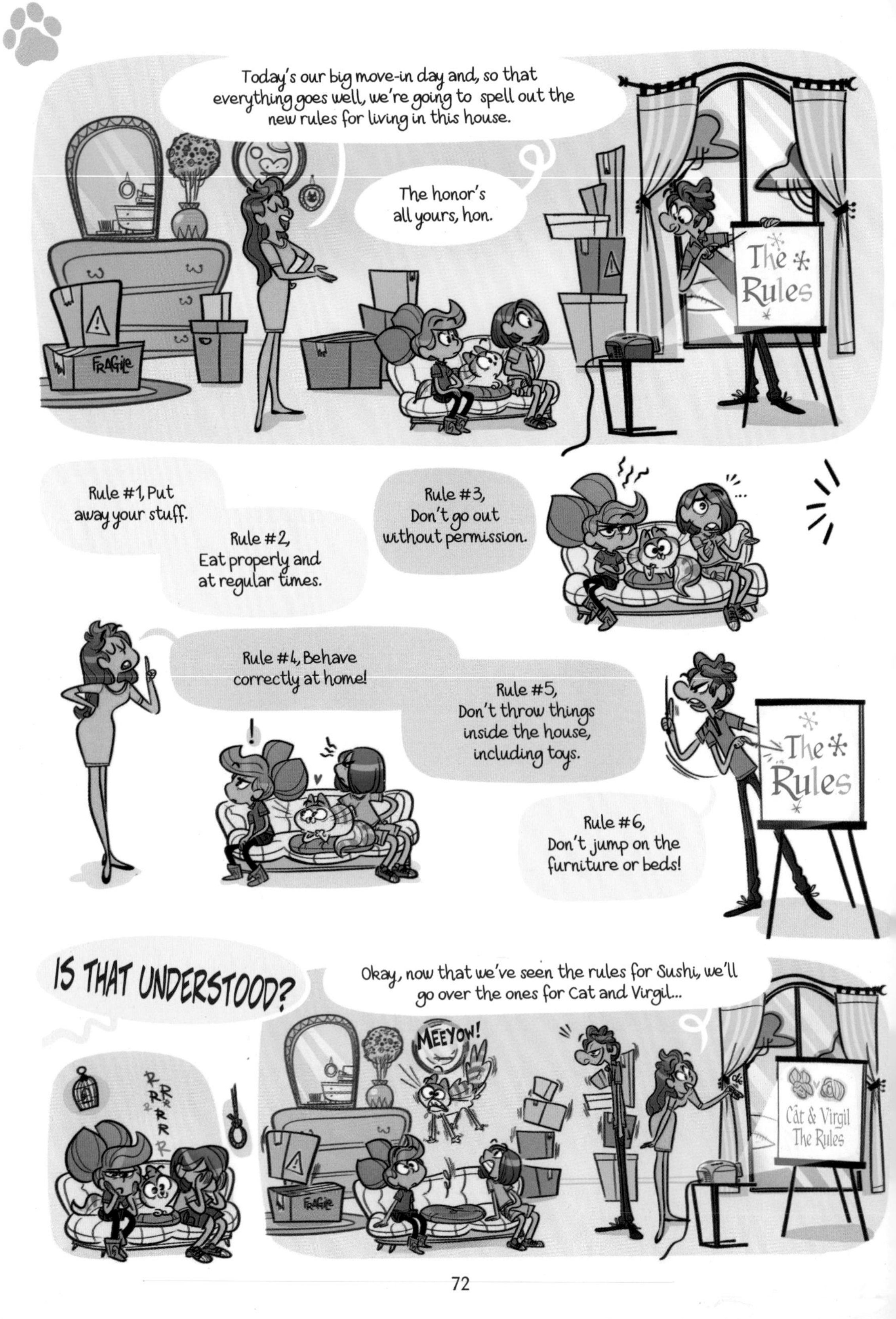
Today's our big move-in day and, so that everything goes well, we're going to spell out the new rules for living in this house.
The honor's all yours, hon.
The Rules
FRAGILE
Rule #1, Put away your stuff.
Rule #2, Eat properly and at regular times.
Rule #3, Don't go out without permission.
Rule #4, Behave correctly at home!
Rule #5, Don't throw things inside the house, including toys.
The Rules
Rule #6, Don't jump on the furniture or beds!
IS THAT UNDERSTOOD?
Okay, now that we've seen the rules for Sushi, we'll go over the ones for Cat and Virgil...
RRRRRR
MEEYOW!
FRAGILE
Cat & Virgil The Rules

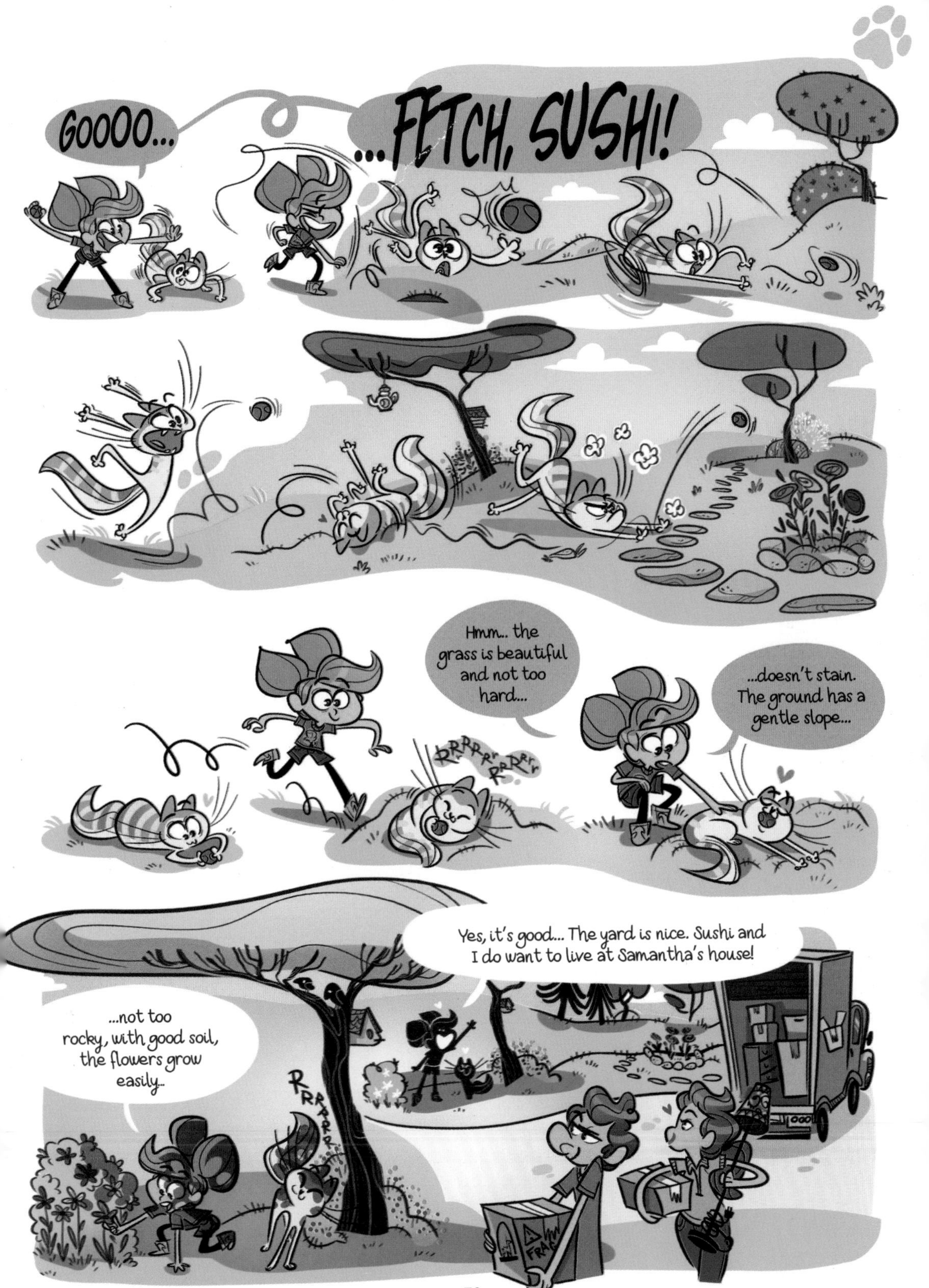
GOOOO...
...FETCH, SUSHI!
Hmm.. the grass is beautiful and not too hard...
RRRRRr RRRRrr
...doesn't stain. The ground has a gentle slope...
Yes, it's good... The yard is nice. Sushi and I do want to live at Samantha's house!
...not too rocky, with good soil, the flowers grow easily...
RRRRRRR

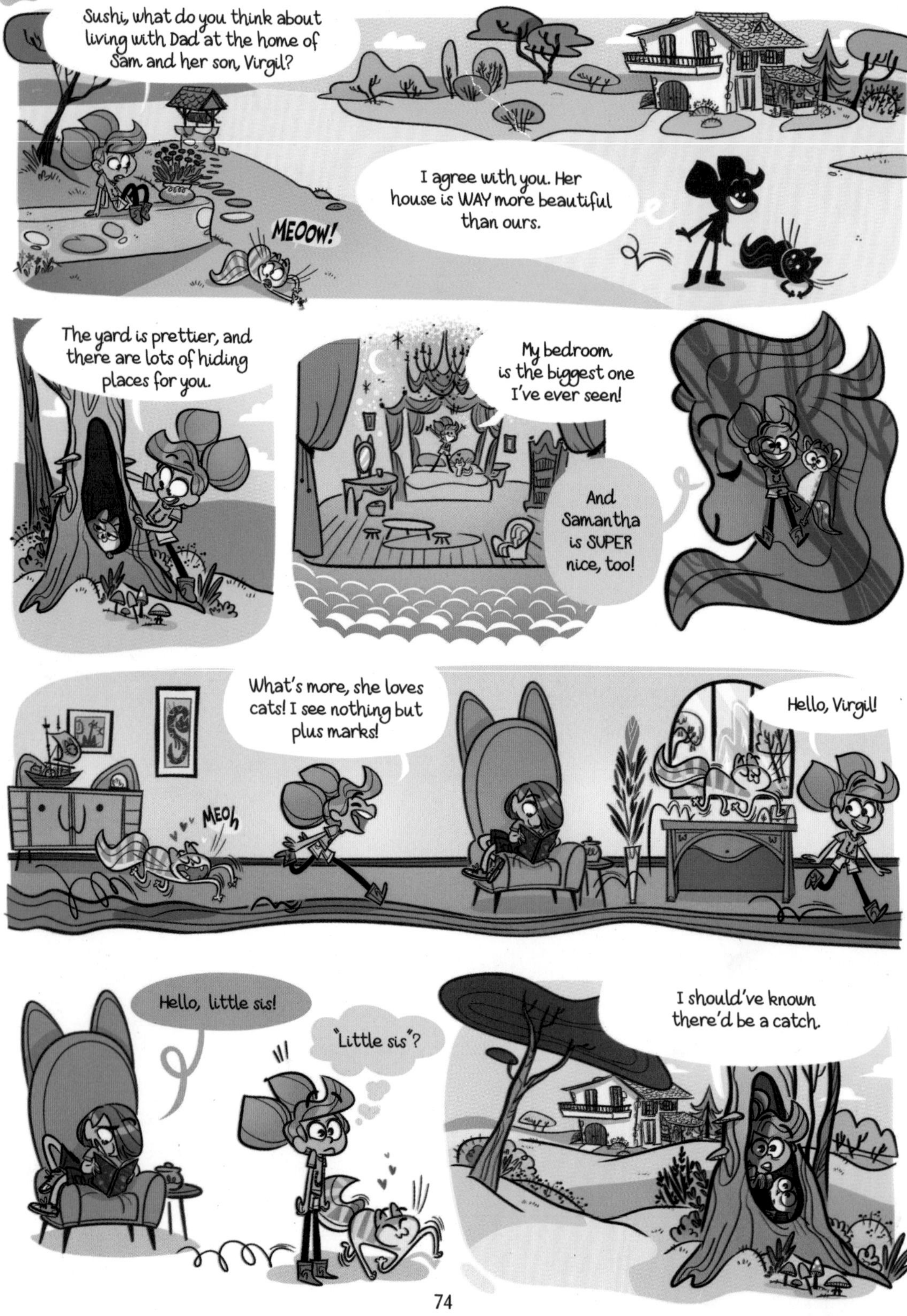
Sushi, what do you think about living with Dad at the home of Sam and her son, Virgil?
MEOOW!
I agree with you. Her house is WAY more beautiful than ours.
The yard is prettier, and there are lots of hiding places for you.
My bedroom is the biggest one I've ever seen!
And Samantha is SUPER nice, too!
What's more, she loves cats! I see nothing but plus marks!
MEOh
Hello, Virgil!
Hello, little sis!
"Little sis"?
I should've known there'd be a catch.

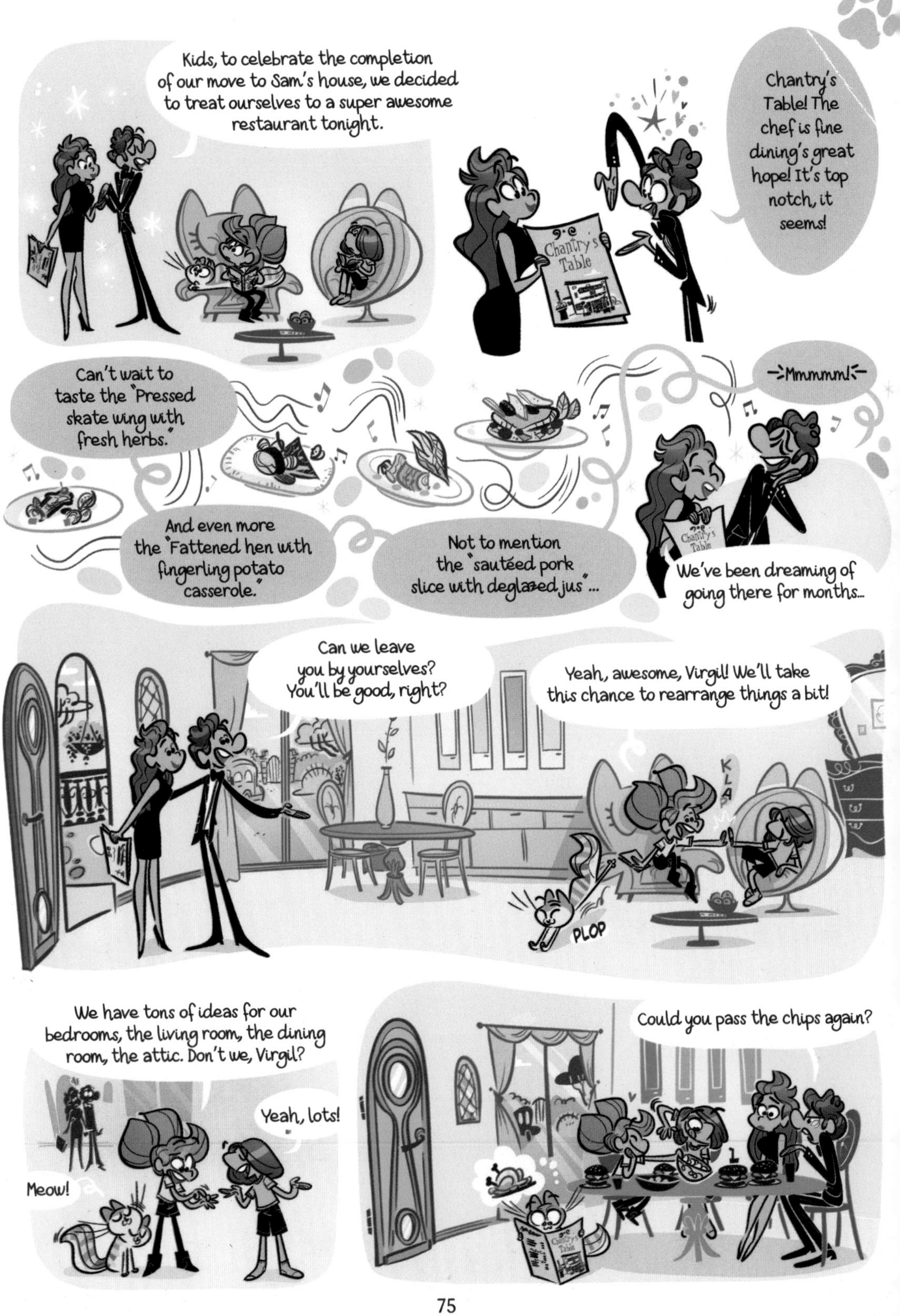
Kids, to celebrate the completion of our move to Sam's house, we decided to treat ourselves to a super awesome restaurant tonight.
Chantry's Table! The chef is fine dining's great hope! It's top notch, it seems!
Chantry's Table
Can't wait to taste the "Pressed skate wing with fresh herbs."
And even more the "Fattened hen with fingerling potato casserole."
Not to mention the "sautéed pork slice with deglazed jus"...
Mmmmm!
Chantry's Table
We've been dreaming of going there for months...
Can we leave you by yourselves? You'll be good, right?
Yeah, awesome, Virgil! We'll take this chance to rearrange things a bit!
KLAP
PLOP
We have tons of ideas for our bedrooms, the living room, the dining room, the attic. Don't we, Virgil?
Yeah, lots!
Meow!
Could you pass the chips again?
Chantry's Table

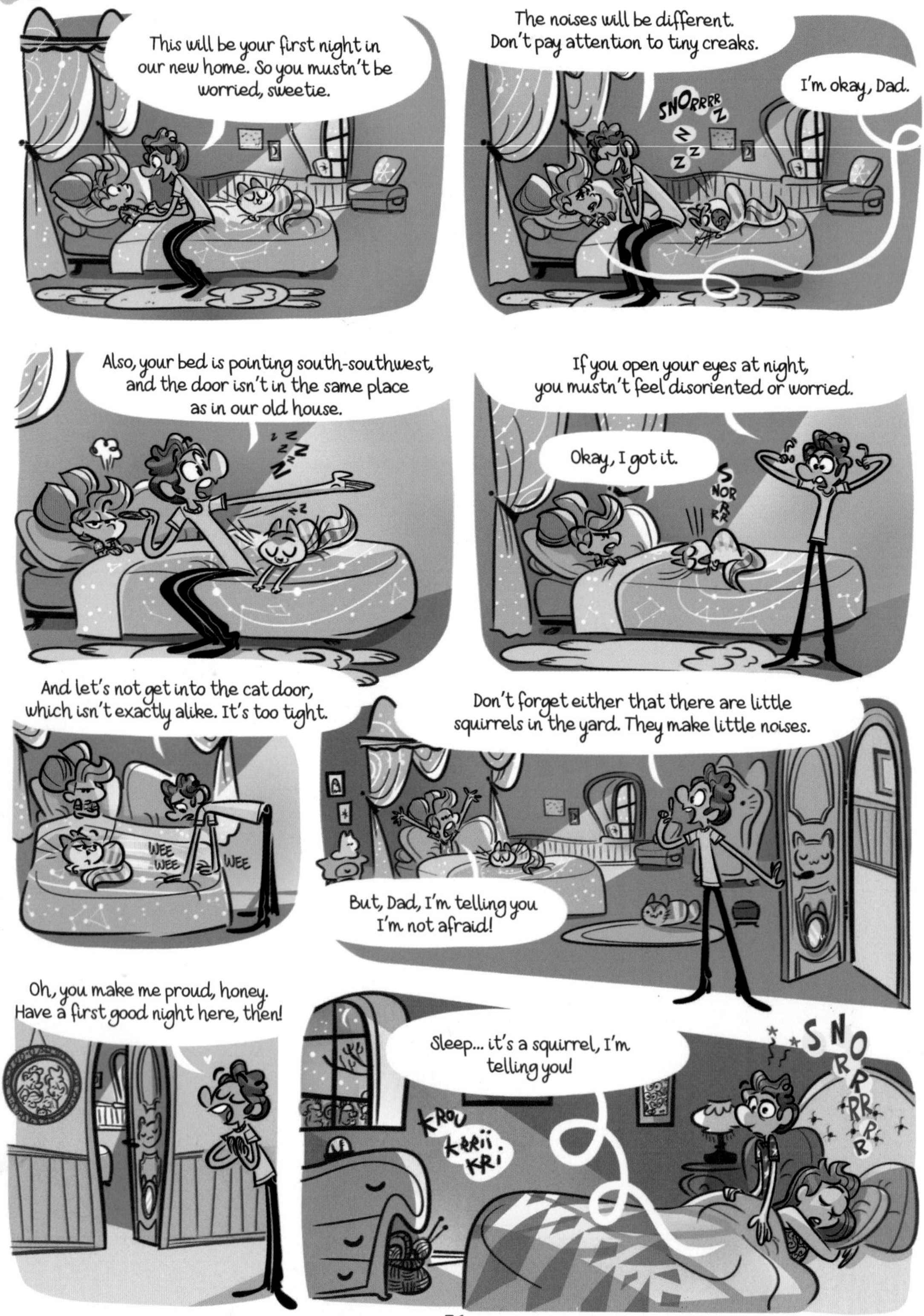
This will be your first night in our new home. So you mustn't be worried, sweetie.
The noises will be different. Don't pay attention to tiny creaks.
SNORRRR
I'm okay, Dad.
Also, your bed is pointing south-southwest, and the door isn't in the same place as in our old house.
If you open your eyes at night, you mustn't feel disoriented or worried.
Okay, I got it.
SNORR
And let's not get into the cat door, which isn't exactly alike. It's too tight.
WEE WEE
WEE
Don't forget either that there are little squirrels in the yard. They make little noises.
But, Dad, I'm telling you I'm not afraid!
Oh, you make me proud, honey. Have a first good night here, then!
Sleep... it's a squirrel, I'm telling you!
KROU
KRRII
KRI
SNORRRRRR

We have to move back!

Why's that? You're not comfortable at my home? Well, OUR home?!

My car doesn't fit in your garage! Your door is too low! That's why!

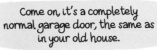

Come on, it's a completely normal garage door, the same as in your old house.

Actually, no. Matter of fact, I had mine custom built!

Custom built? Now that I think about it, you have the same kind of car as mine.

That's right... But you don't have a cat!

And if I have to wait till Mr. Sushi finishes his nap, my car might spend the whole winter outside!

Therefore, the door's got to be higher so I can get it inside!

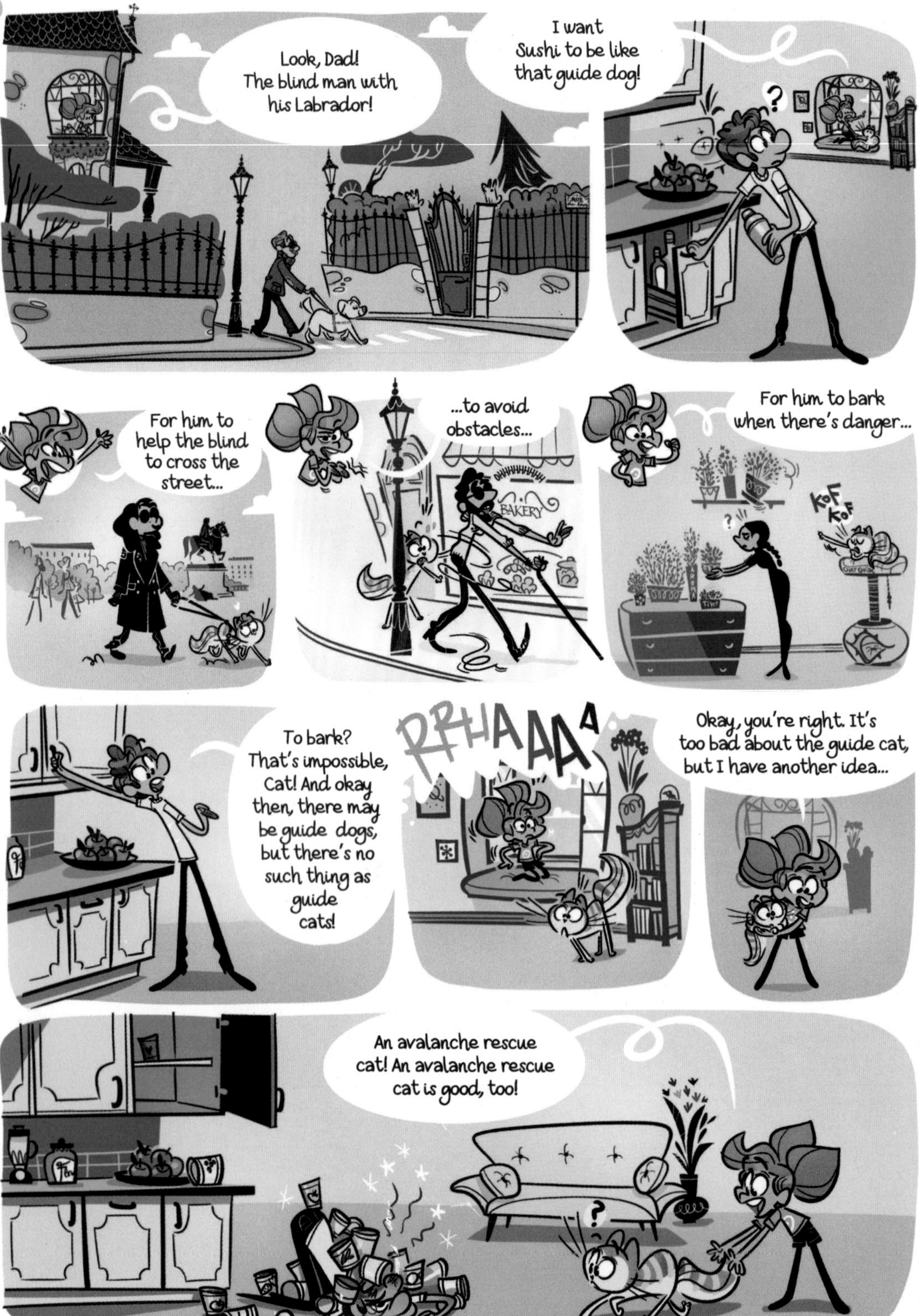
Look, Dad! The blind man with his Labrador!
I want Sushi to be like that guide dog!
For him to help the blind to cross the street...
...to avoid obstacles...
BAKERY
For him to bark when there's danger...
KOF KOF
To bark? That's impossible, Cat! And okay then, there may be guide dogs, but there's no such thing as guide cats!
RRHAAAA
Okay, you're right. It's too bad about the guide cat, but I have another idea...
An avalanche rescue cat! An avalanche rescue cat is good, too!

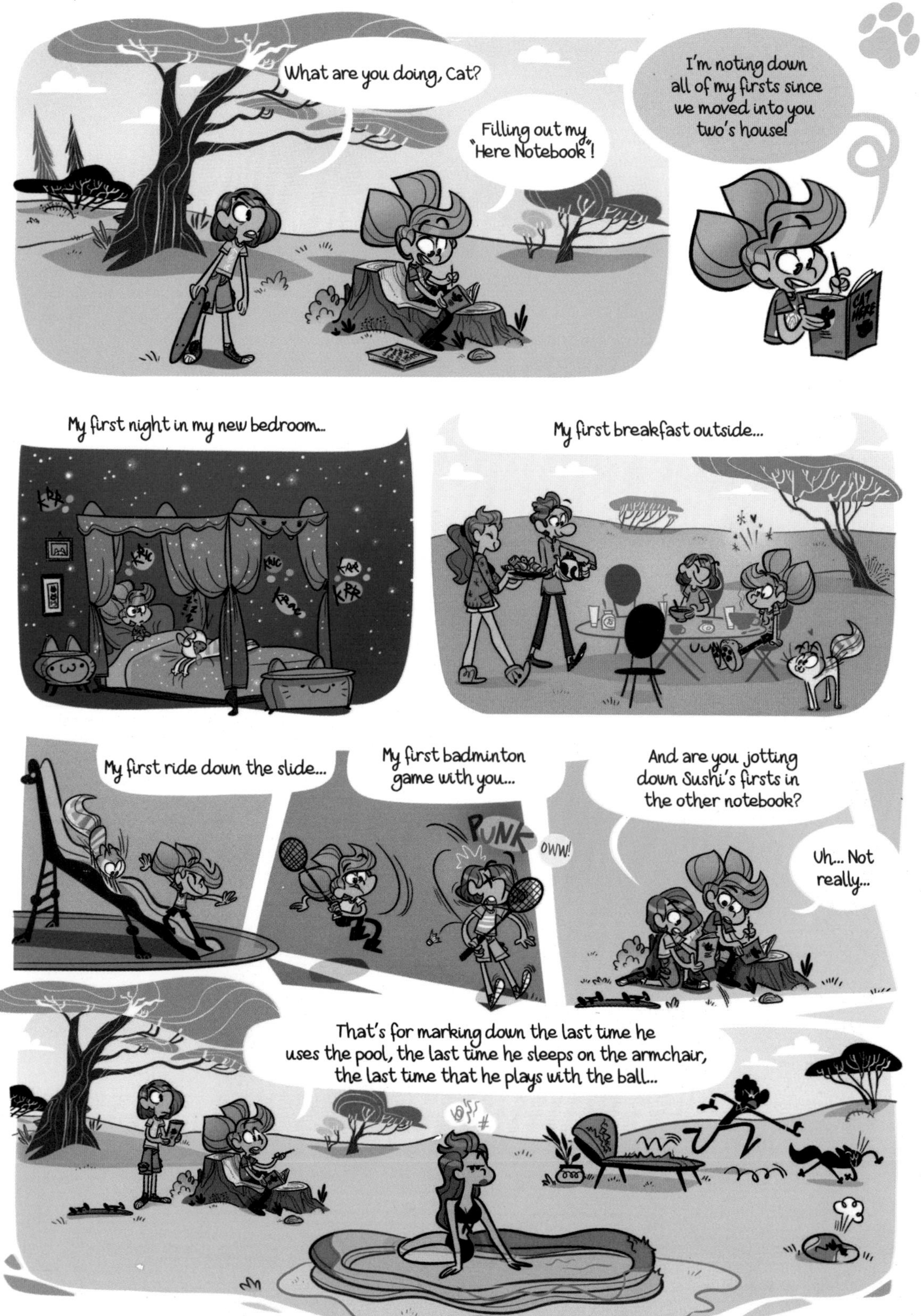
What are you doing, Cat?
Filling out my "Here Notebook"!
I'm noting down all of my firsts since we moved into you two's house!
My first night in my new bedroom...
My first breakfast outside...
My first ride down the slide...
My first badminton game with you...
PUNK
OWW!
And are you jotting down Sushi's firsts in the other notebook?
Uh... Not really...
That's for marking down the last time he uses the pool, the last time he sleeps on the armchair, the last time that he plays with the ball...

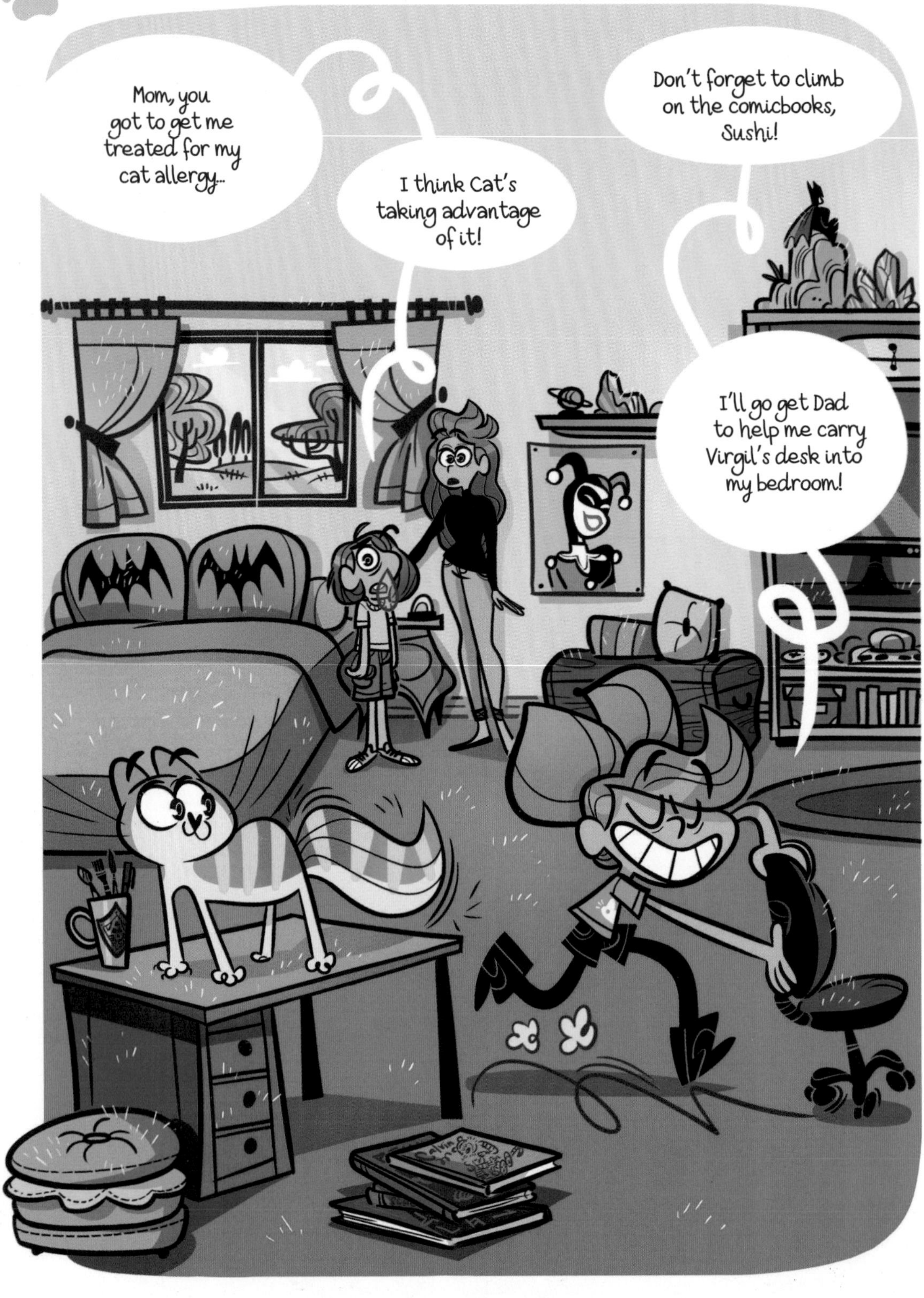
Mom, you got to get me treated for my cat allergy...
I think Cat's taking advantage of it!
Don't forget to climb on the comicbooks, Sushi!
I'll go get Dad to help me carry Virgil's desk into my bedroom!

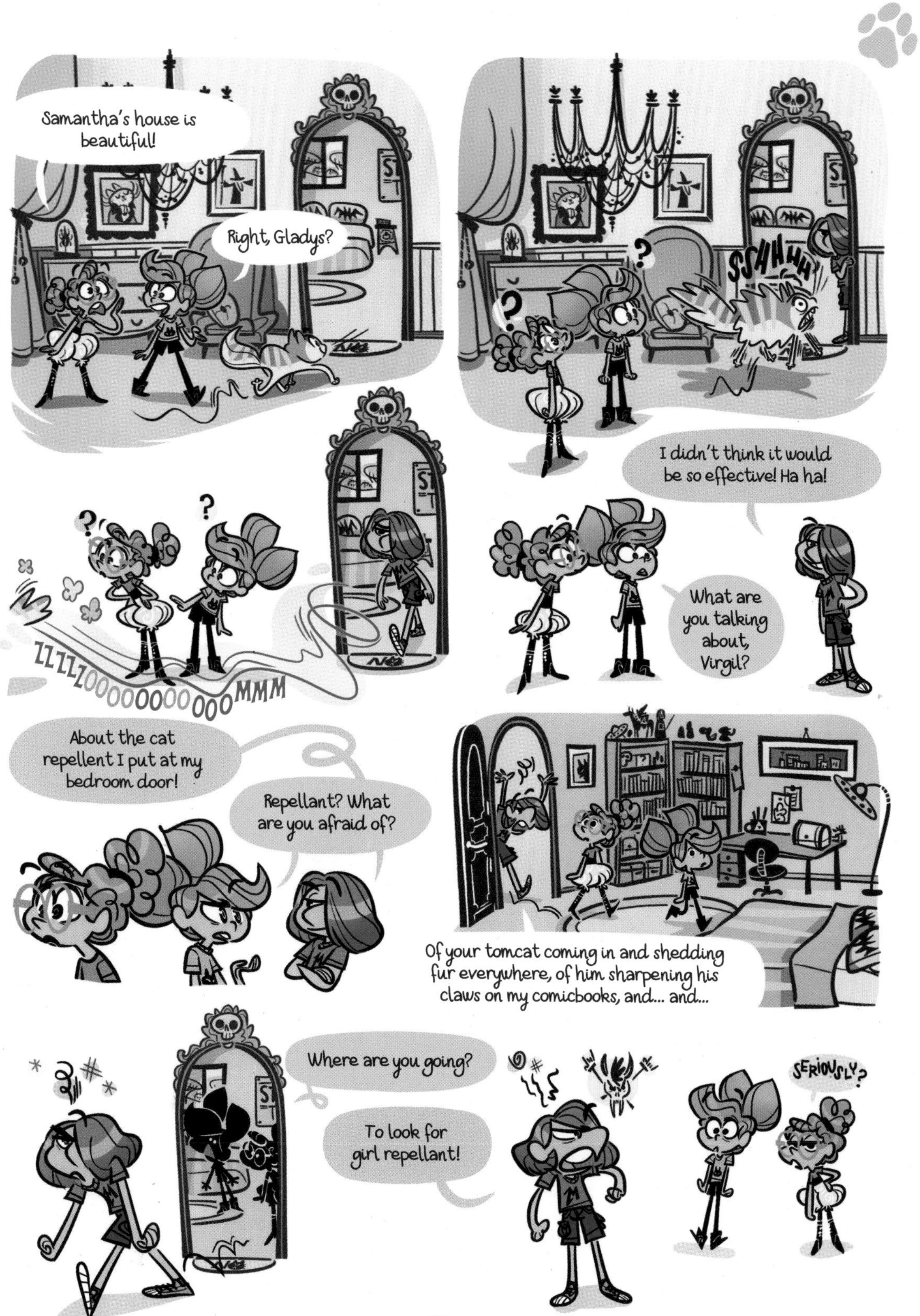
Samantha's house is beautiful!
Right, Gladys?
SSHHHH
I didn't think it would be so effective! Ha ha!
ZZZZZOOOOOOOOOOOOMMM
What are you talking about, Virgil?
About the cat repellent I put at my bedroom door!
Repellant? What are you afraid of?
Of your tomcat coming in and shedding fur everywhere, of him sharpening his claws on my comicbooks, and... and...
Where are you going?
To look for girl repellant!
SERIOUSLY?

Samantha, it's funny how you've put all those locks on your wardrobe, drawers, and--

What? You put them on the fridge, too?!

And the cupboards!

How come?

Because, even if I have nothing against anyone going into the rooms of my house...

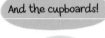
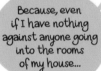

...I'm not so much a fan of your cat's "deep dive" exploration!

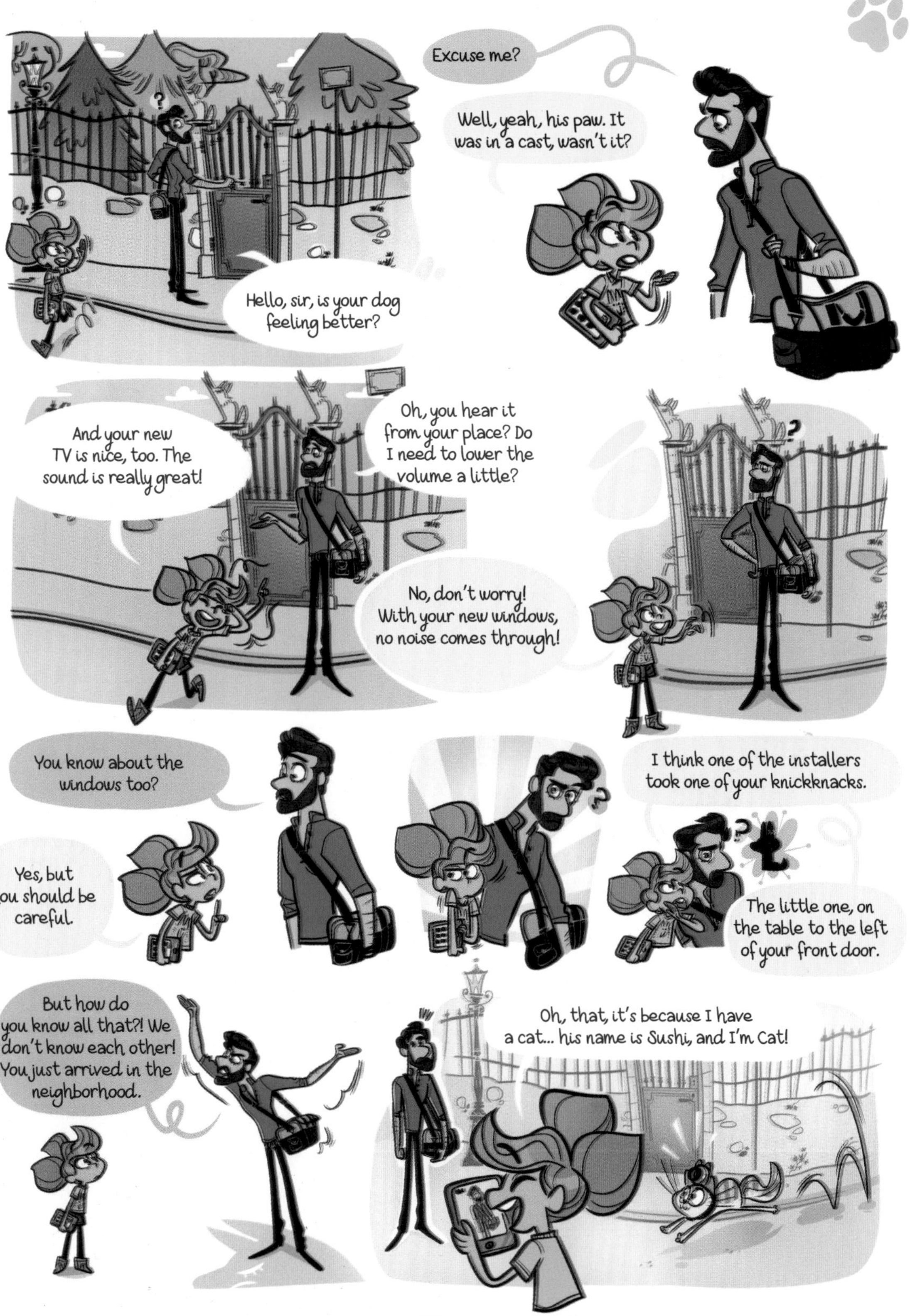
Hello, sir, is your dog feeling better?
Excuse me?
Well, yeah, his paw. It was in a cast, wasn't it?
And your new TV is nice, too. The sound is really great!
Oh, you hear it from your place? Do I need to lower the volume a little?
No, don't worry! With your new windows, no noise comes through!
You know about the windows too?
Yes, but you should be careful.
I think one of the installers took one of your knickknacks.
The little one, on the table to the left of your front door.
But how do you know all that?! We don't know each other! You just arrived in the neighborhood.
Oh, that, it's because I have a cat... his name is Sushi, and I'm Cat!

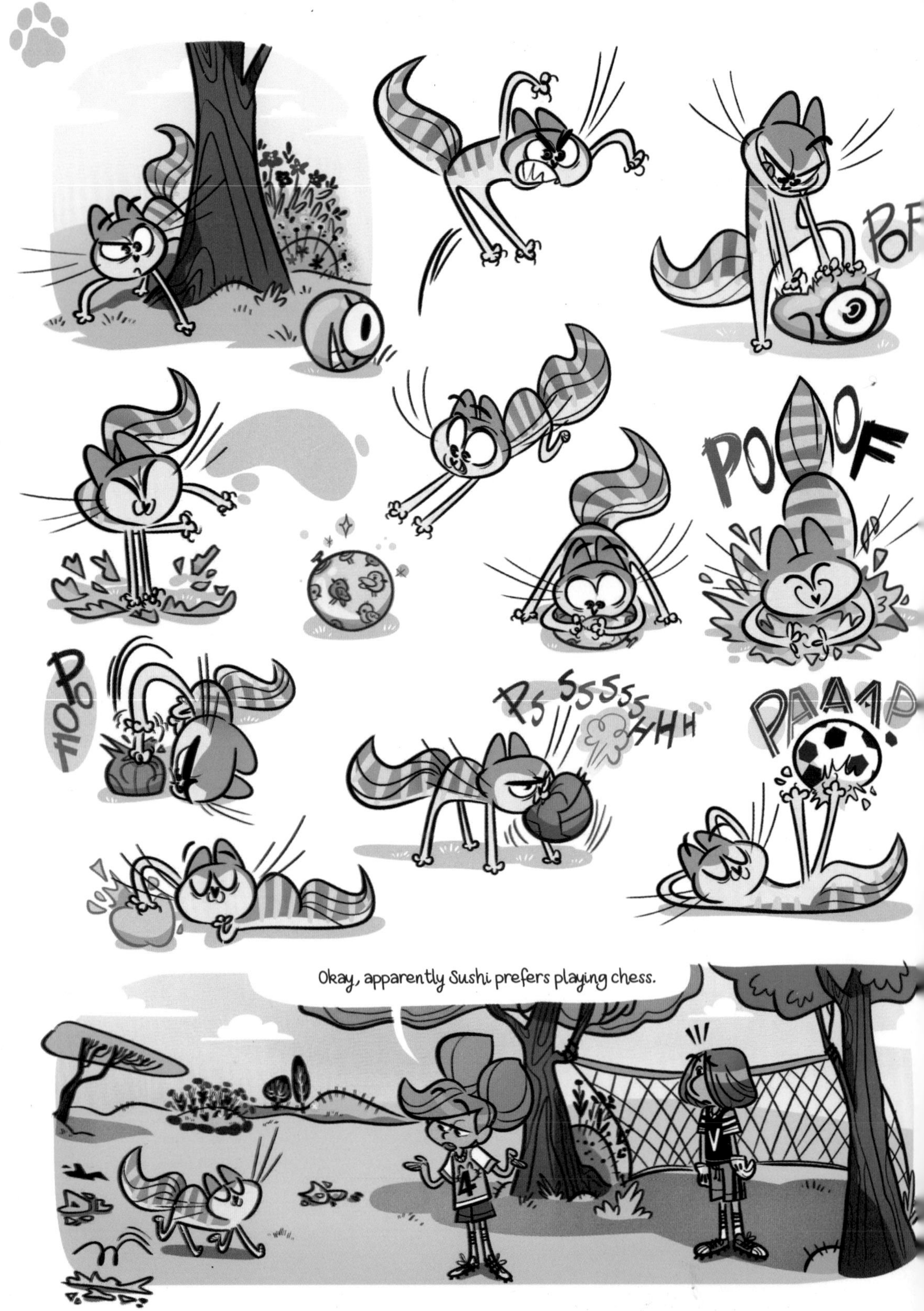
POF
POOF
POOF
PSSSSSSHH
PAAAP
Okay, apparently Sushi prefers playing chess.

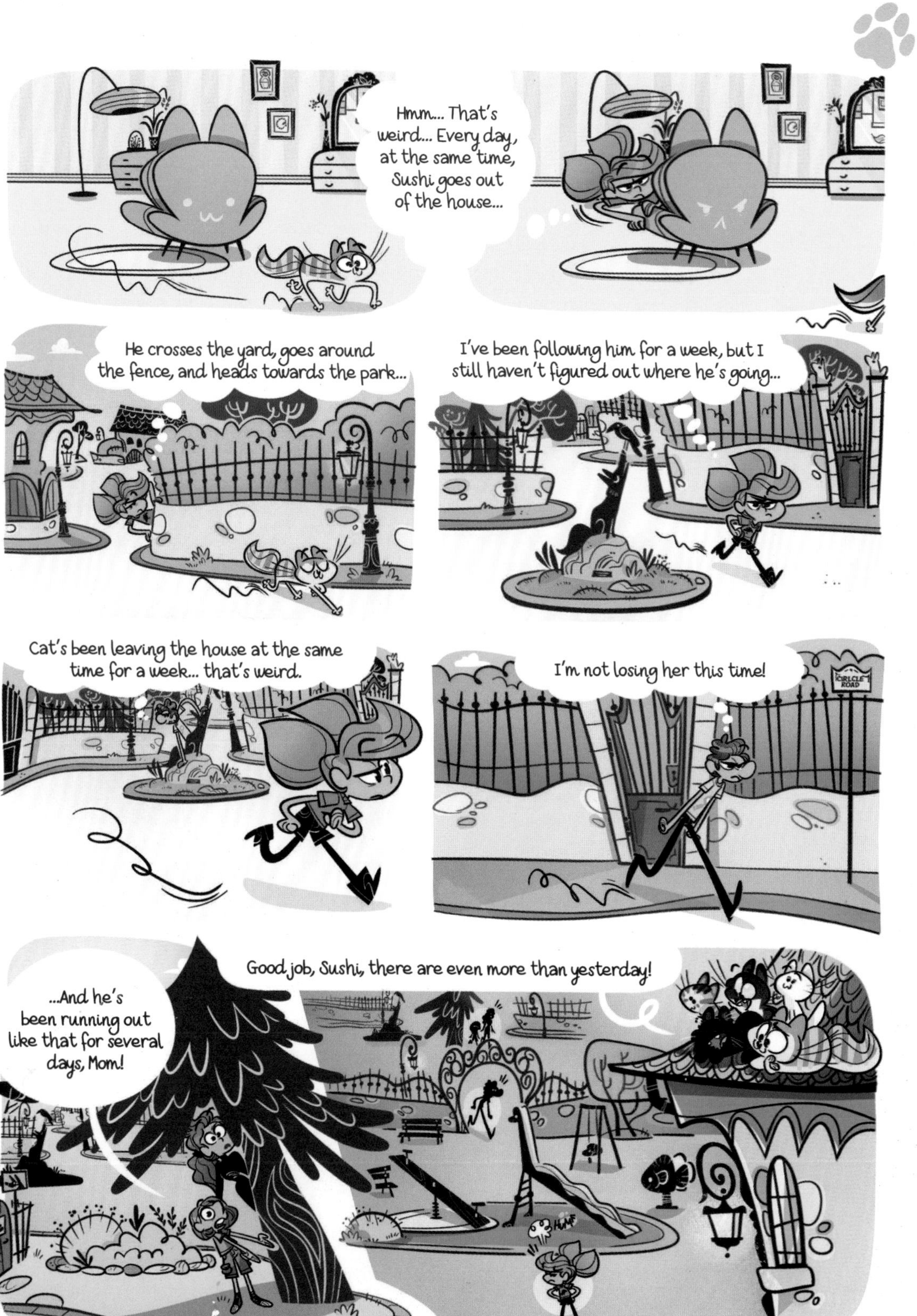
Hmm... That's weird... Every day, at the same time, Sushi goes out of the house...
He crosses the yard, goes around the fence, and heads towards the park...
I've been following him for a week, but I still haven't figured out where he's going...
Cat's been leaving the house at the same time for a week... that's weird.
I'm not losing her this time!
CIRCLE ROAD
...And he's been running out like that for several days, Mom!
Good job, Sushi, there are even more than yesterday!
HUMF

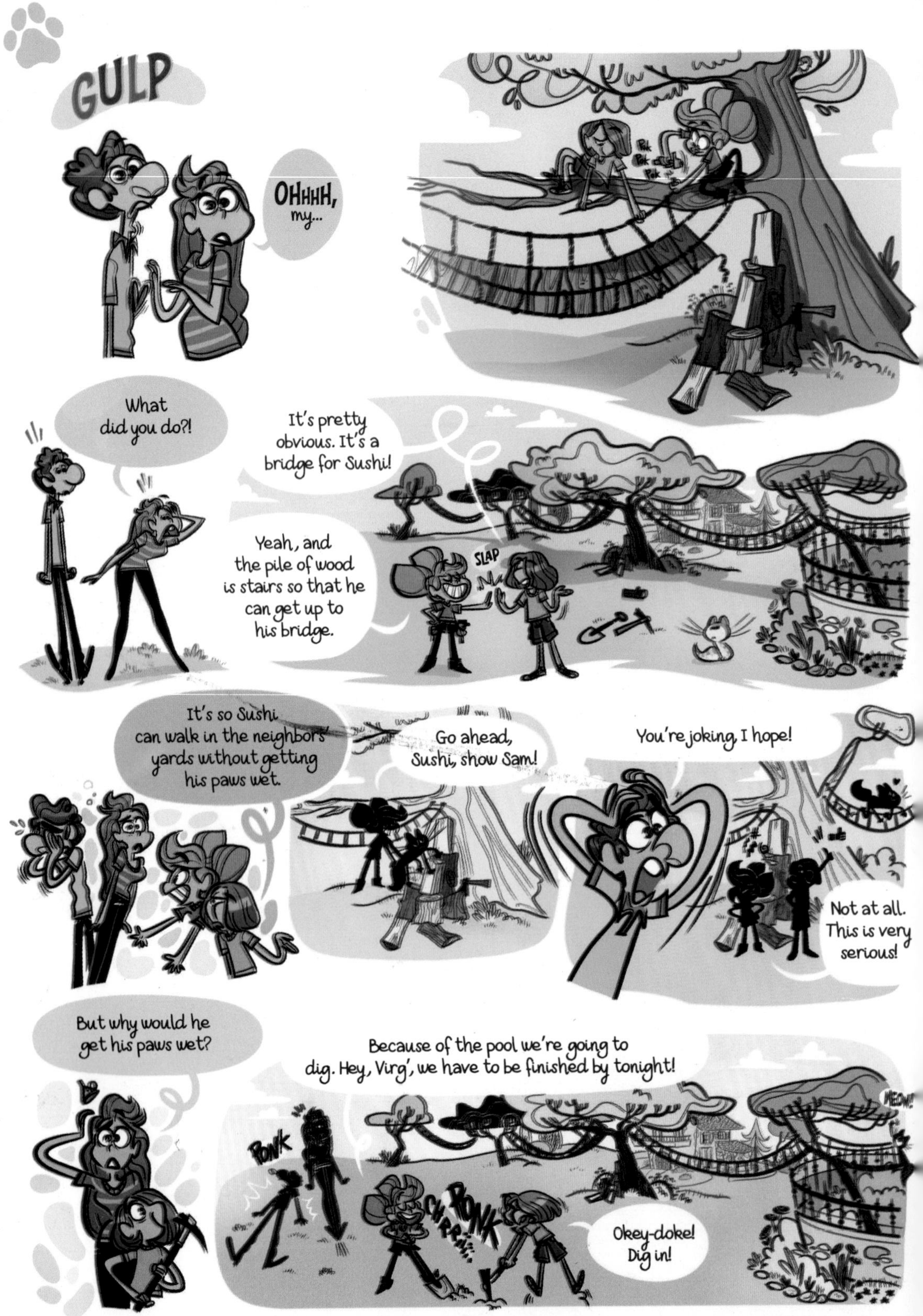
GULP
OHHHH, my...
What did you do?!
It's pretty obvious. It's a bridge for Sushi!
SLAP
Yeah, and the pile of wood is stairs so that he can get up to his bridge.
It's so Sushi can walk in the neighbors' yards without getting his paws wet.
Go ahead, Sushi, show Sam!
You're joking, I hope!
Not at all. This is very serious!
But why would he get his paws wet?
Because of the pool we're going to dig. Hey, Virg', we have to be finished by tonight!
PONK
PONK
Okey-doke! Dig in!

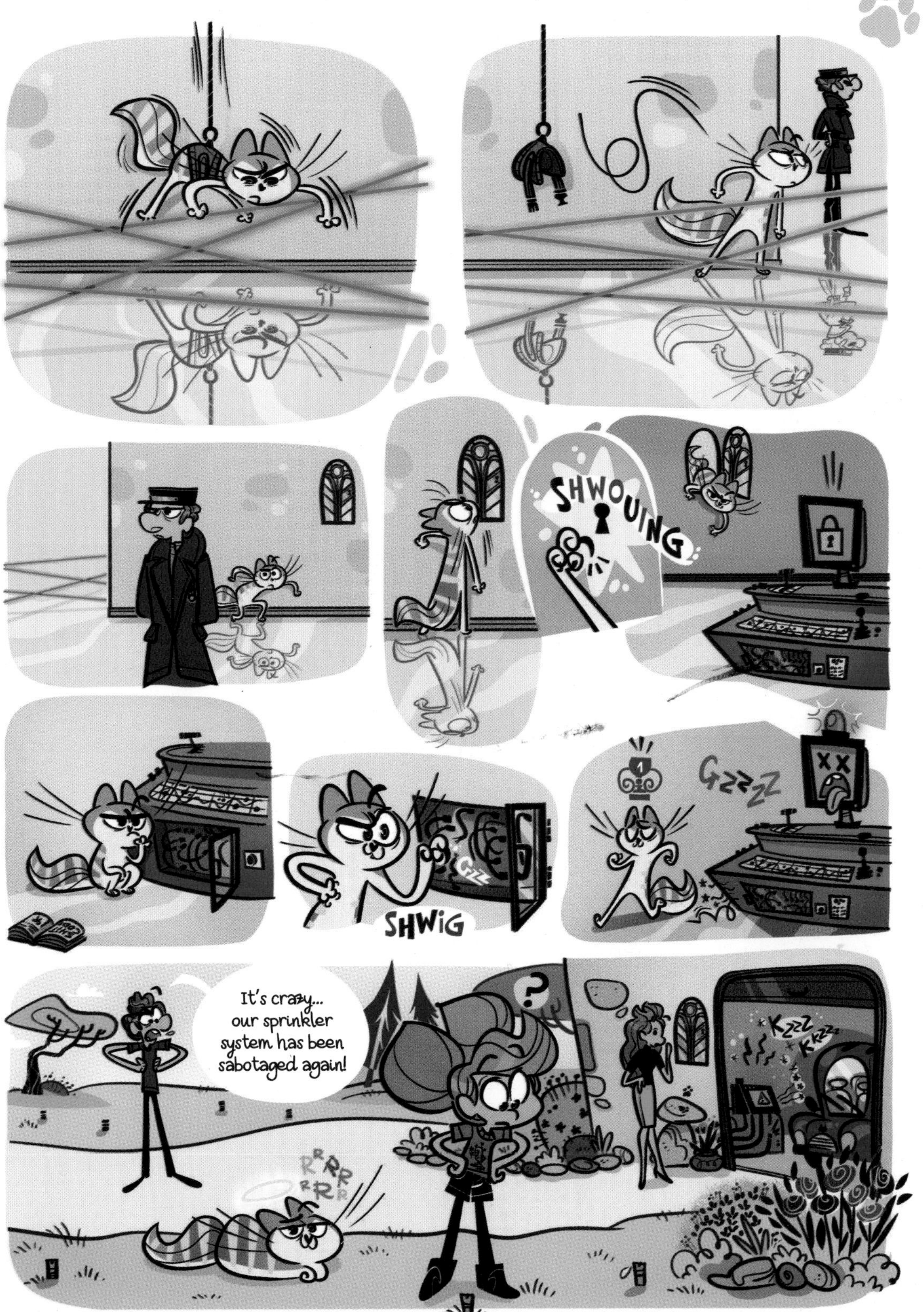
SHWOUING
SHWIG
GZZ
GZZZZ
It's crazy... our sprinkler system has been sabotaged again!
KZZZ
KZZZ
RRRRRR

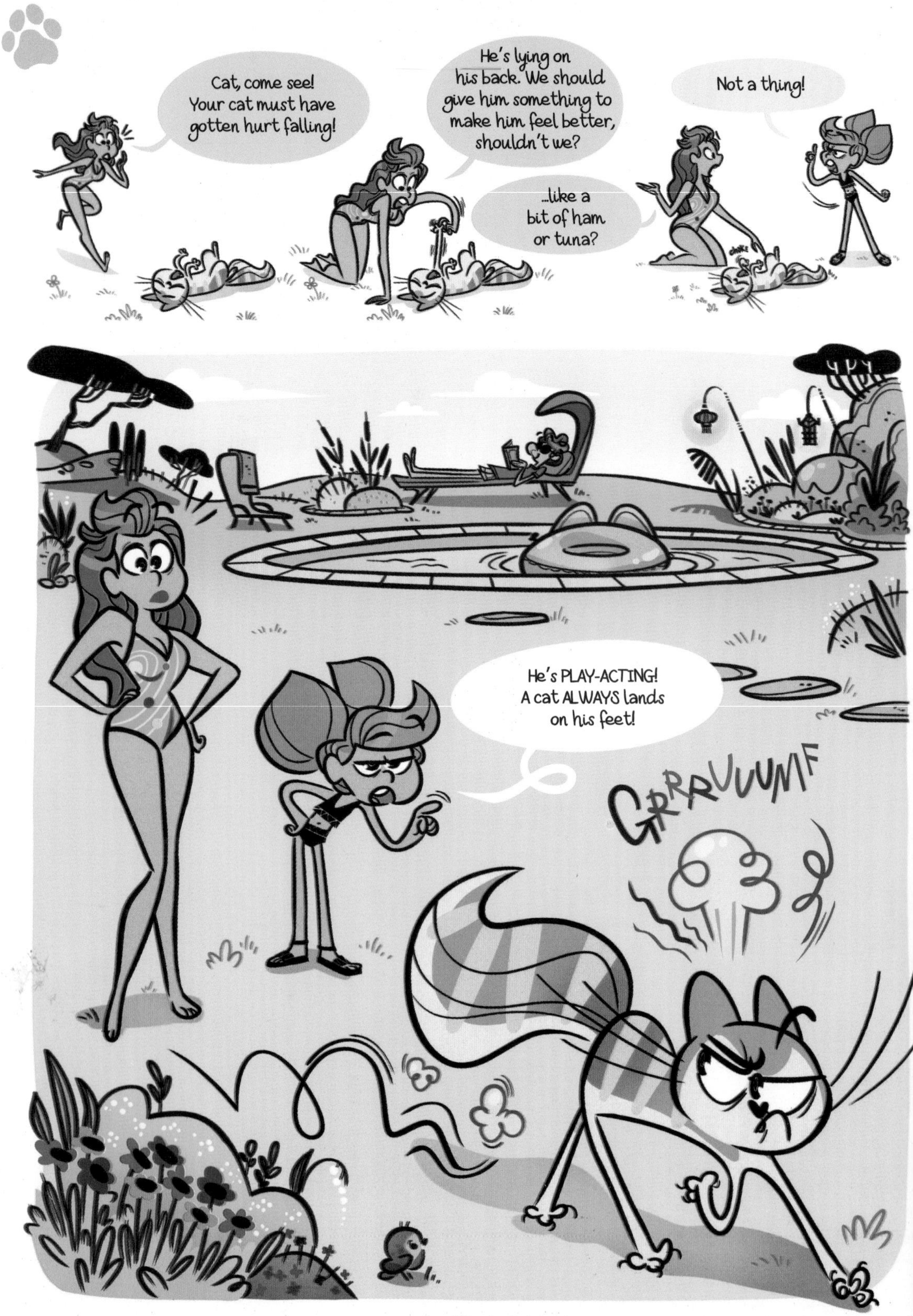

Cat, come see! Your cat must have gotten hurt falling!
He's lying on his back. We should give him something to make him feel better, shouldn't we?
...like a bit of ham or tuna?
Not a thing!
He's PLAY-ACTING! A cat ALWAYS lands on his feet!
GRRRUUUMF

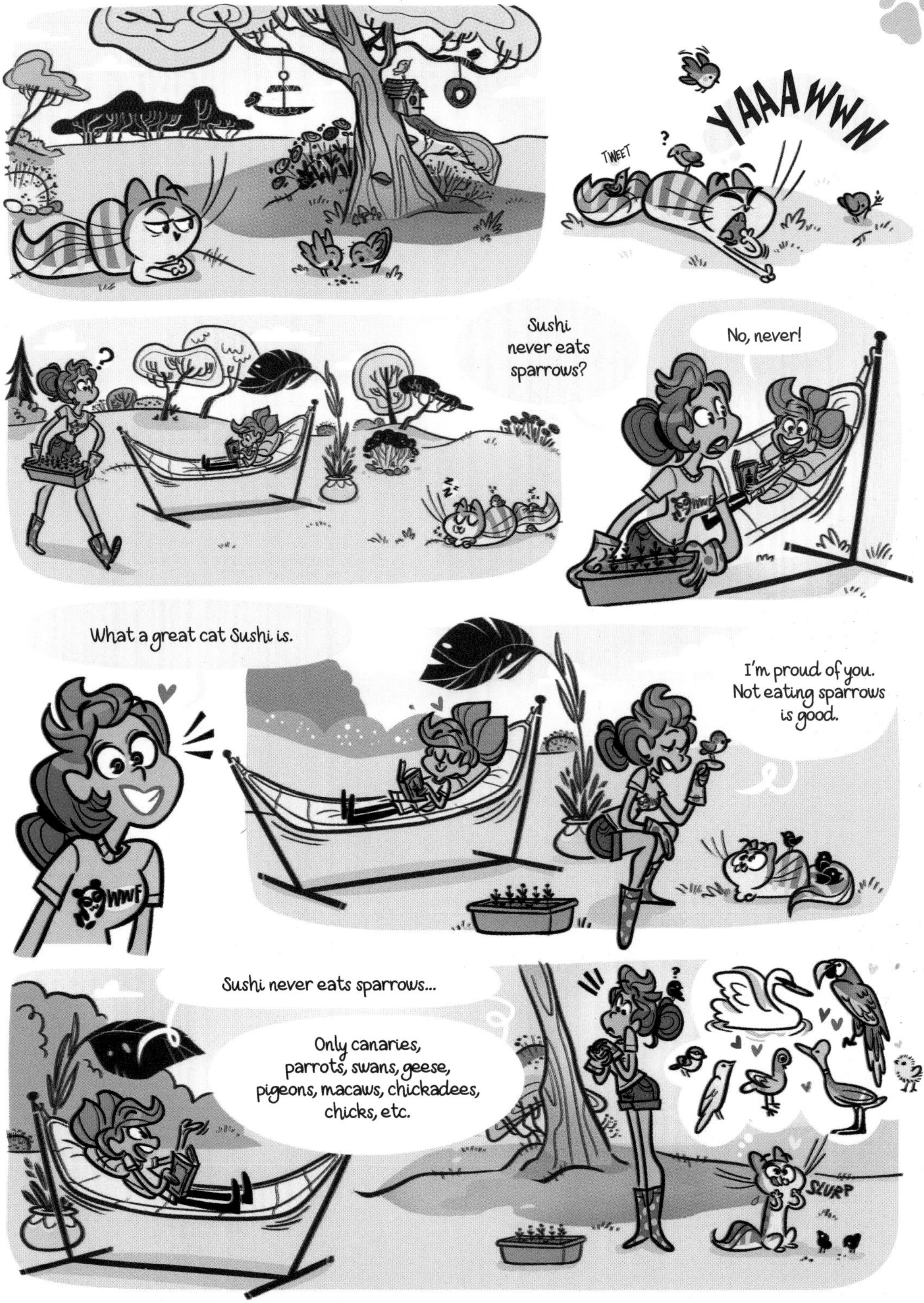
TWEET
YAAAWWN
Sushi never eats sparrows?
No, never!
What a great cat Sushi is.
I'm proud of you. Not eating sparrows is good.
Sushi never eats sparrows...
Only canaries, parrots, swans, geese, pigeons, macaws, chickadees, chicks, etc.
SLURP

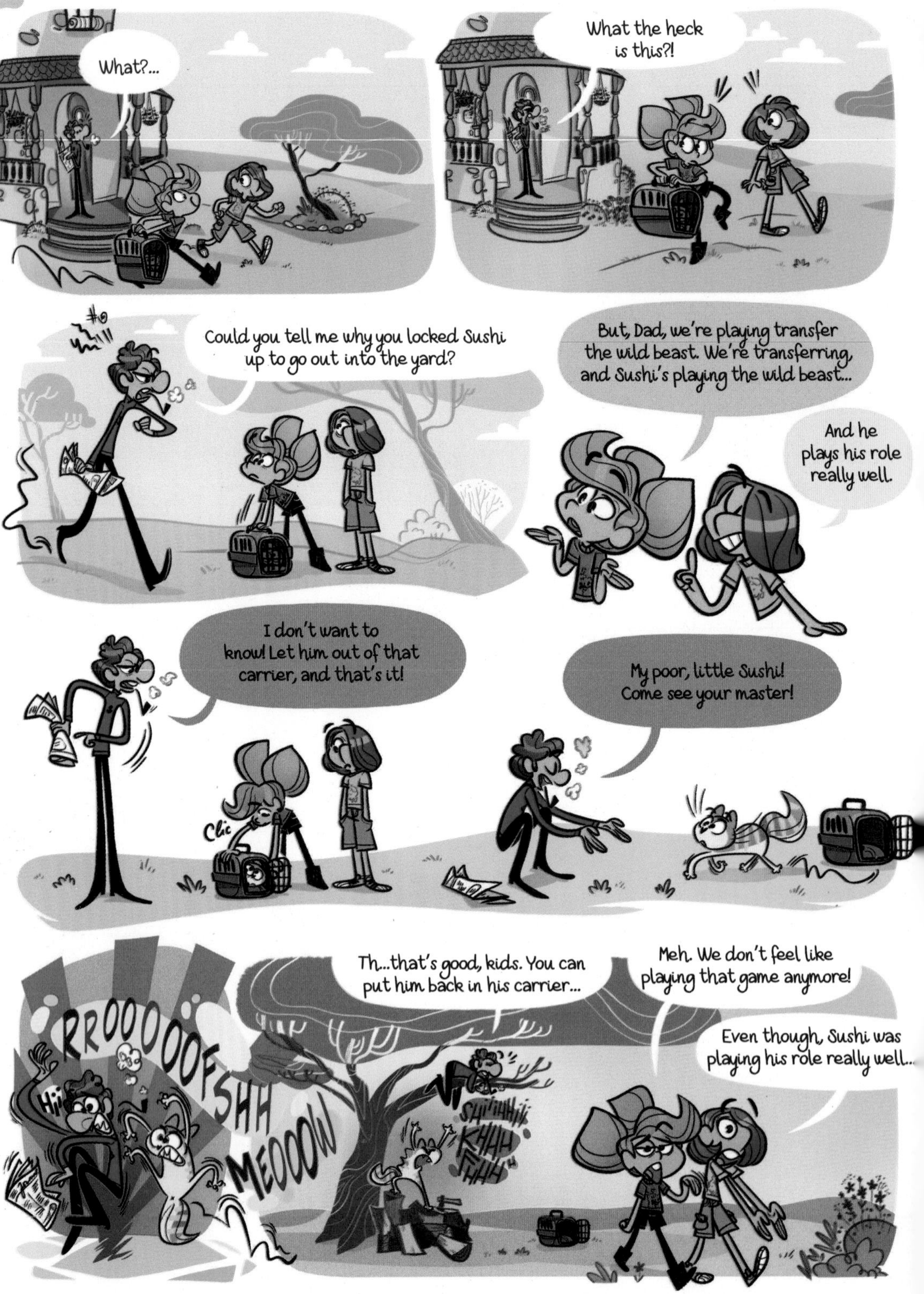

What?...
What the heck is this?!
Could you tell me why you locked Sushi up to go out into the yard?
But, Dad, we're playing transfer the wild beast. We're transferring, and Sushi's playing the wild beast...
And he plays his role really well.
I don't want to know! Let him out of that carrier, and that's it!
Clic
My poor, little Sushi! Come see your master!
RROOOOOFSHH
Hi
MEOOOW
Th...that's good, kids. You can put him back in his carrier...
Meh. We don't feel like playing that game anymore!
Even though, Sushi was playing his role really well...

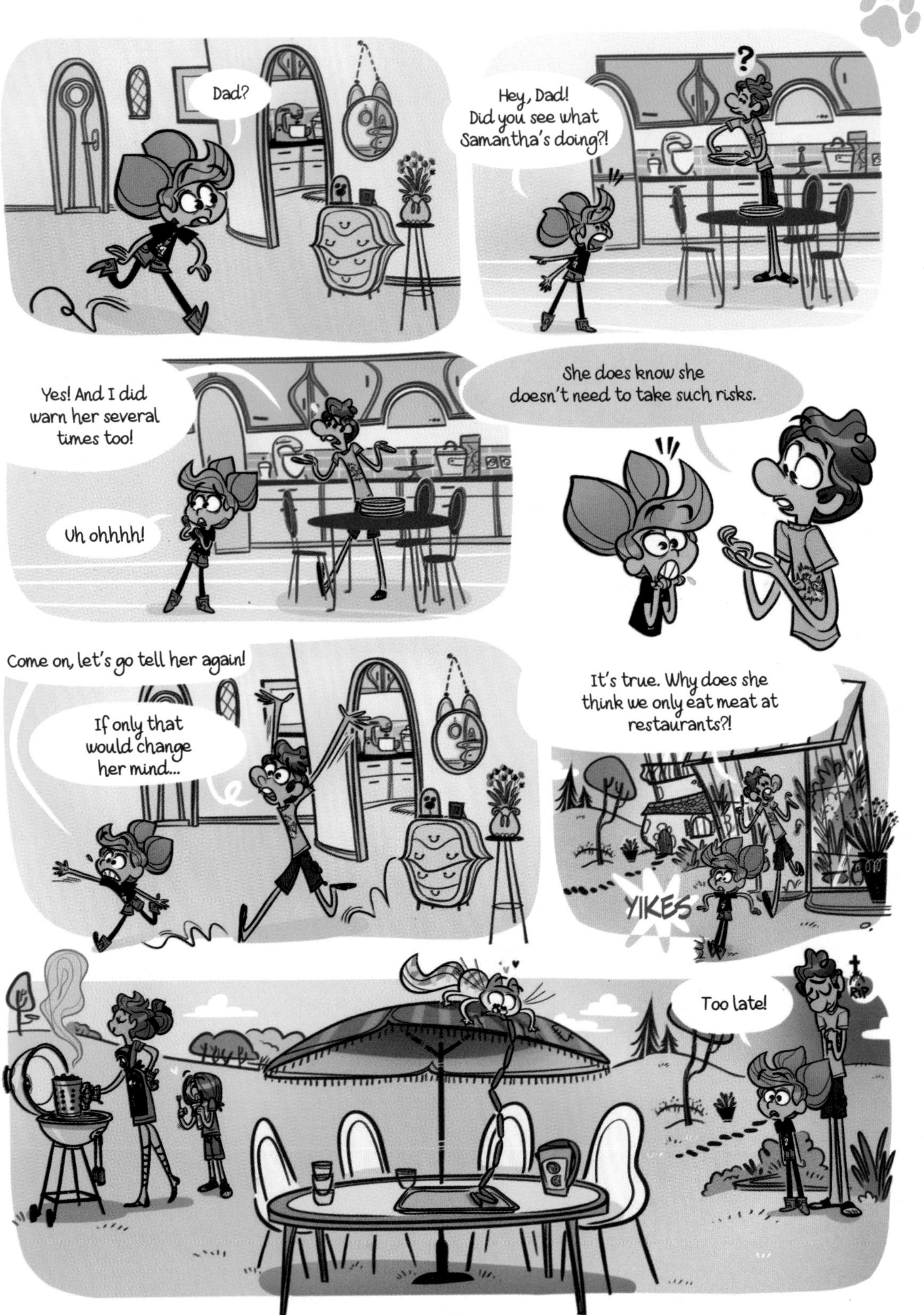
Dad?
Hey, Dad! Did you see what Samantha's doing?!
?
Yes! And I did warn her several times too!
Uh ohhhh!
She does know she doesn't need to take such risks.
Come on, let's go tell her again!
If only that would change her mind...
It's true. Why does she think we only eat meat at restaurants?!
YIKES
Too late!
RIP

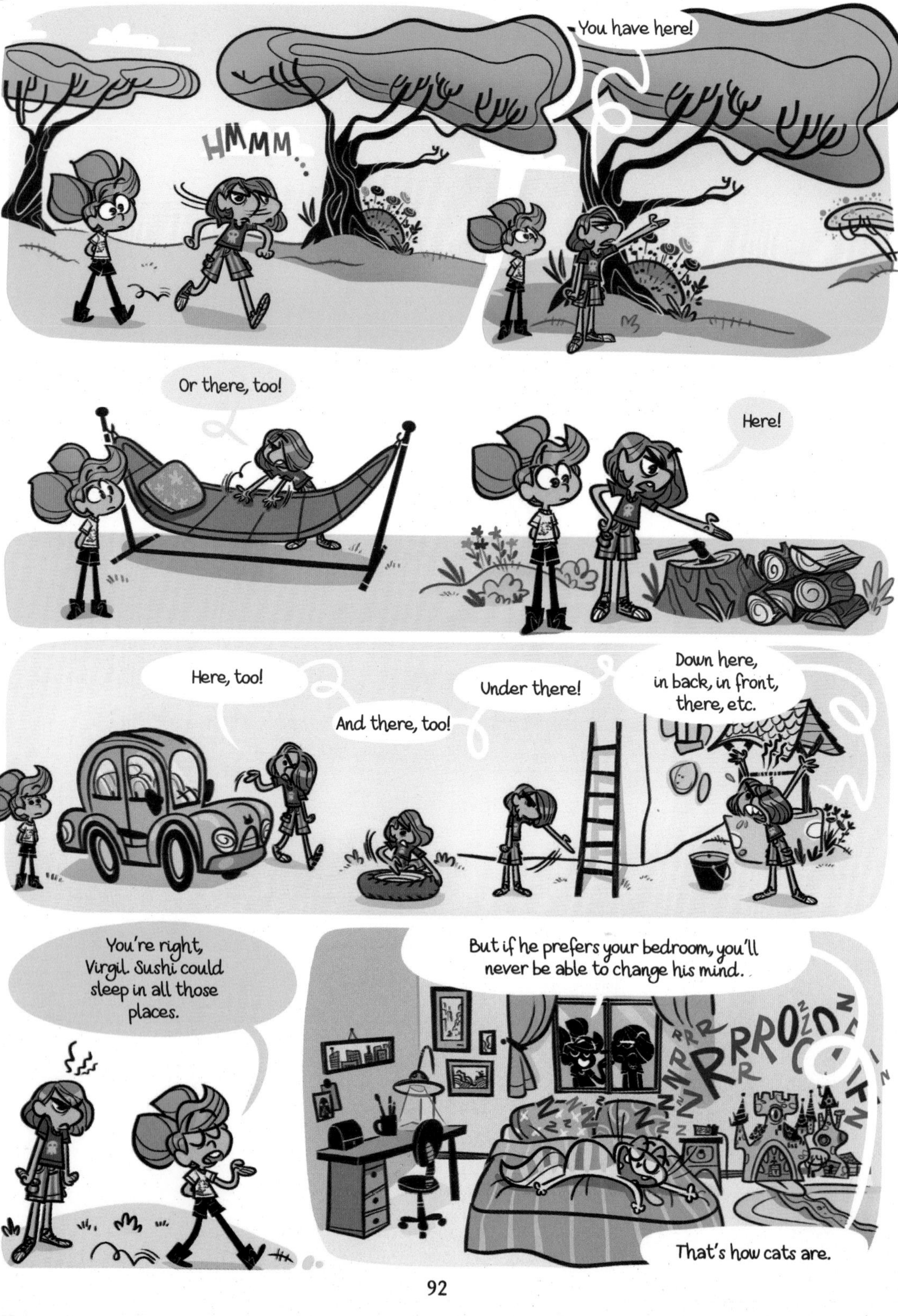
HMMM
You have here!
Or there, too!
Here!
Here, too!
And there, too!
Under there!
Down here, in back, in front, there, etc.
You're right, Virgil. Sushi could sleep in all those places.
But if he prefers your bedroom, you'll never be able to change his mind.
RRRRRO
That's how cats are.

WATCH OUT FOR PAPERCUTZ

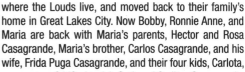

Welcome to the temporarily transient third CAT & CAT graphic novel by Christophe Cazenove and Hervé Richez, writers, and Yrgane Ramon, artist, from Papercutz, those mostly sheltering-at-home-bodies dedicated to publishing great graphic novels for all ages. I'm Jim Salicrup, Editor-in-Chief, holding down the fort alone at the palatial Papercutz offices, here to pontificate on a very moving subject: moving!

Lucy & Liz Lareau Ryan Jampole
geeky f@b 5
Zara
Marina
Sofia
AJ
Lucy 4 Hubble
It's Not Rocket Science
PAPERCUTZ

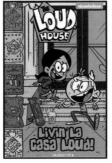

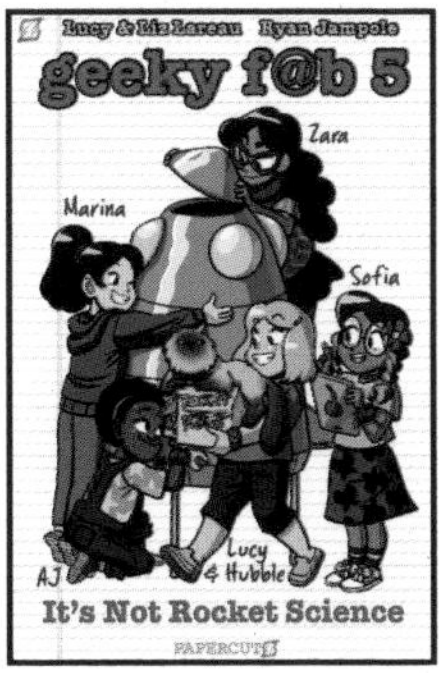

While Cat, her dad Nathan, and their cat Sushi, move into Samantha and Virgil's home, my daughter Cortney was in the process of moving back into my home while I was editing this volume of CAT & CAT. Although it all worked out well in the end, moving can be very stressful. My daughter was actually a bit overwhelmed a couple of times by the enormity of it all. Packing up boxes and boxes of my countless books to make room for her was truly a daunting task, but she persevered—slowly but surely, book by book, box by box—and got it done. Fortunately, we were helped by her boyfriend Joe and my brother Bill with the heavy lifting involving moving some rather big beds around. While it may not have gone as smoothly as Cat's move, one of the nice things about Cortney moving back in, aside from being able to see more of her, is that her cat Baby moved it as well! Unlike Sushi, Baby has been super-shy and has only recently stopped hiding under Cortney's bed and come out to let me pet her.

nickelodeon
THE LOUD HOUSE
Livin' La Casa Loud!
PAPERCUTZ

Another big move that seemingly went without a hitch happened in GEEKY F@B 5 #1"It's Not Rocket Science," when Lucy and Marina Monroe's family, including their cat Hubble, moved into a new home in Normal, Illinois. But it was this move that lead sisters Lucy and Marina to attending Earhart Elementary School, where they meet new friends Zara, Sofia, and A.J. and together they become the Geeky F@b 5. They quickly learn, as they're able to overcome various problems, that when girls stick together, anything is possible. In the latest GF5 graphic novel, yet another girl moves into town, but the girls suspect something's wrong when they discover the girl and her family are living in a motel room. Find out what's really going on in GEEKY F@B 5 #4 "Food Fight for Fiona."

Recently in THE LOUD HOUSE graphic novel series, as well as on the hit Nickelodeon TV series, Lori Loud's boyfriend, Bobby Santiago, along with his mother, Maria Casagrande Santiago, and his sister Ronnie Anne Santiago, moved out of the suburban town of Royal Woods, where the Louds live, and moved back to their family's home in Great Lakes City. Now Bobby, Ronnie Anne, and Maria are back with Maria's parents, Hector and Rosa Casagrande, Maria's brother, Carlos Casagrande, and his wife, Frida Puga Casagrande, and their four kids, Carlota, CJ (Carlos Jr.), Carl, and Carlitos Casagrande. While Lori and Bobby are still a couple, and Linc is still friends with Ronnie Anne, we don't see as much of the Santiagos on THE LOUD HOUSE, but that's okay, because they and the rest of their family are starring in the new hit Nickelodeon show THE CASAGRANDES, and coming soon from Papercutz is a special CASAGRANDES graphic novel: GRANDE SPECIAL!

Actually, I really shouldn't complain about the hassles of moving. Instead I should be grateful that I have a home no matter how cluttered it may be. There are far too many people who do not have a home and that's a serious situation that needs to addressed. And yes, there are even Papercutz graphic novels dealing with such loss… In SCHOOL FOR EXTRATERRESTRIAL GIRLS, Tara Smith loses not only her home, but her life as she knew it when she's suddenly shipped off to super-secret school for female aliens! It's even worse in THE ONLY LIVING BOY and THE ONLY GIRL graphic novel series. Erik Farrell and Zee Parfitt, two children who have lost seemingly everything and find themselves on a strange, often hostile patchwork planet and must work together if they hope to survive. Kind of makes concerns about getting along with your cat seem far less dire, no?

Fortunately, Cat, Nathan, and Sushi seem to be fitting in fine with Samantha and Virgil, but who knows what can happen next for them? Well, you will, if you pick up CAT & CAT #4. In the meantime, check out the preview of GEEKY F@B 5 #4 on the very next page. Until then, I'll be unpacking books and, if I'm lucky, I may even get to read a few!

Thanks, JIM

STAY IN TOUCH!

EMAIL: salicrup@papercutz.com
WEB: www.papercutz.com
TWITTER: @papercutzgn
INSTAGRAM: @papercutzgn
FACEBOOK: PAPERCUTZGRAPHICNOVELS
FANMAIL: Papercutz, 160 Broadway, Suite 700, East Wing, New York, NY 10038

Special Preview of **geeky f@b 5®** #4

CHAPTER ONE: A SPARKLY BLAST

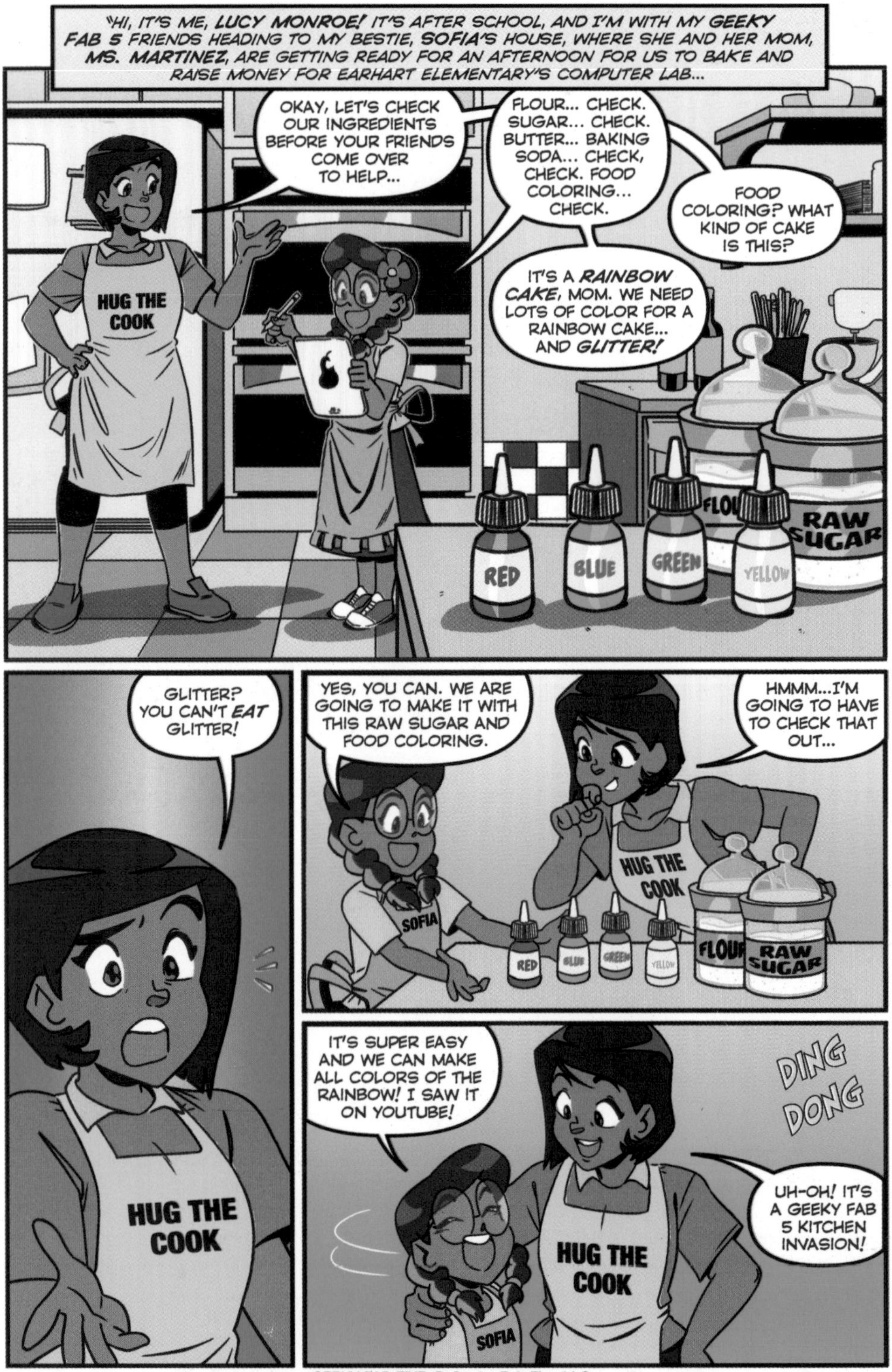

"HI, IT'S ME, LUCY MONROE! IT'S AFTER SCHOOL, AND I'M WITH MY GEEKY FAB 5 FRIENDS HEADING TO MY BESTIE, SOFIA'S HOUSE, WHERE SHE AND HER MOM, MS. MARTINEZ, ARE GETTING READY FOR AN AFTERNOON FOR US TO BAKE AND RAISE MONEY FOR EARHART ELEMENTARY'S COMPUTER LAB...
OKAY, LET'S CHECK OUR INGREDIENTS BEFORE YOUR FRIENDS COME OVER TO HELP...
FLOUR... CHECK. SUGAR... CHECK. BUTTER... BAKING SODA... CHECK, CHECK. FOOD COLORING... CHECK.
FOOD COLORING? WHAT KIND OF CAKE IS THIS?
IT'S A RAINBOW CAKE, MOM. WE NEED LOTS OF COLOR FOR A RAINBOW CAKE... AND GLITTER!
HUG THE COOK
RED
BLUE
GREEN
YELLOW
FLOUR
RAW SUGAR
GLITTER? YOU CAN'T EAT GLITTER!
HUG THE COOK
YES, YOU CAN. WE ARE GOING TO MAKE IT WITH THIS RAW SUGAR AND FOOD COLORING.
HMMM...I'M GOING TO HAVE TO CHECK THAT OUT...
SOFIA
HUG THE COOK
IT'S SUPER EASY AND WE CAN MAKE ALL COLORS OF THE RAINBOW! I SAW IT ON YOUTUBE!
DING DONG
UH-OH! IT'S A GEEKY FAB 5 KITCHEN INVASION!
HUG THE COOK
SOFIA

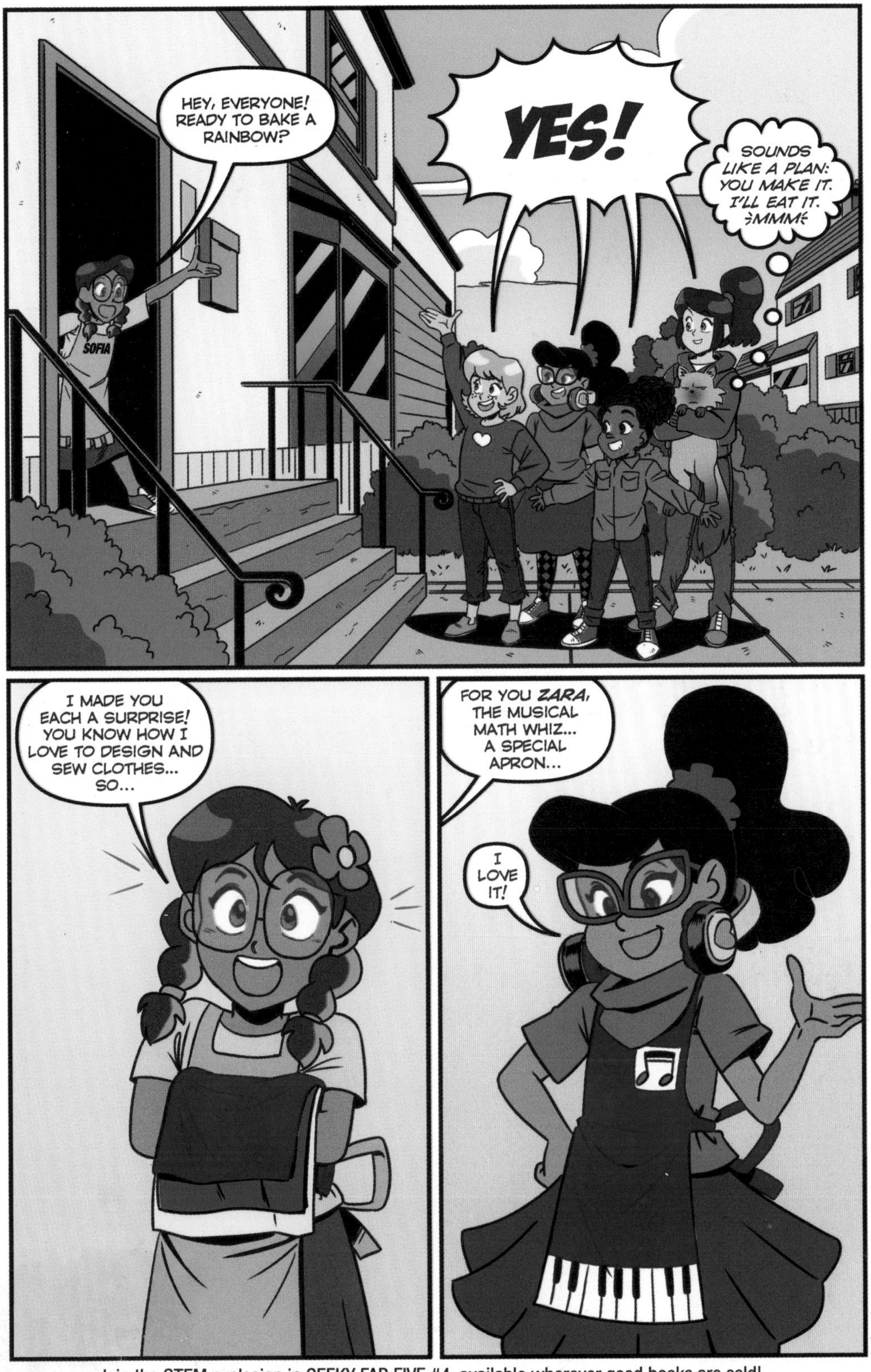
HEY, EVERYONE! READY TO BAKE A RAINBOW?
YES!
SOUNDS LIKE A PLAN: YOU MAKE IT. I'LL EAT IT. MMM
SOFIA
I MADE YOU EACH A SURPRISE! YOU KNOW HOW I LOVE TO DESIGN AND SEW CLOTHES... SO...
FOR YOU ZARA, THE MUSICAL MATH WHIZ... A SPECIAL APRON...
I LOVE IT!

Join the STEM explosion in GEEKY FAB FIVE #4, available wherever good books are sold!

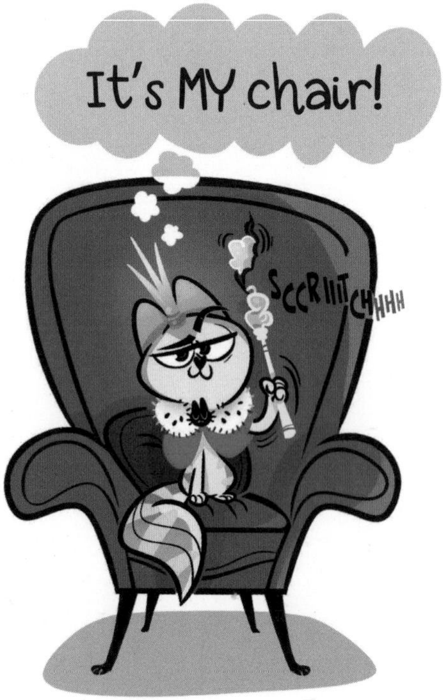
It's MY chair!
SCCRIIITCHHHH